A Mancunian through and through, H. V. KERSHAW has been intimately connected with *Coronation Street* since its inception in 1960. He was the serial's first script editor and acted in that capacity and as a writer until 1962 when he became Producer. He remained as Producer and, later, Executive Producer until 1972 when, on returning to freelance work, he became one of the programme's contract writers. Apart from his work with *Coronation Street* and Granada he has written extensively for the BBC, ATV, ABC and Thames Television. His list of credits is too substantial to quote in full but it includes: *Armchair Theatre*, *Shadow Squad*, *Skyport*, *The Verdict is Yours*, *In Court Today*, *The Odd Man*, *Knight Errant*, *Biggles*, *City 68* (as writer / producer), *Family at War*, *The Villains* (as writer / producer), *Crown Court*, *Love Thy Neighbour*, *Life of Riley* (as deviser / writer) and *Village Hall*.

Coronation Street: Early Days
H. V. Kershaw

Mayflower

Granada Publishing Limited
First published in 1976 by Mayflower Books Ltd
Frogmore, St Albans, Herts AL2 2NF

A Mayflower Original
Copyright © H. V. Kershaw 1976
Made and printed in Great Britain by
Hazell Watson & Viney Ltd
Aylesbury, Bucks
Set in Times Roman

CORONATION STREET: EARLY DAYS

CHAPTER ONE

She decided to close the curtains.

Not from any sense of loyalty – there'd never been anything more than a dull, dutiful, mother-and-daughter relationship involved – but for the sake of peace and quiet. She needed that above everything now. And for the sake of peace and quiet she must do all the proper, expected things. Leave the curtains open, and as sure as God made little apples, that hairnetted old bitch from across the road would be banging on the door.

'Christine Hardman, you may have thought nowt about your mother while she was living but you could at least have the decency to show a little respect now she's dead and gone.' And all delivered in one violent, vitriolic breath.

What in God's name had curtains to do with death? Were they meant to shield the body from the public gaze? Because if so, they wouldn't be doing that job at no. 13, Coronation Street. May Hardman's mortal remains were in discreet repose at A. J. Hollister's Chapel of Rest, and had been within an hour of Christine's telephone call to Mr Hollister the evening before. Not that that would cut any ice with Ena Sharples.

Thankfully it had been sudden . . . They'd been listening to the radio. It was like any other New Year's Eve. The usual motley collection of Scots had commandeered the Light Programme to pipe, sing and drink their unintelligible way into 1961. The mixture as the year before. And the year before that. Even down to her mother's interruptions.

'Eh, I don't know how people can enjoy themselves while I'm feeling like this! If only God could take pity on me and I didn't have to see another New Year!'

And He had. At five minutes past eight May Hardman had straightened suddenly in her chair, clutched her breast and slipped to the floor. By the time Christine bent to her, she was dead.

7

She'd telephoned the doctor from the Rover's Return. Jack Walker had answered her hurried knock at the side door, sparing her the ordeal of explaining her way across the public bar. He'd made no fuss, just led her to the telephone, tactfully disappeared while she made the call, come back as soon as she'd finished. She was back in her own house before she realized that she was carrying a half bottle of brandy.

The doctor had wasted no time. It seemed only minutes later that death had been confirmed, the certificate made out, a sedative and prescription left and a promise made to call at the undertakers on his way home. So Christine had been spared another trip to the telephone. Half an hour later the grey, unsmiling Mr Hollister had come, completed his business, and gone.

Christine, dazed, had been left alone, with just one thought in her head; that one could come into this world with so much fuss, and leave it with so little. She remembered though that she'd apologized to doctor and undertaker for bringing them out on a New Year's Eve.

The bitter self-questioning came later that evening. Had she been wrong about her mother with her endless wingeing, her pains and complaints, the interminable headaches, always at their worst when Christine had been at her most tired herself? Had it all been true and had Christine been unfeeling, dismissing her with weary resentment, every thought ungenerous? Even hypochondriacs must someday die. And when they do, those who are left behind look back and accuse themselves. Blame themselves. Eventually she slept.

Next morning she'd woken up surprisingly refreshed. The happenings of the previous night flooded instantly and vividly into her mind. But she'd washed, dressed, fried some bacon and egg and actually eaten it. It was as she was sitting over her second cup of tea that she started to think of the world outside her front door.

Had Jack Walker spread the news? A considerate man, he'd have thought it helpful to her to warn the neighbours.

8

Though, at the same time, a considerate landlord wouldn't want to depress his customers with news of death on New Year's Eve. From consideration her thoughts drifted to protocol and from protocol to curtains.

She decided to close them.

Outside, Harry Hewitt had been on the point of knocking when he saw the curtains drawn to. He moved away, glad that the decision had been made for him. He was tired. New Year's Eve was always an ordeal for him. As ceremony decreed, his black hair had forced him out into the cold street just before midnight. First footing, they called it. And then afterwards the party at Len's had moved en bloc to the Rover's for the last hour of the extension.

As soon as he had walked in Jack had taken him on one side and told him the news. Told him quietly because the pub had been full: Elsie with daughter and son-in-law, the three old biddies in the snug, the Barlows, that new woman from the shop . . . His thoughts strayed. The new woman from the shop – what was her name? There it was on the newly painted sign: 'FLORENCE LENA LINDLEY'. What a name to go to bed with! And would she? She'd not looked averse to the idea. Len had had a word or two to say on the subject. 'Watch yourself, Harry boy, she's after you, that one . . .' He smiled to himself when he remembered his reaction. Not that Concepta could have heard. Or if she had she had given no sign. Didn't really matter if she had. Nothing between them – yet . . .

He was still smiling when the shop door opened and there was the new woman herself. She caught his smile. Smiled back nervously and wiped her hands on her pinafore.

'Did you want something?'

'Er . . . no! No thanks. I was just, er . . .'

'Only I was in the shop and I . . . I saw you and . . . I don't mind if you *do* want something, New Year's Day or not.'

'No, really, I was just going to knock next door. Mrs

9

Hardman died last night. You probably didn't know.'

'Oh dear.' Her voice deepened, saddened for the repetition: 'Oh dear!'

She looked kind he thought. A bit on the soppy side perhaps, but kind, and gentle. A little soppiness can be forgiven by a widower, especially one who's helpless about the house, trying to cope with an eleven-year-old daughter. Because a little soppiness can bring with it kindness and gentleness, and can mean homemade steak and kidney pie and a snug home waiting at the end of the day and . . . He smiled again, at his own thoughts, not at her. Man the hunter – in a bus inspector's uniform!

'It wasn't exactly unexpected,' he said. 'I know it's an easy thing to say, but it could have been a blessing.'

She agreed. 'Yes.' And qualified the agreement. 'Not that I knew her but I know what you mean.' That nervous smile again. 'You're working then?'

'Oh aye. New Year's Day means nowt to us. Nor Sunday. The buses still have to run.'

'Is . . . is it right? That you've just been promoted? Somebody was saying last night in the pub.'

So she *had* been talking about him.

'That's right! In fact today's the first day.' He looked down at his brand-new uniform.

She looked too, admiringly. 'You must be very pleased!'

'Well, we'll see. I've talked about "them" long enough. Now I'm one. It'll be funny finding out what it feels like!' They laughed together. 'I'd best be off then. Just give Elsie a knock and take myself off to work.'

'Elsie?'

'Tanner, at number eleven.'

'Oh, yes!' Two words but they spoke volumes.

'You've met her I see?' He smiled, inviting frankness.

'A couple of times, yes. She's been in the shop. She's a bit . . .'

She let the inference drift away on the cold wind.

'She's a *lot*! That's why I'm giving her a knock. The daughter's with her and they get a bit noisy at times. Specially when they're rowing – which is most of the day. And night. I'd best warn her.' He hesitated. She didn't

10

answer and the opportunity was there. 'Right then! See you down the road perhaps?'

'Yes.' Reluctantly, 'Bye. Oh, and if you should want anything . . . She glanced back into the shop. 'Don't hesitate.'

He smiled: 'I'll give you a knock.'

A last smile and the door closed.

He walked past Christine's guarded windows and rapped crisply on the peeling door of number eleven. A pause followed and he put his ear to the scarred panel. Obviously he was doing the right thing. The day's rowing had begun already. Raised above the bedlam he heard Elsie's voice:

'It'd look better of the pair of you if you'd get off your fat behinds and answer that door!'

Harry found a smile and lost it again as the door opened. The command hadn't worked and it was Elsie herself who faced him. Elsie in a dressing gown, today's make-up on top of yesterday's, her cleavage bidding welcome to the New Year. She pulled her dressing gown more tightly round her and only succeeded with that uncanny knack of hers, in revealing more. Not that Harry was grumbling. But this was not the time for suggestive comment or neighbourly intimacy.

'Oh, hello!' She noticed his uniform. 'Oo, get you! Very posh!'

He permitted himself a ghost of an acknowledgment. 'Sorry to bother you, Elsie, but I don't know if you know or not. May Hardman died last night.'

Genuine sadness: 'Oh, no!'

'Aye. Heart, apparently.'

'Oh, well! It's an ill wind . . .'

'Aye.'

Behind her, voices rose. She sucked in her breath ominously.

'Hang on a minute.' She disappeared into the house. The odd phrase drifted back to him. 'Just keep your voices down, can't you . . . These flaming walls are like tissue paper . . . Go and do your rowing somewhere else . . .'

And then she was back with him. 'There's nowt we can do is there?' And meant it.

11

'Not that I can think of.'

'I'll give her a knock later on. Take her in a cup of tea.'

'Aye, she'd appreciate that.' A sad smile. 'Just what you need at New Year isn't it?'

'Who needs New Year!'

It wasn't a question. He smiled faintly and walked away. She closed the door.

Linda Cheveski, née Tanner, had inherited much from her mother. It included the knack of carrying on a blazing row at all voice levels. At the moment she was down to a violent whisper.

'You go back! Nobody asked you to come! What d'you think I left you for – so you could come chasing after me? I don't *want* you here – I'm sick of the sight of you.'

'In Poland a husband and wife stay together.'

'In case you've not noticed, we're not in Poland! We're in Lancashire! And they only stay together in Lancashire if they get on with each other. And I don't get on with you!'

Ivan Kazimierz Cheveski was devastated. He would never properly understand these people. Never fully feel at home in the country of his adoption. His parents, Polish refugees, let into a sympathetic Britain after the war, knew they were lucky. They had survived. Survived German invasion, deportation, forced labour on German farms. It was enough that they had kept the family together.

But Ivan wasn't sure that *he* was lucky. Ten years old when he arrived in the country, he had coped with his English classmates at school, endured his workmates at the Stockport steelworks which gave him his first job and accepted the company of his compatriots at the local Polish club. He had got by but no more. Not truly Polish, he would never be fully English.

And one day, in this uneasy, unhappy state, Linda Tanner had walked into his life. Walked in on the arm of one of his friends at an Anglo-Polish Friendship League dance at the Ritz Ballroom in Manchester. By the end of that evening Ivan had lost a friend, the friend had lost Linda, and Ivan had gained a girl.

Linda was beautiful. Dark-eyed, dark-haired – her mother's auburn had not been inherited, a fact not surprising to those of the neighbours who had long believed that Elsie's hair colouring owed more to the bottle than to birth – she was blessed with those voluptuous good looks bestowed so rarely by Nature and then in the strangest places. The father had been wildly handsome. His mother had a favourite story of how she had caught the eye of Edward VII himself as he rode down Market Street one turn-of-the-century afternoon.

'. . . Took one look at me, waving my little flag, and I could see by the gleam in his eye that he'd forgotten all about Lily Langtry! Then he turned down Cross Street and I never saw him again.'

They had a sense of humour as well, that family!

And a temper. All of them. A great family for rowing. Generations of them, quick to anger and stamina-filled, brought up on rows, thriving on them. To Ivan, a strange, terrifying, alien breed.

'Don't just stand there gawping! You heard what I said. I don't get on with you! And don't kid on you don't know what I'm talking about!'

The stricken Ivan turned away from her and found himself facing Elsie.

'Don't tell me you're still at it,' said Elsie.

Linda's eyes flashed. 'Take him out of my sight. For God's sake get him away from me!'

Elsie turned to the wretched Ivan. Why did he have to look like that? Hell's Bell's, it was only a family row. They were ten a penny. He didn't have to look as if it were the end of the world.

'Go on, love, make yourself scarce.'

He was obstinate, if nothing else: 'I don't know . . .'

'None of us know, love. Just leave us alone, it'll sort itself out. Have you made your bed yet?'

'No.'

'Go and make your bed then.'

He hesitated, his agonized eyes turned on Linda. Then,

13

wordlessly, he went out. The lobby door closed quietly after him. Elsie turned to Linda. 'You're a right devil, you are!'

'Don't you start!'

'Look, Madam!' Elsie jabbed a red-nailed forefinger at her glowering daughter. 'As long as you're in my house, sleeping in my bed, eating my food, I'll start when and where I like! So put that in your pipe and smoke it!'

Linda spun away, slammed her hands down on the mantelshelf. Elsie softened. 'Come on, chuck, fair's fair. It's not that long since you married the lad and if my memory serves me right, you were all over him.'

Linda didn't turn. Her voice was all contempt. 'And I suppose you weren't all over my Dad. And how long did he last?'

Elsie settled for the soft answer. 'All right, I asked for that. But at least your Dad wasn't foreign.'

But this time the soft answer didn't work. Linda whipped round.

'Do you know what you're saying?' she spat. 'Do you know about foreigners? Hasn't anybody ever told you? There's only one thing they believe in! The family!' She turned it into a dirty word. 'They sit at home night after night. Daft grins on their faces! Chuffed to little mint balls at having nowt! I've seen 'em! In Warrington! Where he took me! Warrington! Not exactly the Venice of the North is it?'

Elsie tried to stifle the smile, failed, but succeeded. Linda's shoulders sagged. The fire died.

Elsie risked another smile. 'I've had some good times in Warrington, by eck, I have!'

'It's not Warrington, Mam.' There was a despairing note in Linda's voice. 'It's . . . it's . . . we don't go out, not even to the pictures. One night, a month ago, I got him to take me for a drink. We hadn't been in the place ten minutes and he started. Let's go! It's smoky here! It'll get on your chest! God help us, I loved it! We had one drink and we're out of the place and you know why? Because I smiled at my butcher, that's why! Fifty if he's a day and like a flaming barrel of lard and my husband's jealous of him!' The

14

despair changed to pleading. 'That's what they're like, Mam! He's jealous if I so much as say good morning to another man. It's killing me, Mam!'

'They don't know our ways, love. Heaven help 'em, they can't even speak our language proper.'

'Oh, come off it! He can speak English as well as I can!'

'That's not difficult.'

But Linda was in no mood for jokes. The fire sprang to new life. 'That's right, side with him!'

Elsie's patience, never a plentiful commodity, ran out. 'I'd side with anybody who had to put up with you! Poor devil!'

Linda's voice rose. 'Don't "poor" devil him! *I'm* your daughter!'

'By eck you'd better be!' snapped Elsie. 'Trouble you've caused me! And shut up, they've had a death next door.'

A silence. Twenty seconds, perhaps as long as half a minute. Sounds from upstairs. Then . . .

'I only smiled at him, Mam. Honest!' It was Linda's little-girl-lost voice.

Elsie was unimpressed. 'I know how you smile at fellers.'

Battle was joined again. 'And who do I get it from?'

'Never mind who you got it from. We're talking about you, not me. And not *just* you.' Elsie looked squarely at her defiant daughter. Linda shook her head, a barely perceptible movement. 'Tell him!'

The answer had already been given. 'No.'

'If *you* don't, I will!'

'Just try it!'

Two resolute paces and Elsie was at the lobby door, the door was open and she was shouting upstairs. 'Ivan! Come down here!'

Linda sighed wearily. 'Thank you very much. In case you don't know, I'm quite capable of making my own mind up.'

'Oh, I know all right! Trouble is you always go the wrong way about it. Like a bull at a gate!'

'That's summat else I get from my mother!'

Elsie didn't bother to answer. Ivan stood in the open doorway. A whipped dog hoping for forgiveness.

15

Elsie broke the silence. 'Go on, put him out of his misery.'

Linda looked dully at her husband. Her eyes held no love, no gentleness, no hint of affection. And her words, when they came, held no feeling, none of the joy such words should hold. They were flat. Informative.

'I'm going to have a baby.' She sat, heavily, with finality.

'Thank you and good night,' Elsie said disgustedly.

Emotions flitted across Ivan's face like sunshine on a heavy sea. Elsie, describing the scene later to Dot Greenhalgh, said, 'You should have seen him! You know them lights made out of bits of mirror they have in dance halls? I thought we'd had one of them fitted. He kept going different colours.'

Ivan settled for the colour of ecstasy. Then he flung himself to the floor, clasped his arms around Linda's legs and buried his face in her lap. He sobbed. Above his bowed, joyous head, Linda had the good grace to look fairly stricken and to mouth 'See what I mean?' to her mother. Her mother said 'Aw! ' very fondly.

Ivan babbled incoherently. 'I work very hard for you and the baby! Please! Please! ' Harder hearts than Linda's would have melted. Her hands found his hair, stroked it soothingly. His arms tightened around her in gratitude.

'Is there any breakfast going?'

Elsie turned from the scene of reconciliation. In the doorway stood her son. Bleary-eyed, his mouth chewing on an unpleasant taste, greasy hair streaking his forehead, roughly pyjamaed. Dennis, the eighteen-year-old problem child. Elsie's expression was standard – a mixture of sadness, resignation and Why-in-God's-name-did-it-happen-to-me?

'By eck, you choose some great flaming moments! ' she said. And turned back to Linda.

'You look after *your* baby,' said Linda, 'and I'll look after mine! '

'Both of 'em?' asked Elsie. 'You've got a couple to worry about.'

Linda smiled for the first time that year.

A little while later and a little way down the street there was another row. A very different family and a very different sort of row. Not the quick-flaring, quick-fading, Tanner-style shouting match, but a smouldering product of a father's resentment of his son, a jealousy that showed itself in habitual derision and leaped to life at any pretext.

It was Ida Barlow who sparked it off when she nervously announced to husband and younger son that there'd be company for Sunday dinner.

Husband Frank could recognize potential bad news when he heard it.

'Who?'

'Susan's coming.' She kept it light and turned to younger son David, turned away from Frank's angry twitch of his newspaper. 'So clear that mess up. I don't want folk thinking we live in a pig sty!'

'Even if we do.' David's words were cheeky but his actions were obedient.

'You watch it, meladdo! You're not too old for a good hiding!'

'He's old enough and good enough to play professional football,' said Frank. His thoughts shifted from his beloved younger son to Kenneth, the elder, whom he no longer understood. 'Which is more than you can say for some in this house.'

But Ida's affections were all-embracing. She smiled at the embarrassed David who had been mending his bike in front of the fire. He made a move towards clearing up. Throwing a guarded look at her husband, she turned to go as elder son Ken came in. Ken who would be, as ever, cause and victim of his father's scornful anger.

'And *you*'d better get yourself cleaned up as well. Dinn . . . lunch in half an hour.' Frank glowered at the correction. David smiled. Ken successfully pretended not to notice.

'I won't be a minute.' He turned to his brother. 'Hey, our kid, have you pinched a piece of cardboard? About this square?' He held his hands two feet apart.

David picked up the last oily spanner and dropped it into his saddlebag. Then he lifted the makeshift toolbench on which he had spread his bits and pieces and said, guiltily, 'This one, do you mean?'

'Yes, I do mean that one! Why the devil can't you keep your hands off other people's property!'

'Sorry!', David apologized, 'I'll clean it up. What's it for?'

'It'll be for his banner!' sneered Frank, 'He's doing his Sister Anna act this afternoon. Haven't you read t'papers?' He thumbed over a page, read a headline. 'Four thousand expected in City Ban the Bomb March. Four thousand mugs! And he's one of 'em!'

'Now, father,' said Ida.

'I suppose that's why Lady Muck's coming for her dinner, is it? Holding your hand, is she?'

Oh, God, not again, thought Ken. It had started, this new attack, less than a month ago. During the previous term he had joined the University Debating Society and there he had met Susan Cunningham. Susan, as far as he could see, took no active part. She listened avidly, gravely acknowledging each point and smiling periodically and tentatively, at Kenneth. This reserved behaviour, together with a certain blonde ethereality, led him into a meditative mood. Perhaps, he had mused one night soon after their first meeting, she was not Susan Cunningham at all. Perhaps she was Natalia Fedorovna, sent by Krushchev to seek out the Marxist element in Manchester University. Perhaps he was destined, on the back row of the Gaumont one night, to accept a doped chocolate and find himself on board a Russian jet, hell-bound for indoctrination. But Susan, daughter of a bank manager with a four-bedroomed detached family home deep in capitalist Cheadle Hulme, contributed nothing to these fantasies. Her needs were basic. She wanted Kenneth for his mind – and for his body. Their affair had stuttered along, played out for the most part in public parks and darkened cinemas but never reaching any satisfactory conclusion. Satisfactory for Susan, that was. As far as Kenneth was concerned, he was perfectly happy to stop an inch short of ecstasy, not through any lack of masculinity but because he had played out in his mind the scene where he went to his father and told him that he would have to get married because he'd been careless. And he decided he would rather forsake ecstasy than play that scene for real. However, if their sexual progress was slow they kept up to schedule socially and, just before Christmas they had decided that as a special treat they would have afternoon tea at the Imperial. The fact that his mother worked there as a part-time washer-up never occurred to him. In a four-star hotel the distance between lounge and kitchen outstripped such considerations. But not as far as Frank was concerned. When Ken, a couple of days before the date, let slip his intentions, Frank had leapt into battle. 'You're not taking no girl to no Imperial Hotel!' Kenneth's perverse attempt to correct his father's grammar had only added fuel to the flames. 'Don't correct me, you cheeky young monkey! I said you're not wasting no money at that place while your mother's slaving away in the kitchens!'

He had taken Susan, of course. Ida not only knew but gave it her blessing though they had felt it expedient to keep it from Frank. Even so, the sneering had continued. And here it was, starting again.

'Or are you holding your so-called rally at the Imperial! Marching round t'dining room, are you!'

'Now I won't have you two arguing!' Ida made it as briskly matriarchal as her lack of confidence would allow. 'I'm not having good food go cold while you play your silly games!'

She had stayed to defend her son. Now she had to consolidate the peace. She moved, with purposeless purpose round the room, plumping a plumped cushion here, straightening a straight chairback there. Frank returned to his paper. David, embarrassed, handed Ken the grimy cardboard. Ken took it and went.

'Now don't forget what I said. Clean yourselves up for your Sunday dinner. And you clever people might be interested to know that on Sundays it *is* dinner!' And with that brave, parting shot she repaired to her kitchen. Ostensibly to her cooking. In reality, to a quiet weep.

19

And as the Barlows got themselves ready for a less than happy Sunday dinner, the doors of the Rover's Return had opened. Bare elbows resting on the bar counter, Jack Walker surveyed his happy customers with lack-lustre eyes and sighed. Getting a bit old for this game, he reflected. An extension to midnight last night and here we are, open again! And to hear them talk about publicans you'd think it was a bobby's job! Well, if it was, what sort of a job had all this lot got? Standing here, supping, while he was working! Len Fairclough over there, he'd shouted enough about wishing he'd got a pub of his own. Well, thought Jack, if he wants to come round this bar he can have my apron! And the big fellow with him. Alf Roberts, Frank Barlow's mate in the Sorting Office. What was *he* doing here? Why wasn't he pushing the mail along?

'Dropping off?' It was Annie.

'Nay, I were just wondering why we're the only silly so-and-sos working.'

'Jack, love, you say that with monotonous regularity every New Year's Day. *And* every Good Friday! *And* every Bank Holiday!'

'And we're *still* working!'

'And will be, one sincerely hopes, for many years to come. See to Mrs Sharples, will you?'

It really was uncanny. Annie had her back to the snug and yet some sixth sense told her immediately Ena wanted attention. And there indeed she was, standing at the bar, her mouth working impatiently, her hairnet clamping close iron waves to that iron head, ready for milk stout or battle, whichever came first.

'Yes, Mrs Sharples?' Jack asked, politely.

'Oh, you are serving then?'

'Not everybody, Mrs Sharples, but I'll make an exception in your case. Seeing you're an old customer.' The slightest emphasis on 'old' accompanied by the slightest smile.

It is doubtful if Ena would have allowed anyone else in the world to get away with that kind of talk. However, she reasoned, Jack was an old adversary and deserved the odd modest victory. And, of course, he had been known to push her money back over the counter.

'Three milk stouts, please. We've got glasses.' She watched him as, expertly, he levered the tops from the bottles. 'I see Christine Hardman's got her curtains drawn.'

'Aye, well, it's only to be expected'. He risked a leading question. 'She told you, did she?'

'Who, that one? Not likely! Driving your mother to her grave's one thing, bragging about it's another!'

'Now, Mrs Sharples!' The bottles were on the counter. Ena paid, violently, almost scarring the bar top.

'Now, Mrs Sharples nothing! She didn't care a toss about her. I've been in that house when May Hardman was an inch off doing away with herself she was in that much pain. And that young madam didn't give a damn!'

'Oh come on now, Mrs Sharples, you know as well as I do, May Hardman was a dab hand at putting it on. Christine's life's been no bed of roses.'

'Oh, yes? Is that what she died of, then? Putting it on?' crowed Ena.

A few hours earlier Christine had smiled with wry bitterness at that very thought. Now it was Jack's turn. 'No, of course she didn't.'

'I happen to have seen her, you know!' said Ena.

'Who, Christine?' asked Jack.

'Christine be blowed! Her mother! I saw Archie Hollister round there last night so I took myself off to his Chapel of Rest this morning. Oh yes, I saw her. As was my right as a near neighbour of many years' standing. Yes, I saw her all right and you can take it from me that poor body was at peace for the first time in years, God rest her soul.'

There was nothing else to be said. Jack picked up the money and headed heavily for the till. Ena, a small smile of triumph on her lips, turned to her companions. She placed a bottle in front of each of them and sat, her back to the bar. On her left, Martha Longhurst, bespectacled, thin-lipped; on her right, Minnie Caldwell, cosy, vaguely smiling, her toque sitting comfortably on her wispy grey hair. An inviolate seating arrangement. As Alf Roberts once said in a rare analogical moment, 'I reckon Queen Victoria'll get up and walk into Piccadilly Gardens before Ena gives that seat up!' And he was probably right. As many a minor official had learned to his cost, Ena's mind could set harder than the stone of any statue. But at that moment she was in a more magnanimous mood.

'By eck, I thought Jack Walker had more nous than be taken in by the Christine Hardmans of this world!'

'He's not one for calling anybody, isn't Jack. It's his nature,' said Minnie.

Ena, wondering if she was being 'got at', turned to her friend but there was no hint of censure in Minnie's bland expression. Not that the censure wasn't there. It was locked deep in Minnie's mind, in recesses no one knew for sure existed.

'I think he's right. I think Christine had a lot to put up with.' This was Martha.

Ena's head swivelled through a hundred and eighty degrees. 'It *is* New Year's Day today, isn't it?' she asked, blandly.

'Aye, course it is,' answered Martha, walking, as she invariably did, straight into Ena's trap.

'By eck, you surprise me!' said Ena, still mild. 'I thought you'd have said it was Whit Monday. Seeing you disagree with me on principle.'

'I do nowt o' t'sort!' said Martha, indignantly. Which was a lie. Martha had never approved of Ena's leadership. Unable by temperament to assume Ena's role she had long ago decided that the only way she could achieve equality with her Churchillian friend was to try, at every possible opportunity, to drag her down to her own level of ineffectiveness. But poor Martha was as ineffective in this as she was in everything else. Invariably she failed. Whereas Minnie, in true feline fashion, kept her minor victories wholly to herself, savoured them and smiled her contented smile. And that smile worried Ena more than a torrent of Martha's words.

'I'm as much entitled to my opinion as anybody else! And May Hardman led that daughter of hers a dog's life!'

'Oh, Martha!' said Minnie reprovingly. 'She's not cold in her grave!'

'She's not even *in* it yet!' added Ena.

'Well, I'm not like some. If I have summat to say I'll say it. You mark my words, everybody'll be having a go at her inside a week so if there's owt to be said it might just as well be said now! And I happen to know what the doctor thought of May Hardman! Him and our Lily's Wilf are both in t'same lodge!'

Ena's eyes narrowed impatiently. That damned son-in-law of hers! A tuppenny-ha'penny clerk in the Council Offices and to hear Martha you'd think he was Harold Macmillan. She reassumed command.

'Drink your stout and shut up!' she said.

Martha bridled, but obeyed.

CHAPTER TWO

January passed slowly as only January can. Grey, damp days, merging into dark, damp nights. Life in Coronation Street went on. Lucille Hewitt went back to the orphanage after a short stay with her father that proved nothing. Old Albert Tatlock collapsed in his kitchen. The milkman found him and Doctor Graham diagnosed blood pressure, ordered rest. Albert refused to go and live with his daughter Beattie. 'Rest!' he said derisively, 'with *her*? I've had more rest in t'Battle o' t'Somme!'

Esther Hayes was sad that January. Even if Harry was relieved to see his daughter back in care, Esther, his next-door neighbour grieved. Grieved because, as long as Lucille was with her father and her future under debate, Harry had been only too pleased to accept Esther's immediate offer of help. Whenever Harry had been on duty of an evening she'd looked after the child. And made a hot drink when Harry had come, yawning home. And stayed to share it with him. And hoped.

She was respected was Esther. Respected for her education. People came to her for advice. Even Ena saw her as 'a sensible enough girl', although that description probably fell a few years short of the truth. For Esther was deep into spinsterhood. Which accounted for her disappointment when Lucille came to say goodbye and the evenings at number seven came to an end. But Esther was, as noted, 'a sensible enough girl' and her common sense told her that the competition was fierce, that the key to Harry's front door was not the same as the key to his heart. She discounted the new woman at the corner shop, refused to take seriously the little clippie, Eileen Hughes – forever appearing on Harry's doorstep with some insupportable excuse or other. But Concepta Riley, ever-smiling, ever-solicitous, was quite another matter. Hers was a subtle blend of vivacity and stubbornness which provoked both

Esther's contempt and envy. And which established her as firm favourite in the Harry Hewitt Matrimonial Stakes.

January saw two other events of local interest, one of which briefly and publicly illuminated the gloomy month. The other took place privately behind closed doors.

The brief illumination suffused the Rover's Return on the twenty-seventh of the month, a Friday evening.

As on most Friday nights the pub was full. In the houses which the men had left, grim-faced wives were bemoaning once again their husbands' escapes with their wage packets, and were taking it out on the kids. And in the Flying Horse and the Drover and the Vic happy landlords listened with pleasure to the music of the till and thanked God for human nature. But not Jack Walker. Blessed with most of the attributes of the good landlord, still he couldn't get away from that nagging fear that some of the money which found its way into his till could have been better spent. He had even been known to lecture a free-spending father of six on his family responsibilities so severely that he lost his custom for ever.

Business then was brisk, keeping Jack, Annie and Concepta on their toes and Jack was bent over the bitter pump, reflecting on the deteriorating state of Jimmy Gillespie, two weeks married but vastly preferring the company of his mates, when the call came from behind him. 'Give us a pint o' bitter, landlord!' Jack stayed bent to his task, and flung a reproof over his shoulder.

'Wait your sweat! What d'you think I'm doing? Knitting a pullover?'

'All right, blow you! There's plenty of pubs!'

The voice was nigglingly familiar. Jack turned and found out why. And, as he turned, the whole pub seemed to turn with him as Concepta finished her business at the till and Annie came back from a brief visit to the living quarters. Friendly pandemonium broke out. 'Hello, Billy lad!' 'Glory be, look who it is!' 'Get the drinks in, Jack!'

The uniformed figure grinned. 'Do I get that pint or not?'

Jack reached over the bar and grasped his son by his shoulders. 'What the eck are *you* doing here?'

'Marvellous! That's what they call a real hero's welcome!' Billy grinned again at the crowd. A thin cheery-faced lad, who had inherited his mother's looks but little else. Although she had never quite forgiven him for being expelled from Mrs Dudley Henderson's Private School at a very early age – 'And for fighting, Mrs Walker! *Fighting*, no less!' – she loved him dearly and her eyes were alight as she made her way to the public side of the counter. 'Here's me, back from defending the Empire single handed and that's all I get!' His mother had reached him. 'Hallo, Mum!'

'Billy! Let me look at you!' She held him at arm's length, took in with one joyous regard his tanned face, his cropped hair, his crooked grin, his baggy uniform bearing the corporal's stripes and the REME flashes. Then she hugged him again. 'Why didn't you let us know?'

'Because I didn't know myself, did I? They flew us in from Aden to some God-forsaken Southern hole that didn't have tom-toms let alone telephones! I've been on trains for about seven hours . . .' his tone turned plaintive, '. . . and I'm *dying* for a pint!'

As Jack happily took care of the order Annie turned to the crowd and addressed them with mock reproof. 'I would like you all to know that he's picked up that bad habit in the Army! He was never so desperate for drink before he left home!'

'Think yourself lucky he wasn't in the Andrew,' chipped in Len Fairclough, 'Or he'd be after a pint of rum!'

'And stop telling 'em drinking's a bad habit, Annie,' said her husband. 'You'll be putting us out of business!'

A derisive chorus and the customers turned back to their chat, their darts and their dominoes. Lost to them for two years, it had taken a minute to re-accept the wanderer into their midst. Billy Walker was back where he belonged and there was good beer to be drunk.

Two weeks earlier another wanderer had returned to the street. His visit – for he didn't stay – evoked no celebration, nor even comment, as no one but the Tanners knew of it. And they, under strict instructions from Elsie, weren't telling.

Elsie had her feet in water when the knock summoned her to the front door. Miami Modes was in the middle of its 'Record Breaking January Sale – Astounding Bargains' and the day had been hard. It had reached crescendo deep into the afternoon when, despite Elsie's advice, a very fat lady had taken six dresses into the fitting cubicle, all of them two sizes too small. When, at last, she reappeared, purple from her efforts, Elsie had lost three good commission sales and wasn't in the best of tempers. 'I was being a teeny bit ambitious!' said the fat lady, 'Perhaps I ought to lose a teeny bit of weight!'

'Yes, perhaps you ought!' snapped Elsie. 'Start your diet tomorrow and come back in a couple of years!'

As was to be expected, the fat lady reported Elsie to the Supervisor and Mrs Dumbarton went through the motions of giving Elsie a public ticking off. During which time Dot Greenhalgh pinched another customer. Then after the fat lady had departed, Elsie went through the motions of telling Mrs Dumbarton what she could do with her job and Mrs D told Elsie not to be daft and Elsie's feet started to throb. Work finished, she waited twenty minutes for a bus, stood all the way home mentally deciding who was going to make her evening meal for her and arrived at number thirteen to find a note from Linda to say that she and Ivan had gone off to first-house pictures. Dennis, as per usual, was nowhere to be found. Laboriously she made herself a corned beef sandwich, brewed a pot of tea and then, the makeshift meal finished, she filled a bowl with hot water, made free with the Radox, unhooked her suspenders, slipped off her stockings and, straddling the bowl with her aching feet, eased herself gently into the easy chair. Slowly, with infinite care, she lowered her feet into the soothing pool. Then, her eyes half-closed with ecstasy, she lit a cigarette and leaned back.

Ten seconds later came the knock.

As soon as she saw him, she opened the door wide and said, urgently, 'Come in!'

For a moment he thought she was pleased to see him but it soon became clear that she was only concerned that nobody else saw him. He stepped into the lobby.

'What the devil do you think *you're* doing here?'

'I've come to see you, haven't I?'

'I can see that!' She led him into the back room, picked up the bowl of water and took it through into the kitchen. When she came back she was wearing a comfortable pair of slippers. He was still standing.

'Well, go on, what do you want?' she asked.

He tried a laugh but it didn't really work. 'A fellow's entitled to come and see his own wife surely!'

She looked at him gravely. If there was a hint of disappointment in her eyes it was aimed at herself for marrying him. He was in his middle fifties and already well run to seed. The flesh around his chin hung loosely, a greying toothbrush moustache sprouted on his top lip, his greasy hair was carefully combed to cover as large an area of bare scalp as possible. His eyes were watery and his tongue snaked nervously around his lips. It could only have been the uniform, she thought. As far as her memory served her he had looked much the same in those early months of the War but the fattening body was trimmer then and he had been wearing not a crumpled, dandruff-spattered tweed suit but a smart Merchant Navy uniform. And that sexy peaked cap had covered the thinning hair. And she had been sixteen years old.

'Aren't I entitled?' He tried another smile.

'What?' She shook herself back into the present.

'Surely a fellow's entitled to come and see his own wife!'

'If he comes every day, he is. Or come to that every week. But I wouldn't say there was much entitlement when he doesn't even bother to come every year!' She sat, leaving him standing. 'You know 'em round here well enough. You know how their tongues'll clack if they clap eyes on you. God forbid, they might even think I was taking you back!'

'Now, Elsie!' The sea-lawyer took command. 'It was

you who chucked me out. It wasn't me as deserted you!'

She smiled sweetly. 'Just try and prove that!'

'Look, there's no point starting off on the wrong foot, is there?' he asked.

'What d'you mean starting off! We've never been on owt else! And stop beating about the bush. What do you want?'

He decided to invite her into the game. 'What do you think?'

'What do *I* think? I think you want shooting!'

'No, seriously!'

'Yes, I think you want shooting seriously!' She let him sweat for a few seconds. 'Don't tell me you've found another sucker! That *is* what you're round here for, isn't it? A divorce?'

'Yes.' It was a sad whisper, marking the end of a historic romance.

Elsie brought him back to earth. 'Don't sound like that about it! God knows, it's not before time!' She smiled at him. He stayed serious, clinging to a shred of dignity he'd uncovered somewhere. 'What's she like?'

'I don't see that's got anything to do with it.'

'Suit yourself,' said Elsie, matter-of-factly. 'End of conversation. Let yourself out and I'll get my feet back in that bowl of water!'

'Now, Elsie!'

'If you've come to talk, we'll talk. And you can start by telling me about Lady Muck. I'd like to know if she's owt like me. She must be daft to start with!'

'She's nothing like you. She's er . . .' He decided a touch of diplomacy wouldn't come amiss, 'She's older than you.'

'I'll bet!' said Elsie drily.

'As God's my witness.' He delivered the phrase with conviction even though God had been his witness to many a monumental lie in the past. 'Couple of years at least. And she's . . . well, on the plain side. But . . .'

Elsie decided to help. 'But she's homely, and kind. And she looks after you. A sort of companion for your old age.' She'd played it well. He was nodding solemnly. 'Get her out of a cracker, did you? Last Christmas?'

Arnold Tanner's eyes closed in pain. How could his motives be so totally misinterpreted? Elsie helped him find the answer.

'Come on, Arnold, love! I'm the one who found you out – remember? So don't give me that "marrying for love" bit! ' A brief smiling pause, then . . . 'Got plenty of money, has she? Is that it?'

'No, of course she hasn't! ' Arnold made it a strong denial.

'Goes out to work then?'

'Well, not as you might say work. She er . . . she's got a little shop.'

'Oh, I see! ' Enlightenment filled Elsie's voice. 'She's got a little shop! Jeweller's, is it?'

'Jeweller's be blowed! It's a little toffee shop.'

'Not to worry. That *will* be a companion for your old age, won't it?'

She had always emerged victorious from these battles. In the past it hadn't mattered. He had packed his gear and gone off to join his ship and within a few weeks he was forgetting Elsie amidst the fleshpots of Singapore or Sydney or San Francisco. But this time was different. This time he had a mission to perform.

Elsie read his thoughts with unerring accuracy. 'Whose idea was this? Hers? Madam Toffee Shop's?'

'No, it was mine.' He answered with a rare touch of chivalry. 'Like you said, it hasn't worked, you and me. It's time we got things sorted out, chuck.'

'I see! ' Elsie's tone was dangerously co-operative. 'It's time we got things sorted out! I'd say it was long past time – *chuck!*' She made an insult out of the endearment. 'What about last year and the year before and all those other years I spent bringing a family up with not a penny from you! Just count yourself lucky I didn't get the police on you, feller-me-lad! And I would have done if I hadn't been too busy shouldering *your* responsibilities! So don't come to me saying it's time we got things sorted out! There's only one reason why you're here today and that's because you want to get your sticky hands on your lady friend's liquorice allsorts! '

Arnold decided to recognize Elsie's talents as a comedienne and smiled appreciatively. 'Elsie! You don't mean that!'

'Don't I? Get out and think about it! I'll show you whether I mean it or not!' Arnold's smile faded. He licked his lips nervously, shattered by the suddenness of defeat. 'Go on, get out! You're getting no divorce from me!'

She glared at him. The front door opened and closed. It was Linda and Ivan, at it again. Linda's petulant tones filtered into the back room. 'Will you be told! I'm not queuing for anybody!'

The lobby door opened. Linda bit back her next vituperative comment at the sight of Arnold. Elsie smiled wickedly.

'Hello, Linda, love, I've got a nice surprise for you! Meet your father!'

Linda picked up Elsie's cue and joined in the charade. 'Oh, hello, Father. How nice to meet you after all these years. I've heard so much about you!'

Arnold looked from his wife to his daughter and back again. He knew he was no match for them verbally and, even if the nervously-hovering Ivan stayed neutral, they would probably have made physical mincemeat of him, had he opted for violence. He glared, snorted, pushed past Ivan and left. The door banged after him.

'You missed nowt,' smiled Elsie. 'Much better than the pictures, that!'

Arnold had come on a Friday night. The following day would normally have seen Elsie hard at work in the Slightly Better Dress Department of Miami Modes. But this Saturday marked Elsie's quarterly visit to the dentist which was why, at ten o'clock in the morning, she was still in her dressing-gown and slippers, slumped in the armchair, a lukewarm cup of tea at her side, her specs on the end of her nose, reading Tit-Bits. She had told Mrs Dumbarton her appointment was for ten o'clock and, as she would probably need fillings, there was little likelihood of her being fit for work that day. Mrs Dumbarton had accepted

31

the news philosophically, sale or no sale. The four-times-a-year visits to the dentists were a recognized perk of the establishment and might as well, in the interest of peace and quiet, remain so. Although Elsie would have been prepared to forego this particular day off. She had had a fairly disastrous week as far as business went and Saturday could have provided rich pickings in commission. Protocol, however, demanded that the 'dental appointment' remained unaltered. The management of Miami Modes weren't averse, if it suited their book, to asking that an appointment be postponed but the staff had long ago agreed amongst themselves that such requests be resisted on the grounds that dental dates could not, under any circumstances, be changed. So Elsie found herself the biter, bit. Oh well, she thought, staring unseeingly at the open pages of her magazine, money wasn't everything. No, her thoughts added, but what it wasn't it could buy. She shrugged mentally and returned her attentions to the Bluebeard of Selly Oak and his Sixteen Beautiful Brides.

Dennis was clumping about upstairs when, an hour later, the knock sounded on the front door. Linda and Ivan had gone off to the market so Elsie, comfortably settled in the armchair, raised her eyes and her voice to the ceiling.

'Dennis!!' No answer. 'Dennis!! Door!!' Still no answer. Grimly she prised herself up and lurched to the lobby door. She shouted upstairs. 'Dennis, are you deaf or summat! Answer that door!'

'I can't!' Dennis's inability to move could have been because he was handcuffed to the bedrail; on the other hand, he could have been combing his hair and feeling too damned idle. Either way, Elsie knew from long, bitter experience the uselessness of pursuing the point. She answered the door herself.

A woman stood outside. A woman with smiling lips and faintly anxious eyes.

'Mrs Tanner?' she asked.

'Yes,' replied Elsie, guardedly.

'Could I have a word?'

'Er . . . yes,' said Elsie, cool, unmoving.

'It *is* rather private,' said the woman.

Elsie cottoned on. 'You'd better come in then.' The woman followed Elsie into the house. During the five or six seconds it took them to reach the back room, Elsie knew the woman had taken in everything in the lobby: the peeling paintwork, the balding lino, the flaking ceiling. She could have written a two-page description of that lobby, correct in every detail. She was that sort of woman.

Elsie closed the door and looked at her visitor. Mid-forties, too much make-up and badly put on at that. So this, she thought, was Arnold's fancy woman She looked a hard bitch with her gold-plated curls and her nylon mink musquash.

'Perhaps I ought to introduce myself,' said the woman 'I'm Norah Dawson.'

Let her work for her living, thought Elsie 'Oh, yes?' she said.

'I'm er . . . I'm Mr Tanner's friend! '

'Oh, *that* one! ' said Elsie, with cheerful emphasis.

'Yes.'

They'd only met two minutes previously and already it was near-checkmate. Your move, thought Elsie.

'I er . . . I believe he came to see you?' said Norah.

'Is that what he said?' asked Elsie blandly

'Er . . . yes.'

'Then you *know* he came to see me, don't you?' declared Elsie with a pleasant smile.

The woman's jaw set. Arnold had warned her that it wouldn't be easy.

'Look, Elsie, let's put our cards on the table! You've got him by law, I've got him every other way.'

'Sounds interesting! ' said Elsie, thoroughly enjoying herself.

'And don't pretend you want him back! You chucked him out years since so you may as well do the job properly! '

'Lovey, I wouldn't dream of pretending I wanted him back,' laughed Elsie. 'I'd rather have the whooping cough!

33

But let's get something straight. I don't know what story he told you but I did *not* chuck him out. He left. I won't tell you how he did it – you'll probably find out soon enough yourself!'

'He tells it different.'

'Chuck, he tells everything different! His age, his bank balance, even his name at times. But what am I saying! If you met him more than a week since you'll know, won't you!'

Norah sniffed damply. 'I don't expect you to understand but I . . . I happen to love him.'

'Lovey, I might be a hard nut to crack but you don't have to go to those lengths! All right, what do you want! You want me to give him grounds for divorce?'

'Well . . . yes,' said Norah.

'And you can go on wanting! What's your second choice? *He* gives *me* grounds?'

Norah stiffened. 'Like what, for instance?'

'Now don't get me wrong, love,' said Elsie piously, 'I wouldn't dream of suggesting you've done anything but hold hands. I wasn't thinking of anything like that! More er . . . desertion! Let's start with desertion.'

'You'll get no money out of him,' said Norah flatly.

'I never did, chuck!' replied Elsie. 'But then, when I was giving birth to his kids, he didn't have all them jars of boiled sweets!'

'Those boiled sweets are mine!' spat Norah.

'I could have you for enticement,' said Elsie.

'Try it!'

Elsie smiled. Ena Sharples apart, there weren't any worthy opponents in the neighbourhood. At least this one had a bit of spirit. Norah looked at her suspiciously from under lowered lids as Elsie continued to smile at her thoughts. She enjoyed a good fight but this one was beginning to pall. Arnold Tanner wasn't worth the full fifteen rounds.

'Tell you what,' said Elsie, 'I'll let you keep your adultery to yourselves! Tell Lover Boy that if he'll let me divorce him on grounds of desertion I won't want any money from him. How does that sound?'

'How do I know you won't change your mind when you get into court?'

'You don't, love. You just have to trust me. Which shouldn't be difficult if you're trusting Arnold enough to marry him!'

Norah thought for a moment. 'I'll tell him what you said.'

'You do that!'

Norah hesitated. Elsie smiled a winner's smile. True, she'd lost a husband but when you considered that that husband was Arnold Tanner, the loss could only be counted as a resounding victory.

'Well, then!' said Madam Toffee Shop, nodded and left.

The banging of the front door brought Dennis downstairs. His hair was freshly Brylcreemed and moulded into deep waves on top of his head. He smelt of very cheap Cologne.

'Who was that?' he asked.

'Just a rag and bone woman,' said Elsie.

'Oh!' said Dennis, not really interested.

'I gave her a bit of my old rubbish,' added Elsie. 'She seemed satisfied enough, God help her!'

CHAPTER THREE

Leonard Swindley was a fussy man. Neat, meticulous, Pickwickian in build, gravely precise by nature, he was thought by many to border on the pompous. Ena Sharples, as she was wont to do, went much further. She had described him, in the heat of one of their many battles, as 'a puffed-up little fish in a dirty little pond!'

Mr Swindley's fussiness started very early in the day. He lived in an aging Accrington-brick semi ten minutes' brisk walk from his Rosamund Street shop and his other sphere of operations, the Glad Tidings Mission opposite Florrie Lindley's shop on Coronation Street. The house had been left to him by his parents in good repair but three bad years in the drapery trade had played havoc with his plans for re-decoration and as he opened his eyes that Wednesday morning of February the first, 1961, flakes of browning paint, loosened by his week-day alarm, the 7.10 to Glasgow, fluttered down on to his puce candlewick bedspread. But precision did not fail him, even at that early hour. Instantly recalling the date, he stared defiantly at the ceiling and uttered the words 'White rabbits!' Tribal mumbo-jumbo of the Swindley clan had long insisted that these words should be the first to be spoken on the first day of each month. If not, the wrath of the gods would surely descend upon the transgressor. Or, in Mr Swindley's case, the wrath of Ena Sharples.

He smiled wryly in his bed, doubting if such powerful ju-jus were powerful enough. Although, he reflected optimistically, the last few days had been reasonably trouble-free. Their last clash had taken place at Christmas when, conveying messages of goodwill in his capacity as Secretary to the Committee of the Glad Tidings Mission, he had found his own resident-caretaker partaking of alcoholic drink in the snug at the Rover's Return. Naturally he had warned her that such action could not be tolerated and, again naturally, she had told him to mind his own flaming business.

His decision to dismiss her was postponed when she collapsed in front of him in the vestry the following day – an action which still gave him room for doubt. Particularly as she had seen fit to discharge herself from hospital and resume her duties. Making sure he realized that any disciplinary action would now be regarded as victimization of an old, faithful, ailing lady.

As the water bubbled around his poaching egg, he planned his day. Early closing meant that money-making was restricted to three and a half hours but no doubt he would carry on for an hour or two behind closed doors. There was stock-taking to be started and some remnants of his January Sale still required to be packed away. And then, say at four o'clock, he mused, he might walk up the street for a cup of tea with Emily in the stockroom at the back of her baby-linen shop.

Miss Nugent – she was only Emily in his private thoughts – was his clerk, secretary, amanuensis, Sancho Panza to his Don Quixote. Together they carried out the will of the Committee; together they had transformed the Glad Tidings Mission from a simple non-denominational chapel into the hub of the area's social life. They had encountered plenty of opposition in their onward march; from other churches, public houses, bingo halls, not least from their own resident-caretaker.

To Mrs Sharples any hint of a Mothers' Reading Circle or a cookery demonstration or a table tennis tournament was the first step in a deep-laid plan aimed at her personal well-being. Every inch in the Pilgrim's Progress of Mr Swindley and Miss Nugent was hard won. Every battle hardened Ena's resolve to die fighting. And that evening Leonard and Emily had been detailed to put to Mrs Sharples the decision that Mr Tatlock's repeated requests for an Over Sixties' Club were, at last, to be implemented.

As he chewed on his egg and slightly burnt toast, he knew what her reaction would be. After months of conflict over the use of the hall by the local Cub Troop she would no doubt use all the same arguments against the over-sixties as she had used against the under-tens. Probably, even, the same adjectives. Thoughtless, noisy, dirty and demanding. Old or young, they were equally enemies and must be repulsed with the same weapons. He sighed and a little dribble of egg ran down his chin.

Two hours later he was behind the polished mahogany counter of his haberdashery, neat as a new pin in his black jacket and striped trousers, his wing collar with its neatly-knotted tie speared by the minutely pearled pin left to him by his Uncle Cedric. Business was scarcely brisk. He had been standing, day-dreaming, for almost half an hour when the shop bell tinkled for the first time. The lady who came in was faintly familiar. She wore a blue nylon overall and a flushed smile. She was also slightly out of breath.

'Morning!' she said.

'Good morning, madam! Can I be of service?'

'I'd like a tie, please. Something . . . quiet. A stripe perhaps.'

'Certainly!' He indicated a rack behind her and, as she turned, joined her from behind the counter. He lifted a discreetly striped specimen and displayed it against his palm. 'A pleasing design! One of our more expensive lines. Twelve and sixpence. Pure Macclesfield Silk, of course!'

'I'll take that one.' She began to fish in her purse.

'Really?' He found himself faintly disgusted at the speed of the sale. The lady was scarcely putting his powers of salesmanship to the test. He lifted another tie. 'Not this one, perhaps? With a delicate shade of mauve?'

'No, I'll take that one. I'm sorry to be in such a rush but I've got a shop to look after myself!'

'Oh, I see!' He was a just man and forgave her instantly. 'May I enquire the er . . . the nature of your business?'

'The corner shop. At the bottom of Coronation Street. Just round the corner.'

'Oh, indeed! Mrs Lappin's old establishment! You'll be Mrs er . . .'

'Lindley.'

'Mrs Lindley, of course! Allow me to introduce myself. Leonard Swindley.' He offered his hand. She took it tentatively. 'Swindley, Lindley! It could be said that between us we constituted a rhyming couplet!'

Florrie wasn't blessed with the most highly developed sense of humour but he was smiling so she smiled too.

'But I digress,' he added. 'You, too, have the pressures of commerce bearing heavily upon you!' He found an appropriate paper bag and neatly folded the tie.

'I'm sure Mr Lindley will be delighted by your taste,' he said.

'Pardon?'

'Mr Lindley. Your husband. Delighted. By your choice of tie.'

'Oh! It . . . it's not for my husband! It's for a friend. I'm . . . I'm a widow.'

His expression flickered from the slightly shocked to the deeply concerned at this declaration of status. 'Oh, forgive me! May I hope that your friend will be equally delighted?'

She hoped he would too. If she ever screwed up her courage sufficiently to give it to him. Still, she had eight days yet. She was sure about the date because she noted it down the moment Lucille left the shop. The little girl had come in for a farewell ounce of tobacco for her father and Florrie had carefully manoeuvred the conversation from presents to birthdays. But, she thought, you can be too clever. This Swindley chap seems decent enough but you never know, he just might spread it round the neighbourhood. It doesn't pay to tell folk too much.

'Oh, I'm sure he will.' And left it at that.

He took the offered pound note and counted her change. As he handed it to her he treated her to a warm smile and said, 'You may have noticed, Mrs Lindley, that from the front window of your er . . . emporium . . .' She guessed he meant her shop. '. . . you can see a small part of my er . . . "realm". The Glad Tidings Mission. Perhaps you weren't aware that I was the secretary.' Her eyes widened with polite acceptance of the news. 'And I would like to say that, if ever you feel the need for companionship, it awaits you some dozen steps from your own front door. Please don't hesitate to visit us. Whatever your creed!'

'Oh! Thank you!' She smiled at him. He beamed back. Between them they formed a tableau which could have endured until eternity but, with a tremendous effort of will, she broke the spell, nodded Good Morning and left.

Later that afternoon he described her to Miss Nugent as 'a pleasant lady but, I suspect, buffeted by the vagaries of life'. They were sitting amongst the matinée coats and bootees which made up Miss Nugent's life and stock-in-trade, drinking tea and eating ginger snaps. Her business was as far from brisk as his and they had chatted, uninterrupted for twenty minutes. Then, just as he rose to go, the shop bell sounded. He followed Emily through the green canvas curtains to find himself facing Elsie Tanner.

'Don't worry!' said Elsie. 'I won't say a word!'

Emily flushed dark red but Mr Swindley smiled indulgently. If there was one thing he prided himself on it was his sophistication. 'There are more things to do in dark corners than hold hands, Mrs Tanner.' Elsie would have agreed with him but he was in full flow. 'One can muse over the weaknesses of mankind. Wonder why, for instance, certain young gentlemen can find nothing better to do than throw stones through Mission windows and then refuse pointblank to pay for the damage.'

This was an old score. It was three months since a dreamy Dennis, in fact walking down Coronation Street, in imagination sampling the delights of Las Vegas as Billy Fury's manager, had picked up a stone and, for no fathomable reason, lobbed it through Ena's front window. He had then stood transfixed, slowly making the return journey from Las Vegas, as a crowd gathered. Luckily Ena had not been at home. When, haltingly, he told Elsie she, to use her own words, 'clouted him round the earhole'. He didn't know what got into him, he said. He wasn't exactly throwing a stone, he was nonchalantly tossing a thousand dollar chip on to the winning number of the roulette table. At which, once again, she 'clouted him round the earhole'.

She re-used the words. 'I clouted him round the earhole!' she said.

'I'm sure you did, Mrs Tanner!' agreed Mr Swindley, 'But unfortunately, clouts round the er . . . earhole don't reglaze windows!'

'Well, if you can get any money out of him, good luck to you!' said Elsie helpfully. '*I* never can!'

Mr Swindley gave up the struggle. He turned to Emily. 'Thank you for the tea and biscuits. Delightful!'

Miss Nugent smiled back. 'Oh, my pleasure! Seven o'clock at the Mission then?'

'Seven o'clock at the Mission,' he confirmed. Then, bowing politely to Elsie, he made his exit, pausing in the doorway to adjust his black Homburg.

'I want one of them little coatees,' said Elsie.

Emily tore her eyes from the vanishing figure of Leonard Swindley. 'Oh, yes!' she said. 'Pink or blue? A girl or a boy?'

'Girl,' said Elsie without hesitation.

'How old?' asked Miss Nugent.

'Oh, about . . .' she did a rapid mental calculation, '. . . about minus six months!'

'Pardon?'

'It hasn't been born yet!'

'But how,' asked Miss Nugent, 'do you know it's a girl?'

'Don't worry!' smiled Elsie. 'I *know*!'

But there were certain things that Elsie didn't know. She wasn't aware for instance that not a hundred yards from where she stood, her evening was being planned. Turn left out of Emily's shop then first left again and you're in Coronation Street. But turn *right* and first *right* again and you're in Mawdsley Street where two gentlemen from the Gas Board were staring into a hole. Nothing unusual in that, you might think. One of the men was artisan, overalled and brawny; the other white collar, dressed in a crumpled mid-grey suit, and obviously lower management. The latter, whose name was Merriman although you wouldn't have guessed it from the expression on his face, spoke.

'You're sure?'

'You can smell, can't you?' asked the foreman.

'Yes,' said Mr Merriman and, to prove it, sniffed. He obviously found the experience distasteful.

'I remember one like this in Ashton,' said the foreman. 'Went up and took fourteen houses with it. Didn't smell as bad as this,' he added phlegmatically.

'I'd better get on to the police,' said Merriman anxiously.

'I reckon you'd better,' said the foreman.

But in the event it wasn't as easy as that. Merriman first telephoned his regional headquarters who telephoned the Group Headquarters and an hour later two more gentlemen arrived in a Hillman Minx. They too looked into the hole, made certain tests, and consulted the local police.

As a result of their consultations Police Sergeant Sowerbutts was despatched to the area with specific instructions. He also took with him two young constables, a selection of barriers and some Police warning signs. Being an old hand, on arrival in Coronation Street he sent the constables to knock on doors whilst he looked after the Rover's Return.

Inside the pub talk had already swung towards the reason (although no one knew of it at that time) for the Sergeant's impending visit.

'Ee, it smelled foul!' Martha was saying. 'Heaven knows we get our fair share o' smells round here but I've never known owt like that. Mind you,' she added knowingly, 'I can't say I'm surprised! They're forever digging that street up. I reckon I'd drop cork-legged if I ever came out of our house and they hadn't got the cobbles up!'

'It'll be a practice hole,' said Len Fairclough, keeping a straight face. 'They're not digging for owt. They just train their new lads on it!'

Martha wasn't taken in. 'Kid all you like! I wouldn't put it past 'em!'

And at that moment in walked Sergeant Sowerbutts.

'Oh, dear, *now* what!' said Annie testily.

'Nothing like that, Mrs Walker!' smiled the sergeant. 'Just a little emergency. There's a gas leak in Mawdsley Street. They're a bit frightened of it.'

'Told you!' cried Martha triumphantly.

'So if you wouldn't mind, lads and lasses! It's against my better nature to clear pubs but it's in your own interests! Just drink your drinks, leave quietly and find yourselves another beerhouse!' He raised his voice as the chatter started. 'Now, hang on, I haven't finished yet! It could take a while to get this lot sorted out so if you live in Mawdsley Street, Coronation Street or this bit of Rosamund Street between the two, go home, pick up a couple o' blankets and a pillow, nothing else, and take yourself down to the Glad Tidings Mission at the other end of the street. That'll be your evacuation centre for the night.'

'Where did you say?' Ena asked, with dread emphasis.

'I know it's not all that much farther away, Mrs Sharples, but the experts have worked it out. It's only the backs of these houses that might get it. That Mission of yours is quite safe.'

'And it'll stay safe!' said Ena, ominously. 'I'm having none o' this lot tramping their muck in my Mission!'

'Correction, Mrs Sharples! It's not your Mission! I've been on to the Secretary and he knows what's going on! In fact he's on his way over.' Ena lifted a finger to him but he brushed it verbally aside. 'Say what you like, Mrs Sharples, it's happening! And if you've got any sense you'll get over there before you get your hairnet blown off!'

Ena's mouth set like a rat-trap. 'I'll have you!' she snapped.

'Suit yourself, love,' said the sergeant imperturbably and turned to find Minnie Caldwell at his elbow.

'Excuse me,' said Minnie, 'I live in Jubilee Terrace. Will I be all right?'

'Oh aye, right as rain, love,' said the sergeant.

'And can I take my friend? She lives in Mawdsley Street.'

'You make your own personal arrangements, love. As long as you do it fast!' The sergeant turned his attention to the general scene. 'Come on, now, ladies and gentlemen, let's get you moving!'

As the customers began to trickle out Minnie turned to the fuming Ena.

'Would you like to come with me as well, Ena?' she asked.

'What, and let that lot do what they like in my Mission? Not likely!' She scowled viciously at Sergeant Sowerbutts. 'I just hope the police'll be as fast to clean the place up as they are to fill it full of rubbish!' And with a parting glare she swept out.

'As soon as you're ready,' said the sergeant to Jack and Annie and with a final look around the public rooms left to see how his constables were making out.

'I suppose you realize this is costing us money?' said Annie. 'And there'll be no compensation from the Gas Board!'

'It had crossed my mind,' said Jack.

As usual, pandemonium reigned at the Tanners. Elsie was frantically searching the sideboard drawers when Linda came downstairs, ready for the night's exile.

'For Heaven's sake, Mam, hurry up!'

Elsie took no notice. 'It must be somewhere!' she said, irritably. 'By eck, they're right! They say things happen in threes. First you descend on me, then it's Arnold and Madam Toffee Shop and now I can't find my flaming lipstick!'

'Oh, come on! You can borrow one of mine!'

'You know very well, yours are too orangey for me!' She slammed one drawer shut, opened another.

'What do you want lipstick for anyway?'

Elsie was outraged. 'You don't think I'm going to let that lot see me first thing in the morning without my face on, do you!'

Linda stood tapping her foot as Ivan popped his head round the door. 'I've brought enough blankets for Dennis,' he said.

'Goodness knows when he'll be home!' Elsie was rummaging through her handbag now, the drawers exhausted. A cry of triumph. 'Here it is! Look at that! A flaming hole in my lining!'

Linda's patience gave out. 'Will you come on!!'

'Stop mithering, will you?' said Elsie. 'I've got to see to the house, haven't I? Like as not half the fire brigade'll be tramping in and out of here all night!' Suddenly she was back at the sideboard. 'Where's my wedding photograph?'

'What do you want *that* for?'

Elsie regarded her daughter with cold dignity. 'Even *I* have memories!'

In the living room of the Rover's Return, Mrs Walker was surreptitiously sliding *her* memories into her coat pocket. They took the shape of a bundle of letters, neatly tied with pink tape. She took a last look round the room and walked into the bar. Jack stood waiting for her. Under his arm were his blankets, on the counter a shiny brown leather cylinder. Annie regarded it balefully.

'I might have known you'd bring your bowling bag,' she said.

'Aye, well, you can't buy woods like them nowadays!' Jack patted the shiny cylinder affectionately.

'And that's all you can think of at a time like this! Bowls! And within an hour this place might be a heap of rubble!'

'Oh, get away with you!' said Jack.

'I suppose I should be thankful I'm not bedridden.'

'What on earth are you talking about now?'

'You know very well what I'm talking about! If you had to make a straight choice between me and that bowling bag, which would you take?'

Jack sighed. 'Now, Annie!'

'I said which would you take? I'm waiting for an answer!

'Annie!!'

Annie smiled bitterly. 'I see! You prefer not to say. Well, I suppose that's better than telling a downright lie!'

Jack's discretion soured into exasperation. 'Oh, give over, Annie, you know very well which I'd take.'

'Do I?' asked Annie fiercely. '*Do I?* Well, *tell* me then!

Don't just stand there! Tell me!'

She was asking, thought Jack. Right, I'll tell her! 'All right! If I thought you were going to carry on like this for the rest of my life, I'd take my flipping bowling bag!'

There was a momentary pause while Annie adjusted her martyred look. 'So it's out in the open at last!' she whispered.

'Now, Annie, you know very well . . .'

Annie cut in. 'Oh, I *do*! I do indeed! There's many a true word spoken in jest and you never said a truer word in the whole of your life!' Jack watched her, open-mouthed, as she played out a sad pause. 'Alright, now we know where we stand,' she went on. 'I'm just thankful the children don't realize what's wrong!'

Jack's cry came from the soul. 'I don't even realize it myself! !'

Billy stood in the hall doorway, grinning at them. He had long refused to take their arguments seriously and history had proved him right. 'This a private fight or can anybody join in?'

Annie composed herself. 'Oh, you're ready, are you? Where's Concepta?'

Concepta answered the question by arriving on the scene. She was carrying a small portable radio.

'What's that you're taking?' asked Annie.

'It's my portable radio. Wherever *I* go *this* goes!'

Annie shook her head doubtfully. 'Oh, I wouldn't take it *there*, love!'

'And why not?' asked Concepta.

'Why not!' said Jack. 'Ena'll go up the wall!'

On hearing Jack establish himself as an ally, Annie immediately changed sides. She glared coldly at her husband. 'Let her!' she said, then, turning to Concepta. 'By all means bring it with you, dear! If necessary I'll be only too happy to face Mrs Sharples for you!' And with that further declaration of war she stalked out. Concepta pulled a face at Jack and followed.

'What's up with Mum?' asked Billy.

'Ee, *I* don't know!'

'Make you sick, women, don't they?'

'Make you sick?? They drive you round the bend! And if you'll take my advice . . .' He suddenly realized he was talking to his son. 'Come on! And don't talk like that about your mother!'

The young policemen, under the watchful eye of Sergeant Sowerbutts, were cordoning off the street when Len arrived from Mawdsley Street. The sergeant smilingly nodded as the stocky, red-haired plumber knocked at Harry Hewitt's door. 'Going on your holidays by yourself then, are you?'

Len smiled back. 'Aye, my wife's taken the kid over to her mother's. I'll have to see what I can pick up over there!'

Harry answered the door. 'Oh, you're ready then?'

'Ready as I'll ever be!'

'Where's Nellie?'

'By eck, you must have had a few!' said Len. 'I told you! She's taken Stanley over to her mother's.'

'Oh aye!' said Harry, remembering.

'So we might as well enjoy usselves! And seeing that place over there . . .' He jerked a thumb at the Mission. '. . . isn't licensed I reckon we'd better catch Jack before he locks up!'

'I'm with you!' grinned Harry and shut the door behind him.

One of the policemen, a fair-haired lad in his early twenties, held up a warning hand as they walked towards the Rover's Return. 'Sorry, gentlemen! Over to the Mission, please!'

'We won't be a tick, laddie,' said Len. 'Just picking our mates up at the pub.'

'Sorry,' the young constable persisted, 'I've had my orders.'

Len turned and shouted to Sergeant Sowerbutts. 'Eh, Sarge! We're just calling at the Rover. Tell this bloodhound of yours it's a matter of life and death!'

A dedicated beer drinker himself, the sergeant summed up the situation in a flash. 'All right, but get a move on!'

He summoned the two constables as Len and Harry hurried down to the pub. 'You take Mawdsley Street,' he said to the fair-haired PC. 'Knock on every door and make sure they're all out. Then stay round there till you're relieved. And go where the Gas Board lads tell you. We don't want you getting blown up! Them uniforms cost money!' He turned to the other young policeman. 'You start at this shop here and work your way down to the pub. And no looting!'

The decision to evacuate had been taken at seven o'clock in the evening and one would have thought that most of the people involved would have brought their blankets to the Mission and then gone off to enjoy themselves in some safe part of town. But such is the effect of any official pronouncement that no one thought of this. Or, if they did, no one acted upon the thought. They had been directed to the Mission and to the Mission they went – and stayed.

Leonard Swindley, very much the man of the hour, was at the door to receive each family as it arrived. First came Annie and Concepta, Annie immediately checking the hall for draughts and choosing the warmest corner. Then the Barlows arrived laden with bedding and, as befitted a well-mothered group, food. Tagging closely behind, obviously anxious to get as near as he could to the source of the luncheon meat sandwiches, came Albert Tatlock and, hard on his heels, Esther Hayes.

'What have you brought?' asked Albert as Esther neatly made her makeshift bed on the polished wood floor.

'Brought? How do you mean, brought?'

'Ee, you might as well save summat from t'wreckage. I've got my coin collection.'

'Oh, Albert, don't be so pessimistic!' said Esther. 'We'll be back home in a few hours.'

'Oh, aye, and how can you be so sure of that? If there hadn't been any risk they wouldn't have had us over here in the first place, would they?'

His logic was irrefutable. David Barlow grinned across him at Esther.

'He's right, Esther! I brought my football boots. I'm surprised you didn't bring yours!'

Esther smiled. 'It is rather like Desert Island Discs, isn't it? I'm afraid my one luxury's nothing more exciting than Agatha Christie!'

'Don't let *her* hear you say that,' said David. He turned and nodded towards the door, 'No prizes for guessing what their luxury is!'

Len Fairclough and Harry Hewitt were at the door, trying vainly to shake the welcoming hand of Mr Swindley whilst carrying between them a heavy box-shaped object swathed in a blanket. The reception over they moved to the far end of the hall and settled themselves against the stage.

Frank Barlow gestured towards the blanketed box. 'What have you got there then? The family jewels?'

'Aye, you might say that!' answered Len. 'Play your cards right and we'll cut you in!' He lifted the blanket and discreetly disclosed a crate of pale ale. 'But not a word to Bessie,' he added, cocking an eye towards the unsuspecting Swindley, 'or he'll have us excommunicated!'

By now the hall was beginning to fill. The families from Mawdsley Street, the last to be alerted, spread themselves around the remaining space, shepherded into position by the ever-willing Miss Nugent. Mr Swindley smiled benignly on all and sundry and was enjoying his new-found power when the normally tactful Emily brought him, rather rudely, to earth.

'Have you had a word with Mrs Sharples about the Over Sixties Club, Mr Swindley?'

'Oh dear!' He hadn't.

'Oh, I'm sorry, Mr Swindley! I didn't want to worry you unduly. Not at a time like this!'

'No, no, you were quite right to alert me, Miss Nugent. There are times when responsibilities tend to pile on one's already bent shoulders. One can only gird one's loins – if you'll pardon the expression – and apply oneself to the separate tasks ahead. Perhaps you would be good enough

49

to make an urnful of tea whilst I apply myself to Mrs Sharples.'

'Yes, of course!' Sadly, she watched him climb on to the stage and knock on the vestry door.

Ena's first words were scarcely encouraging. 'I wonder you have the brass face to come knocking on my door, Leonard Swindley! Man of the Lord?? If *you* served an apprenticeship it was to Old Nick!'

'Now, Mrs Sharples, we mustn't be like that!'

'I don't know who "we" is, but *I'm* being like that! That scruffy lot tramping all over my clean floors! And for what?'

'Now, you know very well, Mrs Sharples. It was a question of need. Permission was sought from me and permission was granted.'

'Well, permission can be ungranted! Shovel 'em off to St Mary's! They don't belong here!'

'They're God's creatures, Mrs Sharples!'

'Well, I'm blowed if He sees much of 'em!' Ena played her trump card. 'Answer me this, Leonard Swindley. How many of 'em can say this is their place of worship? Go on, how many?'

Swindley lifted a restraining hand. 'That is hardly the point.'

'Of course it's the point!'

'Mrs Sharples, you force me to say this! The fact that we don't number *you* amongst our congregation doesn't stop you living here in this vestry!'

Ena bounced back. 'That's right! Twist it round to suit yourself! It doesn't matter to you if a poor old woman has to get down on her hands and knees and scrub after 'em, does it? And her just out of hospital herself *and* just back from the bedside of a sick friend!'

Swindley found himself, as he invariably did, weakening under Ena's sustained onslaught. Both he and Ena knew that he couldn't clear the refugees out of the Mission but they were both equally aware that, under special circumstances, he could authorize Ena to take on extra cleaning help. Not that the Committee liked it. On each of the few occasions they had been presented with the bill for extra

50

help, comment had been made on the fact that four hands were not only more expensive but apparently much slower than two. And when Mr Swindley explained that it was not in Mrs Sharples' nature to keep a dog and bark herself and that she gleefully grasped the opportunity to supervise in a way no reputable Trade Union had tolerated since World War One, it was poor Leonard who was instructed to explain to Ena the error of her ways. And then to find some other willing lady to step into future breaches. Which meant a long trip to some region where Mrs Sharples was unknown. None of which thoughts brought any relief to the suffering Secretary. For he was, in spite of his pomposity, a Christian gentleman. And it was true that Mrs Sharples was only a few weeks out of hospital herself and if, as she said, she had only that night come back from a mission of mercy to a sick friend . . .

Jack Walker could not have chosen a more opportune moment to poke his head round the vestry door. Opportune for Swindley, that is.

'Sorry to butt in!' He smiled at Mr Swindley, turned to Ena and held out two shapeless woollen objects in her direction. 'Your gloves, love! You left 'em on t'bar!'

He'd known Ena long enough not to expect too much in the way of thanks but nor did he expect her to snatch them from him in the way she did. With a puzzled smile on his face, he left them.

'I know what you're thinking!' said Ena.

'And you're probably right!' replied the victorious Mr Swindley. 'You're probably right!'

Space had been at a premium when Jack and Billy Walker staggered into the Hall. They had missed the reception committee, Mr Swindley being locked in combat with Ena at the time, and had taken the places saved for them by Len and Harry. And just as well, as Annie had reacted more than unfavourably to Concepta's suggestion that they should spread themselves in order to leave room for the men of the house.

'Spread them out for us, Billy lad,' said Jack as he dumped his blankets and the bowling bag on the floor. 'I've got summat for Ena!' He headed for the vestry.

'Aye, right,' said Billy. 'Just watch how the Army do it, Hewitt!' And he proceeded to demonstrate the art of military bed making.

Jack returned from his unwitting errand of mercy, sat heavily and looked around the hall. He leaned over to Harry and lowered his voice. 'Eh, d'you reckon we can smoke in here?'

'I shouldn't think so,' said Harry, 'I can't see anybody lighting up.'

'No, neither can I,' said Jack. He nudged Harry as Mr Swindley, looking very pleased with himself, appeared through the vestry door. 'Go and ask him!'

'Who, me?'

'Aye, go on! He can but say no!'

'What if he does?'

'Think he might?' asked Jack.

'You never know. I think the best thing we can do is get us heads under us blankets and have a crafty draw!'

'You're probably right,' said Jack.

Annie had been watching the exchange with growing suspicion. She leaned over Billy. 'What are you two whispering about?'

'Nothing,' said Jack.

'Well, that's a subject you know plenty about!' And, her point made, she switched on a victor's smile and settled back into her place.

Miss Nugent noticed Mr Swindley's satisfied smile as soon as she staggered from the kitchen under the weight of an enormous tray laden with cups of tea. 'Did everything go all right?' she enquired.

'Oh, indeed yes! I think I can say without fear of contradiction that I was in command of the situation!'

This struck Emily as unusual, to say the least, but she decided not to diminish an obvious moment of triumph by pursuing the subject. And besides, the tray was very heavy. She switched to more mundane matters. 'Shall I serve the tea?' she asked.

'In a moment, Miss Nugent. Allow me a few words of welcome.' He moved down to the front of the stage and spread his arms expansively. 'If I could have your attention for a moment, ladies and gentlemen! I'd just like to say a few words before Miss Nugent serves tea!' He gazed benevolently round his audience, blissfully unaware that they were, to a man or a woman, wishing the silly old fool would shut up and let his girl friend pass the tea round. 'It gives me the greatest pleasure to welcome you all to the Glad Tidings Mission Hall even though the circumstances are, to say the least, somewhat unusual!'

An anguished 'Aah!' rose up from the crowd and he was wondering if perhaps his rhetoric had been too much for simple citizens when he realized that everyone's attention was riveted to his left. He turned too late to see Miss Nugent performing prodigious balancing feats with the mammoth tray but in time for her to throw him a flustered smile as, with a supreme effort she righted the precarious tilt and brought the tea back on to an even keel. Once again he turned his attention to his welcoming speech. His audience sighed, whether in relief that their tea had been spared or because he hadn't finished speaking, no one but they will ever know.

'However, it has always been my firm belief that there is good in everything and what has happened tonight has given all of you the opportunity to see the inside of our little meeting place. Feel free to use it as you would your own homes!'

A violent coughing broke out at his feet. Fortunately Mr Swindley couldn't see the source of the outbreak, due to the overhang of the stage but nothing prevented Annie's view of Jack's purple face as it appeared from underneath his blanket. Jack took a gulp of fresh air, caught sight of Annie's basilisk eye and smiled apologetically as a wisp of smoke curled up and around the edge of the blanket and hung in the air.

'Everything all right down there?' asked Mr Swindley, still unaware who was suffering.

'Yes, fine, thanks!' said Jack and curled up into as small a space as his not inconsiderable bulk would allow.

'Good, good! Now, as I was saying! ' His audience sighed again. The tea was getting cold. 'Whilst you are here you are my guests. If there is anything that either Miss Nugent or I can do to make your stay more pleasant, please don't hesitate to ask! '

'Shurrup and give us a cup of tea,' muttered David Barlow from a safe distance.

'Sh! ' said his mother.

'May I say how deeply I appreciate your joint predicament! ' Mr Swindley was beginning to enjoy himself which was more than could be said for anyone else under that roof. Miss Nugent was far from alone in wishing fervently that she could get rid of her burden. 'To be torn from one's home, one's hearth, is a frightening experience but let me, if I may, soften the blow. Let me, as it were, comfort you in this desperate hour. Think not of what you have lost but of what you have gained. Remember that though you may have said goodbye to your worldly possessions you have gained here this evening a precious gift. The offering of fraternity, good fellowship and brotherly love! '

'By eck, I thought we'd never make it! '

The cry came from the entrance doors and all eyes swivelled in that direction. Elsie stood there, beaming, her arms loaded with bedding and bric-a-brac. Behind her stood Linda, similarly laden, and Ivan, and it was obvious that however much Elsie may have fancied a spot of brotherly love she wasn't saying goodbye to her worldly possessions without a struggle. Ivan carried the television set.

Lukewarm tea had been served. Everyone, including the Tanners, had staked their claims to a patch of floor and had spread out their blankets. Ida Barlow, much to Frank's disgust, had also brought clean sheets but then Ida, had she belonged to a higher income group, would have gone round with a duster before the daily help arrived. Albert was regaling the two boys with selected stories from World War Two.

'Oh, aye, it brings back memories, all right!' He was saying. 'Mind you, in them days, it were every night! About seven o'clock, me and the missus used to make a flask o' tea and cut a few sandwiches and then off we'd go to t'shelter. When we got there like as not there'd be a sing-sing going on and we'd get usselves settled down and then we'd join in. And then you'd hear it. I've never heard a banshee but every time that siren went I used to say to myself "there's that banshee wailing again!" I reckon that was t'worst sound o' the lot! You know, many a time we've sung us heads off while t'bombs were dropping but when that siren went, by eck, it'd quieten you down! You'd lie there, just listening, then somebody'd start a song going and it'd be all right again!'

'You make it sound as if there were some good in it.' It was Kenneth, the smiling pacifist.

'And so there was, lad,' said Albert. 'I reckon I had more kindness done to me during the Blitz than I ever had before or since. And I did more myself. There was more sharing and less grabbing in them days. That's what happens when you throw folk together. And that's why this isn't such a bad thing. If it's done nowt else it's brought this street together for t'first time since VE Day!'

David smiled. 'You sound like Swindley!'

Albert lifted a warning finger. 'I'll tell you summat, young feller-me-lad! I don't mind sounding like anybody as long as he's talking sense!'

In the vestry, Mr Swindley and Miss Nugent were learning one of the facts of life which Ena had embraced as part of her philosophy many, many years ago – that attack is the best means of defence. Magnanimous in victory, Mr Swindley had called to bid her good night. Far from being chastened by his discovery of her deceit she had launched herself with imperishable gusto into a blistering counter-attack.

'I've told you before and I'll tell you again! A gas main going up's an Act of God – it's nowt to do with me! And if you expect me to be a ministering angel to that lot you can think again!'

Swindley fought back. 'Oh, I don't expect it, Mrs Sharples! In fact I've reached the point where I expect nothing but the bare minimum from you!'

'I'm not at all sure I like that sort of talk in a holy place,' Ena protested.

'What I meant, Mrs Sharples, is that the Committee gets no co-operation from you! None whatsoever! Not long ago I had to issue you a warning...'

'Don't you go warning me!'

'I had to issue you a warning,' persisted Swindley, 'that the Committee does not like its caretaker visiting licensed premises.'

'That's right!' said Ena. 'Heap coals of fire on my defenceless head!'

'I have no wish to do that, Mrs Sharples, but at the same time it is my bounden duty to report the fact that tonight you left Miss Nugent to set out the hall alone whilst you visited a public house on the pretext of calling on a sick friend!'

Ena made a flank attack. 'So I was! Martha Longhurst's had bronchitis for years. I only went to give her a bit of company!'

'That was a fabrication, Mrs Sharples. A gross fabrication!'

'Never mind what it were! I heard what you said to that lot about good fellowship and brotherly love! It's about time we had some of that in this here vestry!'

Mr Swindley turned to the harassed Emily. 'There's nothing to be gained by staying here.'

Ena hastened the retreat. 'That's first sensible thing you've said!'

Swindley turned at the door. 'And at the same time, rest assured that your conduct will be fully reported to the Committee!'

'You can report it to t'Prime Minister! And don't think I'm doing owt for that lot! They can freeze to death out there for all I care!'

Miss Nugent, appalled by such unchristianity, spoke for the first time. 'Mrs Sharples, how could you!'

'Don't *you* start! ' threatened Ena.

'Come along, Miss Nugent,' said Swindley, 'I'll take you home in my car.'

He ushered Miss Nugent through the outer door but not quickly enough for her to miss Ena's parting shot.

'And if you've got any sense, you'll watch him! ! '

The door closed behind them. Ena stamped to the stove, picked up a pan, banged it down on to the appropriate ring and reached for the milk. But her hand never reached the bottle for as she stretched towards it the faint strains of music floated from the hall. Grim-faced, Ena headed for the inner door.

Concepta was lying on her side, smiling at Harry over the top of the portable radio when Ena reached centre stage.

'You can turn that thing off for a start! ' All eyes turned to Ena. 'And you needn't all gawp at me – I live here! '

'We know! ' It was Elsie preparing for battle. She and Ena were old enemies, their hostility dating from long before their classic encounter on the night of May 14th 1944.

On that occasion three lovesick GI's, in search of the legendary Elsie Tanner, had been directed by a mischievous Billy Walker to Ena's vestry. The three brave allies had gone away to plan their campaign, become very drunk in the process and had dragged Ena from her bed in the middle of the night. Ena, outraged beyond endurance at this terrible smear on the street's good name, had pounded on Elsie's door until she was forced to leave the loving arms of Sergeant Lee Kuhlman, United States Army Air Force, and join Ena in the street. There, according to eye-witnesses, one of the truly epic battles of World War Two was played out. Could this, thought Jack Walker, be the start of World War Three?

'Did you say something, *Mrs* Tanner?' said Ena, with dreadful portent.

'Yes, I did, *Mrs* Sharples, and while I'm at it I'll say summat else! Being chucked out of your own house is bad enough and having to spend the night here is a damned sight worse but when you start chucking your flaming weight about, it's a bit more than flesh and blood can stand! So put this in your hairnet and strain it! If we feel like a bit of music, we'll *have* a bit of music!'

A ragged cheer went up. Ena quelled it with an evil eye.

'Oh, will you! We'll see about that!' She skipped nimbly down the steps from the stage and advanced on Concepta. Quick as a flash, the Irish girl was on her feet.

'Were you wanting something, Mrs Sharples?' The brogue was soft which was more than could be said for the jawline.

Jack Walker and Harry were also on their feet.

'Because if you were,' said Jack, 'we might get the idea we weren't welcome here. And if we did get that idea *you* wouldn't be welcome in *our* house!'

Ena decided, like many a politician before and after her, that in the interests of continuing comfort, compromise was greatly to be preferred to confrontation. 'If that thing disturbs me in my vestry, I'm having the police in!' And she marched up the stairs and back to her door where she turned and fixed Jack with a stony stare. 'And don't you get big headed, Jack Walker! I can soon find myself another pub!'

The door bang frightened the life out of the Gas Board engineers working two streets away. In the hall, it triggered off a gust of laughter.

'Ee, I enjoyed that!' said Jack. 'Come on, let's show her!' Arm waving, he launched into song. 'Roll out the barrel, We'll have . . .'

He got no further. He had forgotten in the joy of the moment that he had more than one antagonist in the Glad Tidings Mission that night.

'Shut up!!' said his wife, coldly. So he did.

The evening passed slowly. Packs of playing cards were produced and men settled themselves into serious quar-

58

tettes. Their women gossiped, knitted, stored away in their memories intimate details of neighbours' bedding.

'Don't look now,' said Linda to her mother, 'but that woman from t'corner shop's having a good dekko at our blankets.'

'Let her!' said Elsie. 'She's got nowt to shout about. Going to bed with her clothes on!'

Linda turned in time to catch Florrie struggling primly under her blankets.

'So what?'

'What d'you mean, so what? You're not sleeping like that, are you?'

'Course I am!'

Elsie was horrified. 'You can't! It's not hygienic!'

'Well, if you think I'm going to do a strip tease in front of this lot,' said Linda emphatically, 'you've got another think coming!'

'You please yourself, but my frock's coming off. I'm not having it all creased. Besides I've got to go to work in it.' She turned her back on her daughter. 'Give us a hand with my zip.'

'Mam, you can't!'

'Can't I just! Do what you're told and make less bones about it.' Hesitantly Linda eased the zip open. 'Now hold that blanket up.'

Linda looked round the hall with agonized eyes. By no stretch of imagination could she be described as strait-laced but there were certain taboos, even if her mother did ignore them, and undressing in public was one of them. She didn't share Elsie's happy philosophy that everyone had seen it all before.

Elsie was on her feet, impatient. 'Come on! Hold it up!'

Linda made certain that no one was actually staring in their direction and did as she was told. Behind the woollen wall, Elsie started to wriggle out of the over-tight dress. She was having trouble navigating it over her hips when Linda's agitated whisper reached her.

'Mam, hurry up! Harry Hewitt's coming!'

Elsie's head appeared over the blanket as Harry reached them.

'Do you mind!' she said, coldly.

'Oh, sorry! I just wondered if you'd got a match.'

Elsie retained her dignity. 'I'm afraid we're in no position to help you,' she said. Harry coloured slightly, muttered an apology and went off to less embarrassing quarters. Elsie, much to Linda's relief, won the battle with her hip-line, wrapped the blanket around her and settled down.

It was a cold, cheerless night. An uncharitable east wind whipped round the corner of Rosamund Street into Mawdsley Street and moulded the blue serge trousers of PC Croasdale to his chilled legs. Standing in Martha Longhurst's doorway, he watched, sourly, the frozen-fingered efforts of the Gas Board engineers to trace and stop the leak. He'd been married only two months and not four streets away, in the neat little bedroom of a neat little police flat, his warm, pink wife lay in a warm, pink bed. He frowned at the thought. He must have been mad to join this lot.

On the other side of Viaduct Street, within earshot but out of damage distance of any possible explosion, lay Jubilee Terrace. And 'lie' it did, for the inconvenient contours of the land had placed the houses on one side of the street below pavement level. An iron railing, strategically placed to save any of the neighbourhood drunks from breaking their necks, was punctuated every pair of houses to allow a flight of three stone steps down to each front door. And each gap was filled by a neat iron gate.

The railing itself was not without history.

In the early months of 1940 when metal embellishments of every kind were ripped from the city streets in the name of the war effort, two workmen and a dilapidated lorry arrived in Jubilee Terrace and proceeded to uproot the iron rail. Minnie Caldwell remembered the day well. A few months short of her fortieth birthday and already five years a widow, she had stood behind her militant mother as the old lady harangued the helpless workmen.

60

'I don't know whose side you think you're on but take them railings down and you'll kill more Englishmen round here than Hitler could! Mark my words, them areas'll be littered wi' bodies!' Whilst not totally accurate as far as numbers were concerned, her prophecy contained more than a grain of truth. The railings were dismantled and the same night, during a moonless black-out, two of the night shift of Weatherfield Steel tumbled into the area in front of her own front door and were lost to the nation for several weeks with a shattered collar bone and a broken leg. The following day the railings were replaced.

Beyond them, on this cold February night of 1961, down the three stone steps and behind the brown front door, Minnie Caldwell sat with her friend Martha, enjoying Mantovani and a cup of cocoa. As the last strains of the sobbing violins died and the programme came to an end Minnie sighed, switched off and looked anxiously up at the ceiling.

'Can she hear?' asked Martha.

'Sometimes,' said Minnie and cocked an ear towards the upper floor. In the front bedroom lay her mother, still militant but now in her nineties and bedridden for the past three years. As Minnie well knew, the old lady had long learned the trick of switching the world on and off, of hearing what she wished to hear and turning a deaf ear to the rest. Minnie waited for the rap of the stick on the bedroom floor – her mother's intercom system. Martha, caught by Minnie's open-mouthed silence, listened too, but no sound came. Minnie relaxed.

'I'm glad you decided to come here.'

'Aye, so am I! I didn't much fancy Ena's bossing! I get enough of her during t'day without putting up with her all night!' A pause, then, 'I wouldn't say no to another cup of cocoa.' Martha's tone was sharp, an order rather than a request. She was apt to assume Ena's dictatorial mantle when Ena herself was well out of the way. Which placed Minnie firmly at the end of the chain of command. Had the old dictum been true, Minnie, kicked herself from all quarters, would, in turn, have kicked the cat. But Minnie would have cheerfully died before inflicting the slightest pain on Bobby, her huge, barred, tom-cat companion. He lay curled on her lap at that moment. 'If you can get that animal off you!' added Martha. There was a touch of asperity in her voice. She had no time for animals. Come to that she had little time for most humans.

With an effort Minnie carefully lifted Bobby down on to the floor. The cat looked venomously at Martha and padded to its basket, considerately placed inside the brass fender close to the still-glowing fire. Gracefully, it arranged itself inside its wicker bed. Martha stared at it distastefully, as Minnie came back with the cocoa.

'Ee, I wish they'd given us another minute or two! I should have brought my statuette. I'd have been a lot easier in my mind.' The statuette – a dancing lady – was Martha's pride and joy. Bought in a Blackpool side street two years ago by her daughter Lily, flushed by a successful session of Golden Mile Bingo, it had since occupied pride of place in Martha's bay window. She tutted angrily and took the proffered cup from Minnie. 'I'll never forgive myself if that gets broke!' Which wasn't quite true. What Martha meant was that she'd never forgive everyone else.

'Don't worry, it'll all turn out for the best.' And then, vaguely, 'They're very good, the Gas men.'

'By eck, where'd you read that? On a sugar bag? Arthur Crump works for t'Gas Board and he's that daft he'd light a match to look for a leak!'

Faced by Martha's scorn Minnie decided to temper her approval. 'Well, I'm sure they'll be careful! You see, you'll all be back home tomorrow morning!'

'We'd better be!' A smile curved Martha's thin lips. 'Eh, I wonder how Ena's getting on! I'll bet they're giving her a dog's life!'

In fact, the opposite was the case. A few moments before, the Mission Hall had been a haven of peace. The last card school, four gentlemen from Mawdsley Street, whispered its way through a game of solo. Esther Hayes was on the point of discovering the identity of the murderer three pages before Hercule Poirot, Len and Harry were secretly but steadily working their way through the crate of light ale. And then the serpent had entered Paradise.

'You'd better all finish off whatever you're doing. I'm putting the lights out!' It could only be Ena.

Florrie sent up a plaintive cry. 'Could we just finish our sandwiches?'

'If you can't find the road to your mouth in t'dark it's time you saw a doctor. It's half past eleven and time decent folk were in bed and asleep!'

'Excuse me, Mrs Sharples.' This time it was Harry daring the wrath. 'I'm on early turn tomorrow. Could you lend me an alarm clock?'

'I could not! But if you lie awake you can hear the Town Hall clock from here!' And to prove that Harry hadn't succeeded in changing the subject, 'Now think on, these lights are out in five minutes 'cos if they're not I'll switch 'em off at t'main!' And she was gone.

A chorus of dissent spread across the Hall. The card school swiftly dealt the final hand. Martha's next-door neighbour, a lugubrious widower, looked at his cards. 'Misere avare,' he called, 'and it'd be just my flaming luck for t'lights to go out before I got it!'

Esther sneaked a look three pages on and sighed with satisfaction as she learned that she and Miss Christie's Belgian detective shared the same suspicions. Concepta, her ear to the radio, turned up the volume in defiance. The Barlows, Albert Tatlock and Florrie bolted their luncheon meat sandwiches as if food were going out of fashion. And Harry hurriedly opened three more bottles and passed one each to Len and Jack Walker. On the other side of Jack, his son, accustomed by Military service to sleeping through shot and shell, slept soundly. Annie glared once more at Jack and twitched her coat more firmly around her.

None of them heard the door open but the shout was sufficiently official to command attention. 'Everybody all right?' asked Sergeant Sowerbutts. A chorus assured him that everyone was indeed all right. 'It looks as if the trouble'll be settled before morning so you've only got one night in this hotel. Make the most of it!'

'Thank the Lord for that!' said Elsie. 'This floor's as hard as iron!'

The sergeant smiled. 'Nay, Mrs Tanner! If you can't get yourself comfy with the covering you've got, what chance have these others got!'

'Cheeky devil!'

'Cheeky or not, you can't say I don't look after you! Your gas may not be on so the WVS are coming round at seven with some breakfast.'

'Charming,' shouted Harry, 'I've got to be out at quarter to!'

But the policeman was already on his way out. His cheery 'Good night!' floated over his shoulder and before the answering chorus reached him the door had banged to.

The odd groan arose as old bones met hard wood. The lugubrious gentleman from Mawdsley Street made his misère avare and with an unaccustomed chuckle swept the kitty into a capacious pocket. Harry Hewitt settled down to find himself blinking at a piece of writing paper lying on the floor not two inches from his nose. He freed one arm from the imprisoning blanket and lifted the paper into the light. It was yellowed and covered with faded, spidery writing.

'Listen to this, Jack!' There was a chuckle in Harry's voice as he nudged his neighbour. 'Sweetheart! I have just got back to camp after a good trip. Things are just the same here. All I can say is roll on the next leave.' Unseen by Harry, two pairs of eyes clicked open. Annie Walker, who owned one pair, slid her fingers carefully into the pocket of her coat. She felt the blood rush to her face as she discovered that the packet of letters in her hand was loose, the ribbon untied. Meanwhile her husband was trying to lever himself up on to one elbow, anxious to catch his wife's expression and so confirm his fears. Harry read happily on.

'I shared the grub with a couple of the lads. That fruit cake you gave me was just the job but not half as tasty as . . .' A note of disgust crept into Harry's voice as he turned the page to find nothing there. 'Would you believe it! And just as it was getting interesting!'

64

'Where'd you get it from,' asked Jack warily.

'It was on t'floor, in front of my face. Must be one of Ena's old love letters.'

'Let's have a look.'

Harry passed the letter to Jack. 'Go on, then! *You* blackmail her! I'm getting my head down.'

He yawned expansively, turned away and pulled the blanket around his shoulders. Jack sat up. His anxiety waned as he gazed fondly at the relic from his past.

March 1940! By eck, it was like yesterday! In spite of Annie's pleas for him to wait until he was called up he'd been amongst the first to volunteer. They'd only been in the Rover for a couple of years but his job was safe enough. Sir William Newton, the brewery's chairman, was himself an old Lancashire Fusilier and he looked kindly on any of his landlords who joined the regiment. And as Jack was only too ready to confess, he'd had a far cushier billet in his early Army days than he ever had in the licensed trade! His first station, Butlin's Camp at Prestatyn in North Wales, had had the great misfortune to open in the summer of 1939, enjoy one season's proper use then surrender itself for the duration to the rough and licentious soldiery.

Let's see, thought Jack. I was sitting in that chalet looking out over t'swimming pool when I wrote this! His gaze wandered with his mind and he found himself looking into Annie's expressionless eyes. She held out her hand. Silently he handed the sheet of paper to her. She took the bundle of letters from her coat pocket, carefully inserted the errant leaf and meticulously retied the ribbon.

'What d'you want to bring *them* for?'

Annie's reply had a fine cutting edge. 'Why shouldn't I? I hadn't got a bowling bag!' She mistook Jack's smile for embarrassment and pressed home an imagined advantage. 'I don't suppose you kept any of *mine*!'

Jack's smile broadened. Quietly and deliberately he pulled the bowling bag from under his pillows, unbuckled the clasp and took from between the polished woods a sheaf of letters. 'It wasn't just a bowling bag I brought.' His eyes weren't too old for a glint of mischief. 'Grand leave that were! Our Joanie should be thankful for it! She wouldn't be here else!'

'Don't be indelicate!' said Annie. But her smile signed the armistice.

The lights went out, as Ena had promised, in five minutes precisely. The evacuees tired by the very novelty of the day, dropped off, one by one, to sleep. Outside, in the cold streets, representatives of the Gas Board and the law worked and kept watch. In nearby Broadhurst Street, half a dozen standby firemen rubbed their freezing hands and waited for the Captain to bring the coffee.

Sergeant Sowerbutts left the station with PC Clarke at five minutes to three. He reckoned that young Croasdale's concentration would be taking a battering, called away, as he had been, from his barely-used marital couch. And it wasn't easy to explain special duty to a young bride. As far as she was concerned, special duty meant staying in bed together for another couple of hours on an off-beat morning.

PC Croasdale was doing a Scott of the Antarctic when his comrades joined him. Five minutes of arm pumping and foot stamping had restarted his circulation but the blood really began to flow when the sergeant sent him off home. He was five yards up the street when the sergeant called him back. He turned to find Sowerbutts pointing accusingly at Martha's front doorstep.

'What's *that*?' *That* was a cigarette end.

'I er . . . I don't know, Sarge!' Croasdale had always been a bad liar and he wasn't due to improve that night.

'Well, I'll tell you!' said Sowerbutts. '*That* is a cigarette end. Where you've been standing! And it doesn't take me to tell you that smoking on duty is against regulations and it doesn't take *anybody* to tell you that smoking a hundred yards from a gas leak is plain bloody madness!'

Croasdale looked wildly at the ground. 'There's er . . . there's a lot of 'em about!'

'There is *not* a lot of 'em about! There is *one*!' The

sergeant picked up the offending article. 'And a lesser brain than Sergeant John William Sowerbutts could tell you it's recent! Now get off home and ponder on your stupidity, lad. And get yourself ready for the morning. Which is going to be a hard one!'

Two hours later, Doreen Croasdale raised herself on one shapely elbow, gazed at her tortured husband and asked the age-old question. 'What's the matter?'

PC Croasdale turned his back on her. If you can't explain special duty to your wife, how do you spell out that nothing in this world saps the virility faster than an angry sergeant?

Sergeant John William Sowerbutts, however, suffered no such misgivings. He posted young Clarke and strolled over for a chat with the Gas Board engineers. They weren't quite as optimistic as they had been but no, they told him, there was no point in changing the information he'd already given out. If they were wrong the evacuees would very soon hear about it. Sowerbutts agreed. Let them sleep. And if they had to stay another day then so be it. He left the excavation and turned into Rosamund Street and past the row of shops which led to the Rover's Return. Automatically his hand strayed to the door handles, turned and checked as he passed. Swindley's, Piggott's the Pork Butchers, Babywear (prop. E. Nugent). He was at the side door of the public house before he reminded himself that he was no longer on the beat. And that his prime concern that night was not whether a shop's door was locked but whether it would still be on its hinges when morning came.

He caught sight of the shadowy figure as soon as he turned the corner. It turned the Mission corner out of Viaduct Street and crossed the road in front of the raincoat factory. He quickened his stride and reached the door of number eleven at the same time as the stranger. It was a young man, bareheaded, wearing a shabby raincoat.

'May I ask what you're doing here, sir?'

'Never mind me, what are *you* doing?' asked Dennis Tanner.

'I did ask first, sir!' He could be very polite could Ser-

67

geant Sowerbutts. He could also be very rough but this was one of his polite nights.

Dennis produced his doorkey. 'I'm trying to get in. I live here! Any objections?'

'Aye, plenty! You're not sleeping in *there* tonight!'

'Who says I'm not?' To say that Dennis didn't much care for policemen was rather like saying that mice didn't much care for cats. Ever since his appearance in Juvenile Court after a juvenile attempt at housebreaking he was convinced that the CID, the Crime Squad, the Vice Squad, the Flying Squad, the Fraud Squad and the assorted police forces were all under strict orders to make his life a misery. And just recently they'd brought in another branch of the Gestapo and called them traffic wardens. Who were clearly waiting for him to buy a car. So, he bristled.

'Where've you been, son?' said the Sergeant.

'What's it got to do with you?'

The sergeant was patience itself. 'Did you come past Broadhurst Street?'

Not again, thought Dennis. I can't move but they're after me. 'No, I never,' he said, 'so you're not going to pin anything on me!'

Sowerbutts smiled benignly. 'Sonny, you've been watching too much television! All I'm saying is that if you *had* have come past Broadhurst Street you might have noticed a couple of fire engines and then when you saw me hanging about you might have asked me what was going on.'

'What *is* going on?' Even Dennis was beginning to be impressed.

'Well, number one, a gas main's in danger of blowing round the back here in Mawdsley Street. Number two, as soon as we found out we turfed everybody out of these houses in case the backs catch it. And number three, they're all sleeping across the road in the Glad Tidings Mission.'

'Well, why couldn't you say so before?' said Dennis.

And still the sergeant could smile. 'Come on, Jesse James,' he said. 'I'll take you over and let you in.'

Sleep had finally claimed Ida Barlow. Her husband and the boys had dropped off within five minutes of the lights going out but Ida's guilty secret had kept her awake, staring into the blackness of the rafters. Frank snored. She had been faced with this problem before. On the beach at Rhyl, in railway carriages, even, once, in the cinema. But never in the immediate presence of all her neighbours. She knew she must keep awake and at the slightest suspicion, the merest murmur, the barest breath of a snore, she must shake him, gently, until the snore died peaceably away. It was only after she had been performing this service for an hour that she realized that practically every other man in the hall was snoring too. At which point the game changed slightly. Now it wasn't that Frank snored but that he snored louder than anyone else. It was during this period that she must have dropped off to sleep. A shake awakened her. David was leaning towards her, smiling. 'You were snoring!' he whispered. Which gave poor Ida something else to worry about. But the orchestration, the harmony, the gentle persistence of the snoring about her finally overcame her resolution and she slept.

It was into this dark orchestra that Sergeant Sowerbutts led Dennis Tanner. As the door closed behind him, Dennis fumbled for his matches, struck one and held it high. Then, cautiously, he picked his way amongst the bodies. He found his mother at precisely the same moment that the flame found his fingers. He dropped the match, cursing softly.

But not quite softly enough.

'Who's that?' asked Elsie in a strident whisper.

'It's me!'

'I might have known! Get yourself into bed before you waken the flaming neighbourhood! There's some blankets for you next to Ivan.'

'I can't see. And I've run out of matches.'

'Heaven preserve us!' A match flared, illuminating Elsie's bare shoulders. 'Over here! And watch where you're treading!'

Dennis picked his way carefully over his brother-in-law's sleeping body and settled himself amongst the warm blankets. Elsie blew out the match, turned over to try to get back to sleep. Dennis's voice floated over his sister.

'Have you got anything to eat?'

'Course I have!' snapped Elsie. 'There's fish and four-penn'orth under your pillow keeping warm! Have I eckas-like got anything to eat!'

'I'm dead hungry!'

'And we're dead tired, so shut up and go to sleep!'

Linda stirred. 'What's up, Mam?'

'Nothing, chuck. It's just the night shift coming in!'

At precisely five thirty two the following morning the engineer in charge proclaimed the emergency at an end, and with three short words to Sergeant Sowerbutts restored Coronation Street to its old peculiar normality.

CHAPTER FOUR

To an eleven-year-old girl rosebay willowherb is a beautiful flower with a beautiful name. So when Harry Hewitt uprooted the pink blossomed plant from between the flagstones of his backyard, Lucille wept.

'It's a weed, love!' said Harry, taking the tear-stained face between his hands.

'It's *not* a weed! It's a flower! And you've killed it!'

'No, don't you see, love? If I'd have left it they'd have spread. They'd have grown all over the place!'

Lucille looked at her father in horror. Not only had he killed a flower, now it seemed he had destroyed the possibility of a magnificent garden. She burst into tears again.

'Don't cry, love! Here!' He handed her the sturdy weed. 'Put it in that green vase. Keep it in your bedroom.'

Rosebay willowherb, fire weed, blitz bloom, marked the season in the back streets of Weatherfield. In late August, on the very threshold of autumn, the myriad, gossamer, puffball seeds floated through the city streets, searching out cracks in the paving stones, gaps in brick walls, the mossy haunts of the rooftops, the smallest foothold of good earth. And there they lay, quietly waiting for the spring when they would come to life and burst upon the world.

Harry, city born and bred, was no gardener. Like millions of his fellows he gave each plant the benefit of the doubt – it was a flower until it proved itself a weed. And the proving time was when the buds burst and Harry realized what he had nurtured.

On that June the twelfth that the rosebay willowherb declared itself and Harry committed the unforgivable, a flower of a different species blossomed in the fertile Tanner soil.

At eleven o'clock that morning Elsie was already halfway through a packet of cigarettes. Ivan had been at the hospital since eight, pushed out the house by his edgy mother-in-law shortly after he had shattered his third cup that week. Softly she began to curse her errant husband. If only he'd shaped himself, if only he'd sent a bit more money home instead of spreading it round the Far East, she might have had a telephone in the house instead of having to rely on the goodwill of neighbours. She just hoped that Ivan would have the sense to ring Emily Nugent. That one'd shut the shop and come scuttling round without any bother. He wouldn't though! He was daft enough to ask Annie Walker to pass on the message. And *she'd* never let Elsie hear the last of it. 'Well, of course, the trouble with being on the telephone in an area like this is that everybody, but *everybody*, takes advantage of you!' She could just hear her. She took a vicious drag on her cigarette. Just let that damned fat husband of hers come round asking to see his granddaughter! She'd . . . the knock brought her to her feet. The glowing cigarette fell to the floor. She picked it up, burned herself, swore softly, took two deep breaths and walked slowly but unsteadily to the door. She was right – Ivan *had* been daft enough.

'Congratulations, Mrs Tanner!' It was Annie, holding her investiture, graciously bestowing grandmotherhood.

'It's come then?' stammered Elsie.

'Indeed it has! All of nine and a half pounds!'

'Nine and a half . . . ! Eh, bless her, she must have gone through it!'

Annie smiled. 'Mother and child doing well was the message!'

'Eh, mother and child . . .' Elsie suddenly realized that one important piece of information was still to come. 'What is it, for Pete's sake?'

'A little boy!'

72

'Eh, I knew it!' lied Elsie cheerfully. 'Bless him! Nine and a half pounds! Er . . . do you fancy a drink? I don't know what I've got but you're very welcome.'

'Thank you, no, Mrs Tanner. Ordinarily I'd be delighted but I'm opening up shortly and . . . well, you know how it is. I'm only too pleased to have brought good news.' Being Annie, she couldn't resist the parting shot. 'And please don't think it was any bother. If one owns the only telephone in the neighbourhood, one expects these little errands!'

Elsie's smile, never really convincing, turned into a sneer as it followed Mrs Walker down the street. Trust her! But the smile was back before she turned into the lobby and closed the door. A lad! A bit of a waste but still, beggars can't be choosers!'

'What are you so keen on a girl for?' Dot Greenhalgh had asked her.

'Well, there's not much I can tell a lad, is there? And when you think of all the mistakes *I've* made it seems a pity not to pass 'em on to somebody as might benefit.'

'Never did your Linda any good!' She was on the sharp side, was Dot. The Martha Longhurst of Miami Modes.

'Well, some things skip generations, don't they?' said Elsie. 'I mean, my mother was blessed with very nice friends but my grandmother was like me – she had shockers!'

Dot smiled sweetly. 'Heaven help your granddaughter!' she said.

Heaven would have to help him, thought Elsie as she settled back in her chair after Annie's visit and lit yet another cigarette. He wouldn't get many of life's luxuries from his father, poor little devil. She remembered the night that Linda had first brought Ivan home, the stiff, formal introduction and then the solemn declaration of his intentions. After which, his nerves in shreds, he asked for the toilet.

'What's he on about?' hissed Elsie as soon as the door closed on him.

'He's telling you he loves me, isn't he? They're like that!'

73

'Is that all?'

'He wants to marry me!'

There didn't seem much else to say so they had waited until the toilet flushed and Ivan's steps sounded on the stairs. Elsie was wearing a vacant smile when, tentatively, he opened the door and rejoined them. She was trapped and she knew it. The victim of her own experience, the mother of her daughter. And the two of them already fighting like cat and dog. Experience screamed at her to send him away, to tell Linda to think again; but she knew her daughter. In spite of everything she might have said to Dot Greenhalgh, she knew that Linda would reject any advice that Elsie offered out of hand. As Elsie herself would have done.

'I would like to marry your daughter!' said Ivan.

'So I believe,' said Elsie.

The floodgates opened again. 'I will work for her all my life! I will make a good home and be a good husband and a good father to our children.'

What could she say? And yet she'd heard it all before. She'd met them during the War. The Americans, the Army Air Force, all carbon copies in their olive drabs but all so very different. The boys from New York City, the men from the sticks. And if it was mink you were after, get yourself a boy. The men were the Ivans of this world. Honest, patient, hardworking, poor. With Ivan, Linda would never go short of bread. But there'd be nowt much else.

She remembered now, the smoke drifting around her, what she had heard herself saying that night. 'I'm sure you'll make her very happy.' And now there was a nine-and-a-half pound lad and a scruffy house. And a marriage which, if not exactly on the rocks at the moment, needed only a squall to blow it back on. Elsie, the realist, didn't subscribe to the theory that nothing cemented a crumbling marriage more firmly than a baby. Two or three weeks of sleepless nights can play havoc with the tolerance of a saint.

Elsie was on the point of pouring herself a comforting drink when Christine Hardman called.

'Can you smell this stuff?' Elsie asked, mock-accusingly.

'Oh, come on, Elsie! I just met Annie Walker on the street and she told me the news! What do you expect me to do? Knock on the wall in Morse code?'

'Don't come it! You heard the bottle clink. Go on, admit it!' Elsie invariably chided the people she liked and she liked Christine. 'I don't suppose you'll say no?'

'You're right, I won't!' Christine sat down and watched Elsie pour her a glass of sherry. And, as she accepted it, 'Thanks, Grannie!'

'Oo, don't!' said Elsie. 'I feel old enough without folk calling me that!'

Christine smiled and cocked her head on one side. 'Fishing for compliments, are we?'

'Do I ever?'

'You never stop!' But Christine's broadening smile admitted the exaggeration. 'And I wouldn't mind but you don't need 'em. You could still get all the fellers you want!'

'Oh aye, three bags full!' mocked Elsie. 'I'm not your age, you know.' And then, hurriedly, 'Mind you, I'm not all that much older!'

'Doesn't do *me* any good, being my age,' said Christine. She was a creature of moods, as Elsie well knew.

'Get that drink down you! And don't guzzle it! It's good stuff, that is – it's Cyprus!'

Christine sipped her drink and nodded appreciatively. She's not had it easy, thought Elsie. She was a good girl, was Chris; a good, honest, straightforward Lancashire lass and Heaven knows there were enough about nowadays who weren't worth tuppence. Elsie knew quite a few true northerners that she wouldn't have trusted with the cat. But Chris was a good girl. She'd have made someone a good wife and here she was, going on twenty-two and not a lad in sight.

Christine's thoughts were running along similar lines. Not two weeks previously she had replied to Joe Makinson's letter and finished with him for good. As she wrote the words she had been appalled by the cruelty which one

75

human being is, at times, forced to inflict on another. A sensitive plumber, she had thought at the time – how daft can you get!

Joe had entered her life after Malcolm, fancy Malcolm, had left it. Even Christine, straightforward Lancashire lass, had been impressed by Malcolm. But by now she realized that she had been impressed for all the wrong reasons. The sports car with the triple tone horn which so infuriated Ena Sharples; the Rugby club dances; the smart friends who, she discovered later, were intrigued to meet 'Malc's bit of rough'!

His loyalty was less impressive. He had stayed away when she had needed him most. Although he had known of her mother's death within hours of it happening, the sports car had not made an appearance in the street until well after the funeral. And she had sent him away. 'Don't come back,' she had said. 'It's no use.' She had regretted the words as soon as they were said. Regretted them for their needlessness. Malcolm wouldn't waste an opportunity like this. His philosophy was simple. If you want to get out and someone opens a door, dive through it. So he had looked at her soulfully, silently, allowed his shoulders to slump a little, sighed deeply, turned and walked tragically back to his car. And had driven off without a backward look. 'Why did I bother!' thought Christine. 'He won't come back!' And he hadn't.

The following day, Joe Makinson had knocked on her door. Shy, hesitant, considerate, Malcolm's opposite in everything except, possibly, weight (he was a well set-up lad), Joe stammered his way through his self-introduction. He was from Shorrockses, the plumbers, and did she remember, they'd done a job a few months back and the bill hadn't been paid. So they'd asked him, as he was passing, if he'd just give her a reminder. No doubt it had slipped her mind.

It hadn't, of course. A paid day-off for the funeral had been the extent of the raincoat factory's generosity but that was the least of her troubles. She had been thunder-struck to learn from little Harry Bailey, the insurance man, that the policy on her mother's life had been taken out only eighteen months previously which made it (it was all Greek to her) a short duration claim. Which in turn meant that, unless the insurance company were satisfied that May Hardman had not, at that time, been suffering from any heart disorder, only the premiums would be returned to Christine instead of the claim being settled in full.

In the event, after two months' wrangling, the claim was settled but the day Joe Makinson knocked on her door, Christine was, to say the least, 'hard up'. She had explained to him, simply, without any hint of excuse or any appeal for charity, that her mother had recently died, that the insurance money hadn't yet been paid and so on and so forth. She could see his face now and remembered how, at the time, she had resented his apparent stupidity, the way he had stood awkwardly on the wet pavement, his brain struggling to catch up with the situation. And then he had stammered a request for the bill itself – 'so that he could have it checked'. She had been too tired to argue. She had given him the bill and he had gone and she had forgotten him. It was a week later that she found herself passing Shorrocks' and called in to ask what arrangements could be made about settlement. But the bill has been paid, she was told. You must have forgotten. The lad we sent round came back with the money.

There are times in everyone's life when a small gesture, which, under normal circumstances would go almost un-noticed, means the world. Christine couldn't put the affair out of her mind. The bill had been for two pounds seven-teen shillings and sixpence but Joe's gesture had been astronomical. He had given her the moon. And why? It would have been contrary to all the rules of romance had they never met again.

It had happened, as it had to, at a dance at Weatherfield Town Hall ten days after Christine's discovery. She had spent the intervening time wondering how best to contact him when, suddenly, there he was, imprisoned in his best

77

suit, pondering the agonizing question of how to ask a girl to dance. She had solved the problem for him.

There was never an affair. A courtship, yes, but never an affair. On the third of March he proposed to her, formally, with the utmost sincerity. She gave a qualified acceptance – it must be a long engagement – but six weeks later she broke it off. Six weeks during which she realized that even marriage to someone like Joe would not bring her the intimacy she needed from a man. He took it badly and she'd neither seen nor heard of him for four weeks. And then the letter came. An imploring, pleading letter, full of stuttering apology. She wrote back as kindly as she was able but she knew how much it would hurt. And now, again, there was no one.

'What's Linda going to call him?' Christine had emerged from her reverie a little ahead of Elsie.

'What, love?'

'The baby. Have they got a name?'

'Oh, aye, love! Hundreds!'

Christine was not the only resident of Coronation Street to live through a stormy spring. Ena Sharples, never the community pet, made herself even more unpopular over the Great Demolition Scare.

The story, like so many, had humble beginnings.

At five minutes to eight on a Friday morning in March, Ena stood shoulder to shoulder in the kitchen of Albert Tatlock's house. They were tempting the proverb-makers by watching a pot and waiting for it to boil. Or in this case, a kettle.

'How long's it been going now?' asked Ena.

Albert glanced at his alarm clock, brought from his bedroom specially for the purpose. 'Thirty-five minutes, I make it.'

'It's a downright disgrace!'

'Mind you, I don't usually boil a kettleful.'

'Aye, but that's when you're brewing tea,' snapped Ena.

'We're brewing trouble! I know that lot down at the Town Hall! Clever heads, the lot of 'em! If I walk in there tomorrow morning and tell 'em it took three quarters of an hour to boil a kettle of water, they'll get that toffee-nosed look on their faces and say "Ah, but there's kettles and kettles!" That's why I want it exact! Four pints of water there was in that there kettle of yours – measured out of a milk bottle!'

'Aye, you've got summat there!' said Albert, stunned by Ena's logic.

'Oh, I'm not short of a bit of grey matter, you know! I like to get my facts straight, I do! And they can use all the mathymaticks they want but they can't hide the fact that our gas pressure is not what it should be! And it's weeks since that gas leak so they can't blame that!' Abruptly Ena shot off at one of her familiar tangents. 'How's that daughter of yours getting on?'

'Beattie? She's all right,' said Albert without much conviction.

'Doesn't get up to see you very often, does she?'

'She was up this morning.'

'Was she?' Ena's voice was heavy with surprise that anyone could have infiltrated the street without her knowledge. 'I didn't see her. I must have been stoking my boiler.'

'She manages to get up about once a week. Does a bit of cleaning for me. And I mean a bit!'

'She's better than that one of mine!' Ena's lips curled at the thought of her thankless child. 'I see her once every Preston Guild! Mind you, that's often enough for my liking. Where's Beattie living these days?'

'That new estate up the Old Road.'

'Oh, aye?' Ena's tone condemned the property. 'Four bedroom detached with a built-in garridge?'

'It's a nice house,' said Albert defensively.

'It might *look* it! I know the chap as put 'em up. You remember old Harper, don't you? Him as went to St Mary's every Sunday morning wearing a top hat?'

'He's dead!' said Albert.

'Let me finish, will you! I know he's dead! And not before time, neither. The devil got his own there, all right!

Well that estate your daughter's living on was built by his eldest lad. I'm saying "lad", he must be getting on for sixty, but if he learned any of the old feller's tricks, those houses'll be down in five years.'

'Get away with you!' protested Albert. 'Norman's got his head screwed on. Him and Beattie had the surveyor round.'

Ena's smile was knowing in the extreme. 'Oh, a surveyor!' The kettle started to sing. 'How long?' she asked.

Albert studied the alarm clock. 'Forty-one minutes!'

Ena was triumphant. 'We'll show 'em!' She pushed a piece of notepaper across the kitchen table. 'There you are! Get it signed! And it wants the time filling in!'

Albert adjusted his glasses, picked up the paper and began, laboriously, to read the crabbed writing. '*I, Albert Tatlock, of number one Coronation Street, do hereby certify that my kettle containing four pints of water took . . .*' He took a firm grip of the proffered pen and, tongue sticking out of the corner of his mouth, wrote in the missing figure. '*. . . forty-one minutes to boil on the large ring on my gas stove. Signed . . .*' His tongue took a little more exercise and the form was complete.

A few hours later a similar experiment came under discussion in the snug of the Rover's Return. The room was set aside for the Walkers' female patrons (woe betide any man who put his foot inside for anything more than a polite enquiry!) and the centre table had long been the undisputed domain of Ena, Minnie and Martha. Even the seating had been worked out as meticulously as at a meeting of foreign Heads of State. Ena always with her back to the bar, Minnie on her right and Martha on her left. On this occasion Ena was missing and Martha's beret nodded at Minnie's toque across the empty space. Martha was reading from a familiar, but not identical, sheet of notepaper.

'*I, Minnie Caldwell, of number fifteen Jubilee Terrace . . .*' She continued in silence, her mouth working until, horrified . . . '*Thirty-two minutes! Is that all it took – thirty-two minutes?*'

'Yes,' answered Minnie, 'I worked it out particular.'

'Well, mine took forty-five!'

'I can't help that, can I?'

'Ena's not going to like it!'

Minnie's eyes clouded with apprehension. 'Not going to like what?'

'Yours only taking thirty-two minutes.'

'Well, I don't see what I can do about it. I'll show you how the clock was when I put it on!' Minnie wet her finger in a small pool of milk stout and drew minute and hour hands on the table top. 'They were like that and then when it started to whistle I looked and it were like that!' More milk stout, another diagram and Minnie looked appealingly at Martha. 'I worked it out most particular!'

Martha was adamant. 'I still say Ena's not going to like it!' She glanced again at the offending form. 'You haven't even signed it!'

'Do I have to?' asked Minnie meekly.

'Course you do! Here! Where Ena's put them dotted lines!' She handed Minnie a chewed ballpoint pen.

'Can I print it or do I have to do it in proper writing?'

'Eh, *I* don't know!'

'I'd rather print it.'

'Wait a minute!' Martha swivelled towards the counter. 'Mr Walker?'

'Yes, love?' Jack paused in his mopping-up operations.

'When you sign a form can you print it or do you have to do it in proper writing?'

'Oh, it's got to be in handwriting. If you can do handwriting, that is.'

'Thank you very much,' said Martha. And then, to Minnie, 'Go on, you heard what he said! Get on with it!'

Laboriously and with even more use of the tongue than Albert that morning, Minnie signed her name. 'There!' she said, and, handing back the pen found herself meeting Martha's pitying gaze.

'Thirty-two minutes! Ena's not going to like that at all!'

And Ena didn't. They were gathered round the same snug table that evening.

'I *told* you!' said Martha, triumphant.

'And well you might!' Ena regarded Minnie balefully. 'Here am I trying to collect evidence and what happens?' Four sheets of notepaper lay in front of her. She picked them up. 'Martha Longhurst – forty-five minutes. Albert Tatlock – forty-one minutes. Ena Sharples – forty-nine minutes. And then we come to this! If this had come from Elsie Tanner I might have understood it!' She glared at the miserable Minnie. 'Have you been got at?'

'I don't know how you mean!'

'Have you been talking? That's how I mean!'

'I've never breathed a word to a living soul!' Minnie's hand was on her heart.

'H'm!' sniffed Ena, unimpressed. 'I suppose you realize how I'm going to look tomorrow? They're going to pick on this. They're going to ask me if I'm sure the other figures are right! Oh, it's going to be wonderful!' There followed a pregnant pause. Minnie looked a picture of contrition, Martha a reincarnation of the Hanging Judge. Ena went on, very slightly more in sorrow than in anger, 'Thirty-two minutes! If it had been *forty*-two, I might have understood it!'

Martha looked sideways at Ena. Was she being given a cue? Ena's face betrayed nothing. Martha decided to trust her instincts. 'I suppose it could be altered?' she said.

'Now I never said that!' It was Ena, looking incorruptible..

Martha sat back in her chair, pleased that her instincts had not let her down. Minnie looked fearfully from one to the other.

'Will I get into trouble?'

'Hear that?' Ena was asking Martha. 'That's all she's worried about! She doesn't value my friendship – that means nothing!'

Minnie looked nervously across the counter, convinced that the forces of the law were gathering to bring about her downfall.

'I haven't got an indiarubber,' she whispered.

'I have!' said Ena and the rubber was on the table and the paper turned to face Minnie in the twinkling of an eye. Another fearful glance and Minnie joined the criminal classes. Ena's eyes narrowed in triumph.

'Just wait till I get in that Town Hall tomorrow! They'll wonder what's hit 'em!'

And that was how it all began.

Weatherfield Town Hall was a squat black building set back from the main Manchester road. It housed, besides all the varied battalions of local government, the branch offices of the Electricity and Gas Boards and the show-room of the Solid Fuel Advisory Council. In short, those agencies which give rise to the vast majority of our day-to-day complaints. Which probably explained why the entrance was so difficult to find. A notice board, strategically placed at the top of twenty steep stone steps leading to the massive front doors, declared to the perspiring climber 'Entrance in Duke Street'. It was calculated that fourteen per cent of all protesters gave up at this point. Those of sterner stuff began to look for Duke Street. A fast recon-naissance disclosed that the Town Hall was flanked by Atherton Street to the left and Birley Street to the right. Where then was Duke Street? By now, a further twenty-one percent had fallen by the wayside. The intrepid ex-plorer, however, would discover that Duke Street was a cul-de-sac leading from Atherton Street. He would also discover that the street nameplate had been defaced by black paint and was unreadable except on the closest in-spection. Whether this was the result of vandalism or quick thinking on the part of the Sanitary Department's junior clerk was the subject of some controversy. Whoever was to blame, the defacement provided an extra obstacle on a hazardous journey. Had our explorer plumped for Birley Street and been forced to retrace every one of his steps, he would have been extremely tired by the time he reached the dim, uninviting entrance and thus been easy prey for the denizens of the Town Hall, fortified as they were by regular tea and biscuits.

No such problems confronted Ena. 'Know Your Town Hall' had long been one of her rules in life and although offices and departments were constantly being moved hither and thither and from one floor to another, the desperate authorities never wholly succeeded in thwarting her and her like. Not that she treated the authorities casually. She invariably dressed up for the occasion and that morning was no exception. The grey princess-line coat was, of course, her normal wear but not so the black cotton gloves, the real leather handbag and *the hat*.

Little Doreen Lostock, gazing out of a first-floor window of the raincoat factory, nudged her friend Sheila Birtles and pointed down into the street. 'Eh up, somebody's going to cop it! Ena's got her hat on!'

A twopenny ride on a 63 bus, an unfaltering walk round the Town Hall to Duke Street and Ena was past the aged commissionaire before he could lift his eyes from his *Sporting Chronicle* and ask what she wanted. Not that she would have stopped. She knew him of old. He was the last, but the toughest obstacle, Cerberus at the gates of Hell. His job it was to confuse by false information, and rumour had it that one determined lady, resolved to see the Town Clerk, had passed old Arthur's booth nine times in her unavailing search and, her resolution sapped, had finally thanked him profusely for showing her the way out.

Ena passed the wide staircase facing the marble statue of William Cobden, marched along the musty corridor and into the office marked, rather uninformatively, Room 22. Facing her was a counter bearing a wooden painted sign which read, simply, 'Meter Enquiries' and, behind it, a thin, fair-haired, nervous young man. The young man's name was Phil.

Ena addressed him.

'My name's Mrs Ena Sharples of the Glad Tidings Mission Hall, Coronation Street.'

'Oh yes?' said Phil, politely. 'Good morning!'

'Well, go on, put it down!' said Ena irritably, 'I don't want to have to keep telling you.'

'Oh yes!' agreed Phil nervously. He pulled a pad and pencil towards him and began to write as instructed. 'Mrs Ena Sharples, Glad Tidings Mission Hall, Coronation Street. Yes, Mrs Sharples?'

'I've come about my gas pressure.'

The clerk's relief could almost be tasted. 'Not about the meter then?'

'I suppose it comes through t'meter but it's the pressure I've come about.'

'Ah, well, it's the District Engineer's office you want! You go out of here, turn to your left, take the stairs at the end of the corridor, turn left at the top and you want room 151.' He had been looking towards the door hoping it would start her on her way but when he turned his eyes to her he discovered she hadn't moved. Moreover there was a pitying smile on her face.

'How long have you worked here?'

'Er . . . five years.'

'Five years, eh?' said Ena. 'Well, I'll have you know that I first walked into this Town Hall the week it were built and that were in nineteen nineteen. So don't you start telling *me* where to go because I happen to know that if you have any complaints about gas pressure you bring them to *this* office!'

'Not complaints, Mrs Sharples. This is meter enquiries.' He pointed to the painted sign. 'Nothing about complaints.'

The pity deepened in her eyes. 'Get away!' she said. 'It might surprise you to know that you can walk the length and breadth of this Town Hall and never on one door will you see the word "complaints". They don't advertise the fact, you know, they might have people coming in making 'em! So either write down what I'm going to say or, if you can't deal with it, fetch someone as can!'

Phil needed no further invitation. 'Right!' he said, and he was off.

Ena, not quite sure if he had genuinely gone for help or had fled to sign on as a deck-hand on some Patagonia-bound steamer, decided to sit and wait. She pulled up a scratched bentwood chair and was trying vainly to make herself comfortable when the door opened and an old lady walked in. Probably no more than a couple of years older than Ena, but decades older in spirit. With a nervous smile she hobbled to the counter and waited, meekly, for attention.

'What did you want, love?' asked Ena, the champion of the oppressed.

'I wanted to pay my water rates,' said the old lady.

'Ee, you're miles off, love! Turn left outside here and follow your nose till you come to the big hall with the stone statues in it.'

'I've come past there,' said the old lady.

'Well you shouldn't have. Carry on through till you come to a feller with a peaked hat on but don't ask him or he'll set you wrong. Walk straight past him and get in the lift and go up to the second floor. Turn left out of the lift and it's on your right-hand side. It's no cockstride, mind. They're after you soon enough if you don't pay but, by gum, they make it hard work! What was it, water rates?'

'That's right,' said the old lady, miserable at the thought of yet another route march.

'Let's have a look,' said Ena and took the bill out of the lady's unprotesting hand. She glanced at it briefly. 'Is that where you live – Pleasant View?' The old lady nodded. 'They're overcharging you then!'

'Are they?'

'They are that! Think on, you see 'em about it before you pay!'

'Oh, I will! Thank you very much!' The old lady took the bill back and went off in search of a sympathetic ear. Ena watched her go, wondering idly if she'd ever be seen again. She waited a couple of moments then stood impatiently and moved to the counter. Her eyes swept distastefully around the drab office, taking in the outdated ink-wells, the untidy scatter of paper, the notice on the wall headed 'Demolition of Property, Borough of Weatherfield' and on to the faded, framed sepia-chrome of some long-dead Mayor. Her eyes returned to the notice and she began, idly, to read the fine black print. 'Order pursuant'; 'as mentioned heretofore'; 'That are bounded by and including . . .'

A familiar word caused her to lean forward for a closer look when the adjoining door opened and another young man, darker, more assured, led the nervous Phil into the office. But, though interrupted, Ena had seen enough and now all she wanted was to get away. Vaguely she could hear the new young man telling her that strictly speaking this was a matter for the District Engineer and she cut in sharply.

'Here, take these!' she said, pushing the four signed declarations across the counter. 'Pin 'em to a General Complaints form and if you don't know what them are you'll find 'em in the bottom drawer of that there cabinet!' She poked a stiff finger towards a battered filing cabinet which occupied one corner of the office. 'And think on I want to hear from you inside a couple of days!' With a final glare she was gone.

The dark young man knelt by the cabinet. Wonderingly he pulled from the front of the drawer a sheaf of yellow forms headed 'General Complaints'.

'She's right!' he said.

'She's the sort who always is!' said Phil.

But he was wrong.

Within half an hour of Ena returning to the street the news was on everyone's lips.

'But why haven't the brewery told us?' Annie asked Jack as they prepared to open for the morning session.

'Eh, don't ask me! Happen because they've nowt to tell!' replied her phlegmatic husband.

'She was very convincing when *I* spoke to her!'

'Now, love, you've known Ena Sharples long enough to realize she's *always* convincing, right or wrong!'

But Jack Walker was alone in his cynicism. He was right in his assessment of Ena. The farther she was pushed into a corner the harder she fought back and the more doubts that were expressed over the news she had brought the more emphatic her declarations became.

'I tell you I saw it with my own eyes. And I don't know how you feel about yours but I can believe mine! Coronation Street's coming down! Be told!'

'What did it say exactly, Ena?' Minnie had asked.

'I've told you a dozen times! That area bounded by and including the north-east side of Coronation Street.'

'And that's the side everybody lives on?' This was Martha. They were in her front room, drinking her tea.

'Everybody bar me,' said Ena, gently stirring her Typhoo Tips.

Martha looked around her apprehensively. 'What about here? Did it say?'

'If it did I saw nowt. Still, if this side of Coronation Street's coming down I can't see you escaping. I mean, you back on, don't you?'

'What about Jubilee Terrace, Ena,' asked Minnie in a still, small voice.

'Eh, *you'll* get away with it!'

'She always does!' added Martha spitefully.

'Aye,' said Ena. 'Push her off the Co-op roof and she'd fall in the divi!'

All over the neighbourhood little groups of worried citizens met to discuss the disquieting news.

In the Rover's Return, Len, Harry and Albert were barely enjoying a lunchtime drink before going off to County's home match with Crewe Alexandra.

'I don't know!' muttered Albert. 'You live in a house all your life and then some jumped-up so-and-so puts summat down on a piece of paper and next thing you know you've got a bulldozer knocking at t'front door!'

'Time enough to start worrying when that happens,' said Len.

'Is it eckaslike! It's too late by then!' Albert's tone was injured. 'Where am I going to live?'

'What about that daughter of yours?' asked Harry.

'I said "live" not "exist"!' grunted Albert and turned back to the comfort of his rum.

The door swung open and Frank Barlow entered followed by burly Alf Roberts, his colleague at the Sorting Office.

Len wiped the froth from his lips. 'Heard the news?' he said.

'Aye!' said Alf cheerfully. 'Frank's been telling me. Not affected myself!' He slapped Frank on the back. 'I'd better get you a drink, you poor old devil, before you get slung out on t'street!'

Harry turned back to the bar. 'How about ringing the Town Hall up, Jack?'

'At this time on a Saturday? You must be joking, lad! Saturday mornings, they start getting ready to come home the minute they get there!'

'Wouldn't the brewery tell you if anything was going to happen?' asked Frank.

Jack put down the glass he had just polished and picked up another. 'I'd have thought so but so far I've heard nothing.'

'According to Mrs Sharples,' said Annie knowingly, 'they don't want us to know! The Town Hall, I mean, not the brewery.' She leaned forward confidentially. 'It's only a few weeks to local elections and they don't want to lose votes, do they? According to Ena the poster she saw was for internal consumption only and not for the information of the downtrodden general public!'

'Now, Annie!' said Jack. 'You know Ena! There's times when, according to her, the earth's flat!'

The men shook their heads gravely, unconvinced. There was smoke and where there was smoke there was fire and it might not be long before the fire was burning the time-worn timbers of Coronation Street.

It was a long, worrisome weekend. Those under sentence met, conferred, weighed every pro and every con and reached no other conclusion than that Ena Sharples had read the official document which sentenced the street to death.

The casual observer might well feel that it was a simple matter to prove the rumour true or false but that was far from the case. Kenneth Barlow, Esther Hayes and Elsie Tanner each made trips to the Town Hall but their identical reports that, according to a variety of officials, there was no substance whatsoever to Ena's story only succeeded in hardening the suspicions of their fellow-residents.

'Mark my words!' said Albert Tatlock. 'First you'll hear

about it is when t'roof falls on top of you! '

Martha nodded. 'They'll be frightened to death now it's out! But it won't stop 'em, you watch! '

It was Wednesday lunchtime and they were in the snug with Minnie, Albert having been granted special dispensation to sit there in Ena's absence at the market.

'Let's go and see if Ena's back,' suggested Minnie. 'Perhaps she's heard something.'

None of them gave a second glance at the dark-suited gentleman who stood back politely and allowed them to pass him at the front door. The gentleman, neat, fiftyish and bowler-hatted, walked purposefully to the bar and introduced himself to Jack Walker as Mr Harper from the Borough Surveyor's Office.

'The brewery have been in touch with us and they've asked me to have a word with you,' he added. 'Could we er . . . ?' Harper glanced significantly towards the door which led to the Walkers' private quarters.

Jack whispered a couple of words to Concepta and led Harper through the bar and into the living room, collecting Annie on the way.

'This is Mr Harper from t'Town Hall. Brewery have asked him to have a word with us.'

'I'll come straight to the point,' said Harper. 'Your Managing Director happens to be a golfing friend of the Borough Surveyor and they were playing together yesterday morn . . .' That innate loyalty which one public official holds for his superior rose to the surface. '. . . yesterday evening when they started to chat as golfers apparently do and Mr Crabtree, that's the Borough Surveyor, was given to understand that some rumour has been circulating that this street is to be demolished. I believe you've been on to the brewery about it yourselves?'

'Aye, we have,' said Jack.

'And several of the local residents have been to the Town Hall,' added Annie.

'So I understand,' said Harper, 'and as usually happens in such cases the enquiry tends to be answered and forgotten but when Mr Crabtree heard . . .' He smiled thinly and allowed the words to hang in mid-air. Without actually putting it into words he was implying that ordinary citizens could batter their heads against the wall of bureaucracy until the cows came home but when one of the Borough Surveyor's golfing friends dropped a word or two the entire system swung into dynamic action. He summed up in ten words. 'It was decided that I should make a few enquiries.'

Jack and Annie looked at each other. After twenty-three years of marriage each knew how the other thought. At times like this there was little need for the spoken word. 'He's going to ask us if we know how it started,' thought Jack. 'I know,' thought Annie, 'and I'm going to tell him!' 'I thought you might!' thought Jack.

'Well, naturally, I hesitate to talk about our own customers but necessity does tend to overcome the normal conventions, does it not?' Annie was one of the Beaumonts of Clitheroe and let no one forget it. Although her education had been sketchy, to say the least, she had been brought up in the bosom of a shabby genteel family who believed in self-education of a specialized kind. Annie had been taught at an early age never to use a word of one syllable when one of four would do. She had also known the intimate histories of each of Queen Victoria's numerous offspring before she could recite 'Little Bo Beep'. Which was why Jack tended to take a back seat on such occasions. Even after twenty-three years he could still find himself impressed by Annie in full flow.

'I agree entirely, Mrs Walker,' said Harper, equally impressed.

'And I think you may find that a good starting point for your enquiries would be the Glad Tidings Mission. At the other end of the street.'

'I see,' said Harper. 'And the name of the er ... person?'

Annie switched on her air of sweet martyrdom and looked soulfully at her husband. Whilst it was permitted for her, as a lady, to sharpen the dagger of deceit it was a man's job to plunge it into the victim's heart. Jack took the point.

'It's a Mrs Sharples,' he said. 'She's the caretaker.'

Harper's first remark to Ena after, eventually, she had let him into the vestry and he had found himself facing

91

not only her but two more ageing ladies and an elderly gentleman, all regarding him with grave suspicion, was to suggest that they should talk in private.

'These are my friends!' said Ena. 'If you've got owt to say to me it can be said in front o' them!' A remark she was soon to regret.

'Very well, Mrs Sharples!' Harper hesitated then opened his briefcase and took from it a large piece of cartridge paper. Even folded into four as it was, it measured eighteen inches by a foot. He went on, making no attempt to open the folds. 'I understand a rumour is rife in the neighbourhood that this street is scheduled for demolition?'

'If you mean have we found out what you've got up your sleeves, yes, we have!' said Ena the implacable.

'I've been doing a little detective work and I'm told you visited the Town Hall at the end of last week to complain about your gas pressure.'

'Five days since and we've not heard a word.' Ena looked at her friends for support and was rewarded with grave nods.

'Could I ask if you saw this on the wall?' Harper unfolded the stiff paper. He held out the wall poster for Ena to see. It was headed 'Demolition of Property, Borough of Weatherfield'.

'I did!' said Ena. 'Decided the game's up, have you?'

Harper ignored the remark. 'May I ask you to read it once again, Mrs Sharples?'

'Why?'

'I'd like you to.'

Ena paused then screwed up her eyes and began to read. Her head nodded slightly as it moved along the lines and back again. And then, with a cry of triumph, 'There you are! It's as plain as the nose . . .' She broke off. There was a moment's stunned silence. Her three cronies looked at her questioningly, Harper levelly. 'Anyone can make a mistake,' she said.

'Very true, Mrs Sharples, but few people take their mistakes to such lengths.'

Martha broke the pause which followed. 'What's he on about, Ena?'

Only on the rarest occasions was Ena annoyed with herself. But then it was only rarely that she would admit to a fall in perfection. At that moment, however, she was very angry with herself. If only she'd had the sense to send her friends away she could have told the street that Harper had come to negotiate but that she had been adamant. And that due to her resolution Coronation Street would live on. But Ena never dwelt too long on the 'ifs' and 'buts' of life. She decided to attack.

'Never mind what he's on about! There's places for this kind of talk and it's not in my vestry!' She turned to Harper. 'Tell us where your office is and I'll come to see you in the morning!'

Harper smiled. 'Oh, I don't think that's necessary, Mrs Sharples! You seemed to spread the rumour easily enough in the first place, I'm sure you'll have no difficulty in putting matters to rights.' He held the poster to face Minnie and Martha. 'It was quite a simple mistake. Mrs Sharples misread Coronation Terrace for Coronation Street. The area this poster refers to is over on the other side of Weatherfield, just off the Rochdale Road. The only pity is that Mrs Sharples didn't query the matter whilst she was in the Town Hall. I'm sure her error would soon have been discovered.' He folded the notice, put it back into his brief case and clicked the catch. 'I won't keep you any longer. Good day!' And with a polite nod to Ena he let himself out.

There had been other silences but this one was deafening. And this time it was broken by Minnie, normally the meek and mild corner of the snug triangle, she had always saved her biting wit for the appropriate moment and when those moments came her shafts had an edge which even Ena envied.

'I think we'd better get back to t'Rovers,' said Minnie in that dangerously soft voice, 'before we're told t'milk stout's contaminated!'

'Aye, I think we'd better!' said Martha and followed Minnie out. Albert hesitated for a second then met Ena's baleful eyes and scuttled out.

Harper had been right although it wasn't Ena who set

the record straight. Within an hour every household had heard the truth behind the rumour. After which it would have been difficult for Ena to set any record straight. The street sent her to Coventry.

Sending Ena to Coventry for her false rumour was rather like stopping the morning papers for crediting Zsa Zsa Gabor with the wrong age. It had the effect of cutting oneself off from the flood of news and gossip which normally entered every household. The street suffered rather more than Ena did.

Martha Longhurst appointed herself the overseer of Ena's ostracism. The first sign of weakening, the merest hint of a smile in Ena's direction brought a blast of invective from the thin-lipped Martha. She knew that the only way she could take over Ena's command was by making sure that Ena stayed out of the way, and she made full use of Ena's absence. Even to the extent of taking over Ena's chair in the snug. This was regarded by some as requiring great courage but Martha knew when she was safe. On being told of her banishment Ena had made it quite clear that until the street came to her she certainly wasn't going to them.

'Blow 'em!' she had told Polly Hardcastle off Bessie Street when they rubbed shoulders reaching for the same remnant on Singh's Silk Stall in Weatherfield Market. 'They're not worth talking to, anyway!'

And, sure enough, the street was forced to go to Ena.

It had been the custom for several years for the pub to organize an outing on Whit Monday. Each year a committee, formed specially for the purpose, held a series of meetings, debated at length the pros and cons of a variety of resorts and beauty spots and, inevitably, chose Blackpool.

Only once, in 1956, had the revolutionaries won the day

and swung the vote to Whitby. The morning of departure had been dull but the party had set off, not only in Charlie Weston's super 24-seater Landcruiser, but in remarkably high spirits at the thought of a change from the Golden Mile, the Pleasure Beach, a tour of a Blackpool rock factory and plaice and chips behind the Winter Gardens. And a change was indeed what they got. The Landcruiser developed some obscure mechanical failure deep into the Yorkshire moors, well out of sight of the nearest habitation and, what was much worse, six miles from the nearest hostelry. As Len Fairclough sourly remarked, 'The only spot in the flamin' British Isles that's six miles from a pub and we've got to hit it!'

The emergency rations of pale ale and milk stout were consumed within the first forty-five minutes and the remainder of the six-hour wait was spent in castigating the committee for their stupidity in flying in the faces of the gods and not choosing Blackpool. In future, it was decided, as the rain clouds scudded over them en route from the North Sea to Leeds, the committee could decide what it liked as long as it didn't meddle with where they went.

And so, on Whit Monday 1961, it was to be Blackpool once again. The weekly collections had been organized well in advance and were in full swing when Harry Hewitt, Committeeman in charge of Transport, brought the news to the Rover's Return that Charlie Weston could only supply a 32-seater that year.

'Eh, we'll never fill a thirty-two seater!' said Jack.

His son, Billy, in charge of Bookings, took out his notebook and did a quick calculation. 'Twenty-two so far,' he said. 'We thought we only had two to find. Now it looks as if we've got to find another ten!'

'Can't we advertise?' asked Elsie, the eternal saleswoman.

All eyes turned to Florrie Lindley who was standing meekly in the corner, minding her own business and devoting herself to a half glass of ginger beer shandy. She gulped and smiled around nervously.

'I could manage a postcard!' she said. 'I don't like taking

up too much window space with notices because . . . well, that's the only way I can advertise my goods! '

The clientele regarded her with an air of faint disgust and returned to the problem.

'We've always put a notice up in the Mission before,' contributed Martha Longhurst.

'Bit difficult with Mrs Sharples in Coventry, isn't it?' Doreen Lostock turned her wide eyes on the regulars as they nodded in agreement.

'You've hit it, kid! ' said Billy Walker admiringly.

Behind him, Annie flashed a sharp glance. Doreen was a pretty enough child – that elfin face and big bright blue eyes. But Doreen was a working-class girl with working-class parents, not at all the sort of young lady one would welcome into the bosom of a family highly placed in the catering trade. Annie had been distressed to learn that Billy and Doreen were 'walking out' and secretly wished that the affair could be short-lived. Meanwhile she wished he wouldn't appear quite so affectionate in public.

Jack noticed the look from Annie and decided to move back into calmer waters. 'I don't know how many I speak for,' he said, 'but I reckon Ena's learned her lesson. I reckon it's time we got her back.'

It was the statement the street had been waiting for. Apart from the fact that Ena's absence left an unaccustomed gap in the street's affairs, they really were missing her for her news value. The curtains had come down in Bessie Hardwick's front room in Inkerman Street two weeks previously and the rumour that she had run away with Ada Blunt's husband remained unconfirmed. Only Ena could supply the relevant information.

Ena let them down lightly. She graciously received the deputation of Minnie, Martha and Albert, hung the hastily drafted poster on the notice board and accepted their invitation to return to the Rover. Honour was satisfied, the gap was filled and the street at last learned the full, unexpurgated truth about Bessie Hardwick and Fred Blunt.

Two days after Ena's unfounded rumour of demolition had hit the street like a bombshell, Ivan had completed the purchase of No. 9, Coronation Street.

'Just our luck!' philosophized Elsie. 'You'll no sooner move into t'place than they'll knock it down!'

It had been, therefore, with a great deal of relief that Ivan and Linda who had given £565 for the house, learned the truth from Minnie and Martha. Within a week they had moved in and once again Elsie was surrounded by her family. Which she considered to be a mixed blessing. At least, she thought, they cancel each other out. If Linda was the 'heavy', the emotional member of the family, surrounded always by the drama of life, Dennis could only be described as the light relief. A role which Elsie viewed with a wary eye. 'Oh, he makes me laugh all right,' she'd say of her loving son. 'Till I cry!'

Dennis flitted from job to job like a bee on honeysuckle. Unlike the bee, however, he rarely collected anything of value. His first venture of 1961 was into the realms of show business which wasn't surprising as, since his early teens, he had enjoyed a series of daydreams, all of which cast him as the sensation of the century. He had electrified an audience of millions with his guitar, thrilled a generation when he elbowed Jack Lemmon off the screen and took Marilyn Monroe in his arms, brought the world cheering to its feet when, with one mighty blow, he knocked out Floyd Patterson.

At the moment it was the night club scene. Dennis had only to close his eyes and he was transported to his own plush gambling club, surrounded by roulette tables, strong-arm men and beautiful women.

His favourite fantasy had him on the telephone, sending a Transatlantic cable. 'It's to *F. Sinatra, Burbank, California* and the message reads – *Frankie, come and sing for me. It's an order. Dennis.*' But that, reasoned Dennis, might take a little time. Everyone had to begin somewhere and Dennis's 'somewhere' was a seedy little clip joint on the fringes of Manchester's night-life, called, for some obscure reason, the Orinoco Club.

Dennis was front-of-house, the welcoming smile over the

97

frilled dress shirt and the black velvet bow. There was a cabaret of sorts and one of Dennis's many duties was to take care of the artistes. Which could hardly fail to lead him into some kind of trouble.

One escapade doubled the number of Elsie's grey hairs in a matter of seconds. One dismal afternoon in mid-February Elsie, bedevilled by a headache since early morning and catching Mrs Dumbarton on one of her sympathetic days, was sent home early. She let herself into the quiet house; pausing in the lobby to listen to Dennis's rhythmic snores floating down from the back bedroom, and trudged wearily into the back parlour bound for a cup of tea and a couple of aspirin. On the table stood a large cardboard box and, idly curious, Elsie lifted the lid . . .

Harry Hewitt, off duty two doors away, swore he had never heard anything like it since the Blitz. Florrie Lindley dropped a carton of eggs. Ena Sharples flew to her curtains. But as Elsie explained later, 'If you'd found yourself face to face with a nine-foot boa constrictor, what would *you* have done? I'll tell you! You'd have done the same as me – you'd have screamed your head off!'

Dennis still swears that the screams vibrated the house so much that he fell out of bed. Flying downstairs he found his mother and the snake regarding each other with open-mouthed concentration. Such was the stillness of the tableau that they appeared simultaneously to have hypnotized each other, Elsie's screams having petrified the poor snake who, rudely awakened from a deep sleep, had reared itself up to peer over the side of the box at this noisy intruder.

With great presence of mind and a courage which given a moment's thought he would never have shown, Dennis clapped the lid back on the box and led his shaking mother to a chair. At that precise moment the door opened and a rather attractive head popped into the room. 'What's wrong?' asked the attractive mouth. 'Get that thing out of here!' hissed Dennis and the rest of the attractive package christened Eunice Bond but known to the patrons of the Orinoco Club as La Composita, stepped into the room.

'This is Eunice, Mum,' whispered Dennis. 'It's her snake. She uses it in her act and her landlady found it in the room and gave her notice to quit and she'd nowhere to go, I mean Eunice not the snake, and she could only find digs for herself so I said I'd look after the snake until she got herself settled and I never expected you back so early because we're taking it away now.' He needn't have bothered. Elsie didn't hear a word he said and he was forced to repeat the whole sorry story when, slowly, Elsie returned to full consciousness.

Meanwhile, Eunice felt she really ought to say something. 'Pleased to meet you, Mrs Tanner,' she said. 'I've heard a lot of you.'

She would probably have heard a lot more had not Elsie lapsed again into a python-induced coma. Dennis, who fully realized this danger, waved Eunice to silence and shepherded her and her nine-foot pet out of the house. Then, bravely, he returned to face the music . . .

Two months later Elsie frowned at Dennis over the break-fast table and, speaking of Arthur Dewhurst, said, 'Why did you have to bring that feller into the house? Why couldn't it have been another flaming snake! '

Arthur Dewhurst was a Detective Inspector on the Weatherfield CID. His success was more the product of doggedness than intelligence, more the result of pain-staking enquiry than the analytical genius which allows more brilliant lawmen to point unerringly at the criminal. His character was best summed up by the name given to him by his colleagues at Weatherfield Central. In the canteens and the offices and the interrogation rooms of that establishment Arthur Dewhurst was known as PC Plod.

He had walked, or, rather, staggered into Elsie's life one dark night in early April. Elsie had fallen asleep in her chair in front of a dying fire and was dreaming of Clark Gable who, for some unfathomable reason was serving behind the counter of the corner shop, when the front door banged and her offspring crept noisily in.

'Oh, sorry!' he said. 'Did I wake you?'

'Yes, love, you woke me! And you could have picked a better time. Clark Gable himself was just about to cut two ounces of boiled ham.'

Dennis was used to his mother's fantasizing. 'Any cocoa?' he asked.

Elsie decided not to embarrass him by asking what a night club tycoon wanted with cocoa. 'Go and get yourself a cup. And make me one while you're at it.'

They heard the scuffle in the back entry as Elsie put down her empty cup. They both listened for a moment to the following silence.

'Fetch that poker!' said Elsie. 'There's summat going on!'

'You stay where you are. I'll go!' And Dennis went.

I must give him more cocoa! thought Elsie but her thoughts would have been less generous had she realized what strange fish her son was about to land. She heard him from the backyard.

'Give us a hand, Mum!'

As she reached the backyard the moon broke from behind a cloud and illuminated her son holding up a limp and obviously heavy figure. Between them they managed to half carry the injured man – there was blood on his face – into the living room. Dennis laid him out on the sofa while Elsie warmed some water and poured a whisky.

It was a simple story. Detective Inspector Dewhurst, called out to investigate a prowling gang of youths, had happened on a couple in Viaduct Street. He had given chase, they had disappeared down the entry behind Coronation Street and he had cornered them. Unfortunately for Arthur that wasn't the end of the matter. One of the young gentlemen had picked up a brick and dealt him a nasty blow. And had then escaped with his companion.

The story didn't exactly please Dennis. It was solidly against his principles to help policemen however grievous their distress but worse was still to come. Arthur Dewhurst, knocked silly by the blow, had opened his eyes to find a ravishing, titian-haired houri tenderly ministering to his wounds. Not only that, the houri was none too securely wrapped in a dressing gown and, as she was leaning over him, she offered an unrestricted view of what Len Fairclough had described as 'the best scaffolding in the North of England' and Ena Sharples often called 'a downright disgrace!' Arthur thought it magnificent and called the following evening to express his thanks. And the evening after that. He would have called the following evening too but as he was on duty he came round in the afternoon instead.

Within a week he had his feet under the table and, much to Dennis's disgust, was calling Elsie 'little flower'.

At first Elsie was flattered. Then she experienced a sense of security such as she had never known before. After all, there weren't many women who had their own private detective-inspector to look after them. The Queen, perhaps, and one or two others. But these heartening realizations rapidly lost their effect. She soon discovered why his pals called him PC Plod. His idea of a great, swinging night was to sit and gaze at Elsie over a pot of tea and a homemade fruit cake. As Elsie was wont to say, 'I'm not much around the house but I'm a dab hand at fruit cake.'

So Elsie was rather less than ecstatic when Arthur happily informed her that he'd so arranged his duty roster that he was free to take her on the Whit Monday outing to Blackpool. As she said to Linda later that night, 'I suppose I could have said no but he looks at me with that spaniel's face of his and . . . well, you know me and dogs!'

For once it wasn't raining. Clusters of grave-faced little girls, clad from head to foot in shining white, met and conversed at street corners, waiting for the buses to take them into 'town'. Standard Two of St Mary's C of E School, complete with proud parents stood patiently at the corner of Coronation Street and Rosamund Street, en route to Manchester. They were to congregate in Albert Square where they would form up into marching order. And at nine thirty, complete with brass bands and waving banners, those grave little girls would walk demurely through the city streets to the cheers and applause of a hundred thousand Lancastrians. For a dying ceremony it was still remarkably lively.

Lucille barely looked at the waiting group as she left her home and walked down to the Rover's Return. She wasn't wearing her dress – it was over her arm. Jack opened the door to her.

'Eh, I'm sorry, love!' he said. 'If you want a drink of beer you'll have to come back later. I can't serve you yet!'

'I don't want a drink of beer!' said Lucille, shyly.

'Oh, I beg your pardon! I thought you did! Come in a minute!'

Lucille followed him into the darkened bar. 'It was Auntie Annie I wanted.'

Jack pretended to be hurt. 'Oh, I see! I thought for a minute it might be me!'

'Well, it's you as well. But I wanted to show Auntie my dress. Is she in?'

'Oh, yes, she's in, love. But she's not really with us yet. You might say she's still getting herself ready. Still, we'll have a try! You stay where you are and I'll see what I can do!' He walked into the hall and shouted upstairs. 'Annie! There's a very important young lady to see you!'

Annie joined in the game. Her voice floated downstairs. 'Would you tell her I won't be a moment, please!'

'The lady said would you mind waiting a moment,' said Jack in his best butler's voice.

'Oh, very well!' Lucille knew how much her 'Uncle' Jack enjoyed playing his little games with her. She was a kind-hearted girl and it cost nothing to humour him.

'Perhaps you'd like to sit down?'

'Thank you!'

They sat facing each other. The schoolgirl and the publican. Separated by two World Wars, four monarchs and a millennium of human achievement.

'Lovely weather for the time o' year!'

This hilarious observation was too much for Lucille. The giggles broke out as Annie opened the door.

'I see! Here's me slaving away making the beds and you two down here enjoying yourselves! '

'It's Uncle Jack! He's funny! '

'He's more than funny,' said Annie, 'he's downright peculiar! '

'Now, Annie, I've told you! Any more of that and I'm going to lock you in the coalshed and marry Lucille! '

'You'll do no such thing! ' said Lucille disapprovingly.

Annie smiled. 'That's right, love, you tell him! Now, what have you come to show me?'

'My dress. For the procession.' Shyly she stood and held the white beribboned dress by the shoulders.

'By gum! That's a frock and a half that is! ' said Jack, more than suitably impressed.

'It's not a frock, it's a dress. And a lovely dress, too, which is just what it should be for a lovely young lady.'

Lucille tucked the collar under her chin and with her free hand lifted the blue satin sash.

'Auntie Concepta made my sash.'

'And who's taking my name in vain?' It was Concepta herself, dressed, rather splendidly, for the day out. Almond-green suit, white, lacy blouse, black patent shoes and handbag and, Annie noticed immediately, white gloves.

'She's being very complimentary,' said Annie. 'She's telling us that you made that lovely sash for her . . .' And without drawing breath '. . . and do you really think white gloves are right, dear?'

'Well, I've got black,' said Concepta, 'but I was thinking they were more suitable for a Wake than a Wakes Week! '

'Oh, no, dear! Always match your gloves to your other accessories! I've got a rather dressy pair of black upstairs. They're not at all funerally. I'll bring them down for you.'

'Oh, that is kind of you! You know, I was wondering about white. Something told me they weren't quite right! ' Which was a downright lie. Concepta had been quite pleased with her choice but she had long since learned that there was little point in arguing with Annie on matters of dress, etiquette and the aristocracy. Particularly, she added ruefully to herself, if you're dependent on her for your job, board and lodgings. And then, being a fair-minded girl, she dismissed the thought as ungenerous. Which it was, for Annie had a soft spot for the Irish girl.

'I reckon they've forgotten about us!' Jack said to Lucille. 'I reckon they've gone off into a world of their own and forgotten all about us!'

'Oh, no, we haven't!' said Annie, turning to survey Lucille's dress with a critical eye. '*Very* fashionable! *Very à la mode* indeed! White gloves, of course?'

'Yes,' said Lucille, 'and a little bouquet.'

'Delightful!' said Annie. And meant it.

Jack took his half-hunter from his waistcoat pocket and held it out to the correct focal length. 'Hadn't you better be getting it on, love? You'll be missing your procession.'

'Oh, we're not walking today! Our lot walks on Wednesday.' She turned to Annie. 'We're coming down Rosamund Street. Right past this corner!'

'Oh, I *am* pleased!' said Annie. 'You know, that's one thing I miss with having our picnic on Whit Monday – going into Manchester for the Walks!'

'There'll be a much better show on Friday!' said Concepta, smilingly faithful to the Church of Rome.

'Now don't get me involved in *that* argument!' said Annie. 'I'd like to see them *all*! I think they're all lovely, bless their little hearts!'

The front door swung open and Harry Hewitt popped his head round. 'Have you got a daughter of mine in here?' His eyes found her and the door creaked further open as he walked through to her. 'I just hope you're not being a nuisance!'

'Nuisance be blowed!' said Jack. 'She's showing us her dress. We're very honoured!'

Harry pretended to see Concepta for the first time. 'By eck, there's some smart uns going on this trip, Jack!'

'There are that, lad! I reckon we've had it! They'll have nowt to do with us!'

'Oh, we might at that!' said Concepta. She looked

appraisingly at Harry. 'This one's not bad for a bus inspector in civvies!'

A tableau formed. Concepta, her head cocked on one side, showing approval of the smiling Harry. Jack, openly beaming, blessing the partnership before it was even formed. Annie, her tongue firmly in her cheek but her thoughts nonetheless straying to orange blossom and receptions and black Rolls Royces. And Lucille, eleven years old but very wise and hoping fervently that her father wouldn't do anything stupid until he'd consulted her.

Detective-Inspector Arthur Dewhurst sat bolt upright in Elsie's best uncut moquette easy chair. Even so, being a big man, his legs still stretched dangerously across the hearth rug as Elsie had discovered on her frequent trips to the fireplace for her bits and bobs.

'Are you quite comfy there?' she had asked as she stumbled over those enormous feet for the third time.

'Oh aye! Fine!' Sarcasm blunted itself on Arthur, the armour-plated male.

'Oh, I *am* pleased!' said Elsie and Arthur thought she meant it. And glowed.

He might have felt less contented with life had he known what had been said about him in that room half-an-hour earlier. It had all started with an innocent happening in the Rover's Return the night before. Ivan had been enjoying a quiet drink with a few of the regulars when the doors swung open and Arthur's not inconsiderable bulk stood framed against the night sky. The pub fell silent as pubs do in the presence of a policeman. Particularly a policeman who is known to be investigating a series of break-ins in the neighbourhood.

'Ivan Cheveski in here?'

All eyes swivelled to Ivan as he stammered out an answer.

'Could I have a word with you outside?'

As Ivan told Elsie a few minutes later, the walk from the

bar counter to the door had been the longest journey of his life.

'But what did he want?' asked Elsie.

'He just wanted to tell me that I had forgotten to register when we moved here. As an alien I am supposed to go to the police station and tell them where I am living. And . . . there was so much to do that . . . I had forgotten.'

'Well, the daft devil!' Elsie was livid. 'Of all the potty things to do! And in front of a pubfull o' people, an' all! Come on, Fanny, get your coat on!'

'Why?' asked Fanny, alias Linda.

'Because we're all going for a last drink before they close, that's why! And Ivan can tell 'em all what he was wanted for. I don't want 'em thinking he's been pulled in for them burglaries!'

That morning, at breakfast, it had all started again.

'Good job we went last night,' mumbled Elsie through a mouthful of toast. 'Half the pub thought you'd been arrested!'

'He was very nice,' said Ivan the peacemaker.

'Oh, he's *very* nice!' said Elsie. 'If he picked you off the floor he'd tread on your toes while he was doing it! And what does it matter anyway? He knows where you live and he's a policeman!'

'It is the law,' said Ivan, switching from peacemaking to upholding the British legal system.

'Them and their laws!'

'Are you going off him?' It was Linda, taking a shrewd look at her mother.

'Off who?'

'Arthur, who'd you think?'

'What's it got to do with you? And go easy on that marmalade, it doesn't grow on trees! And think on, this breakfast lark's not going on for ever! I might have fallen for that trick of yours once! – about it being daft making two pots of tea when we live next door to each other, but it cuts both ways! I'm coming to you tomorrow morning!'

'Suit yourself! And it *does* grow on trees!'

'What does?'

'Marmalade. Well, the oranges do! And stop changing

the subject. I asked you if you were going off him!'

Elsie thought it over and decided on simple honesty. 'Wouldn't be difficult, would it!'

And, by eck, it wouldn't, she reflected, sitting in that armchair like Lord Muck with that daft look on his face. She decided to broach the subject as she faced the mirror and applied another coat of lipstick.

'Aren't there any nice policewomen down at your place?'

'Aye, one or two. Why?'

'Oh, I was just . . . wondering if you wouldn't be happier with one of your own kind! You know how most people are about policemen!

'They get some daft ideas, don't they!'

'Well, yes,' said Elsie reluctantly, 'but you can hardly blame 'em, can you? I mean, you going in the Rover last night after Ivan! They all thought he was your burglar!'

'Eh, you wouldn't credit it, would you?' said Arthur, shaking his huge head in disbelief.

Elsie decided he wasn't deliberately misunderstanding her. He wasn't clever enough for that, she reasoned. His next words proved her right.

'It's nice of you to worry about me! Thinking I might be better off with a policewoman!' He shuffled himself more deeply into the easy chair.

'I wonder what would have happened if me and Dennis had left you to suffer in our back entry the night you got coshed?'

'Well, I wouldn't be here for a start!' said Arthur happily.

'No, you wouldn't, would you!' said Elsie. But not happily.

Charlie Weston's thirty-two seater, spick and span for the trip to Blackpool, turned the Mission corner out of Viaduct Street and rolled to a halt outside the Rover's Return. Wally Prentiss, who had been driving for Weston's for over twenty years, swung open his door and climbed stiffly down to the pavement. A small knot of trippers stood on the corner, eager for the best seats.

'Morning!' said Wally. 'Just hang on a minute and I'll open the door for you!'

'Is this that chara that stops at every pub?' asked Ena.

'Hard to say, Mrs Sharples.' Wally knew Ena of old. 'Why? Feeling thirsty, are you?'

'No, I'm not!' replied Ena sharply. 'And it might interest you to know that some of us pays us money to spend an hour or two in Blackpool, not visit every four-ale bar between here and Central Pier!'

'I'll bear it in mind, Mrs Sharples!' Wally stood back from the open passenger door. Ena, first in the queue, paused on the steps.

'And I hope your driving's improved since last year!'

'Nowt wrong with my driving, love!'

'Oh, no? What about that coal cart you nearly hit going through Moses Gate?'

'What coal cart?'

'Aye, I suppose as far as you're concerned, some things is best forgotten!'

It took a good man to wrest the last word from Ena but Wally felt on top form that morning. He waited until Ena reached the top of the steps.

'I'll try and do better this morning, Mrs Sharples! If I see another coal cart in Moses Gate, I'll hit it!' And then, before she could turn and deliver another withering blast, 'Right, on you get, please! Keep moving!'

Ena found herself pushed down the bus by the boarding passengers. She carried on to the back seat and tucked herself in a corner. Then she spread her belongings on the two seats next to her, fixed the oncoming fellow travellers with a malevolent eye and dared them, silently, to complain at this illegal reservation of seats. Not that it was necessary. No one in his right mind would start a pleasant day out by sitting next to Ena uninvited.

Martha was outside the coach, looking anxiously towards the Mission when she heard the rapping on the window. She looked up to see Ena signalling to her.

'What were you doing out there?' asked Ena as Martha joined her.

'I was waiting for you! I looked on t'front seat and when you weren't there I thought you hadn't come yet.'

'You know why I'm not sitting at t'front, don't you?'

'No.'

'Because it's *him* again! Wally Prentiss! He put the fear o' death in me last year!' She craned her neck to look down the coach. 'Where is she?'

'Ee, *I* don't know!' From the disgust in Martha's voice, they could only be talking about Minnie. 'Perhaps she forgot to set her alarm!'

'Nowt'd surprise me about that one!' Ena sniffed and set her sights on the approaching figure of Len Fairclough. True to form he was staggering under the weight of a crate of beer.

'That's what gives these trips a bad name, you know! Can't you keep away from that stuff for five minutes?'

Len dropped the crate thankfully on to a seat. 'Me? I can keep away from *this* stuff for ever! It's milk stout!' He grinned at Ena. 'Shall I take it back?'

Ena's scowl sent him on his happy way and he was still grinning cheerfully when he reached the door of the coach and stood back to allow a flustered Minnie Caldwell to climb aboard.

'Made it then, love!' said Len.

'Just about!' Minnie paused to take breath and prepare herself for the meeting with Ena.

'Where'd you think *you've* been?' It was milder than Minnie had expected.

'I couldn't get the fire to light.'

Martha joined the attack. 'Whatever do you want a fire for this weather?'

'It's mother. She likes a fire to look at!' Minnie smiled tentatively. 'Do you want me next to t'window?'

'By eck, she's come!' said Ena. 'No, we don't want you next to t'window! That's my place! I don't want anybody kicking my bad ankle!'

As they sorted themselves out, Wally Prentiss navigated

the aisle nodding and smiling to his passengers as they settled themselves in their seats.

'Which way are you going, Wally?' asked Len.

'I'm easy. Which way do you want to go?'

'Could we go on that new motorway?' Wally turned to his questioner. It was Doreen Lostock. Peppy little Doreen from the raincoat factory out for the day with Billy Walker. They sat together, their hands entwined under cover of Billy's raincoat. Great idea, Billy had thought, bringing that raincoat! If I play my cards right and we get straight off the coach on to a tram we can be in the sandhills at South Shore inside quarter of an hour!

'Aye, if you like!' said Wally. 'I'm licensed for motorways!'

Len chipped in. 'We don't want motorways! Go the old road — through Bolton and over Belmont! See some nice country that way!'

'See some nice pubs you mean!' It was Ena from the back seat. 'I'd have thought you'd got enough booze with you without stopping every five minutes!'

'That's for coming back, not going!' said Harry.

Elsie decided to add her weight to the argument. 'Look, are we going to sit here all day arguing? Put it to t'vote!' All in favour of Belmont, hands up!' Her hand went up and a dig in Arthur Dewhurst's ribs and a wink at Dot Greenhalgh added two more votes for the scenic route. Then, ever aware of the power of lobbying, she leaned forward to two of Jim and Mabel Hawksworth's four kids sitting in the seat in front. 'Put your hands up!' she said. 'You can have a lemonade going this way!'

Wally Prentiss counted hands and declared an overwhelming preference for the old road. Elsie smiled, Ena scowled again and Wally settled himself in his driving seat. His finger was on the starter button when Harry's voice stopped him.

'Hey, don't go without Jack and Annie Walker! They won't be a minute!'

In the public bar, not seven paces from the waiting bus, Annie was by no means as optimistic about their imminent departure.

110

She looked at the clock for the hundredth time that hour. 'It might be fairer to all concerned if you went out there and told them! Just explain that the landlord and his wife are unable to come on their own picnic because the landlord's brother is quite incapable of showing any consideration for his own kith and kin!'

'Nay, Annie, stop worrying! He'll be here!'

'Oh, he'll *be* here!' Her tone was highly derisive. 'But when! I *knew* we shouldn't have asked him again but no, you would insist! And after the trouble we had last year!'

Annie never had accepted Jack's younger brother, Jim, as a member of the family. To her, he was an outsider, some strange mutation who had strayed into their lives for the sole purpose of disrupting their peace of mind and thwarting their rare chances of happiness. Like today.

'He *knows* how much I look forward to this trip! Which is probably why he's late!'

Jack found his brother's contrariness hard to deny. Jim, the joker, liked nothing more than to annoy his sister-in-law. When told, twenty-four years earlier that his brother was to marry Annie Beaumont, Jim, apparently awestruck, remarked, 'By eck! Who's organizing t'wedding? Duke o' Norfolk?' But Jim was a kindly man and could never be spiteful. Which was why Jack knew that, sooner or later, Jim would arrive. But he wished it could have been sooner and saved him all this bother.

Annie looked at the clock for the hundred and first time. 'We'll give him two more minutes! And then you can present our apologies and send them on their way!'

Jim made it by fourteen seconds. His arrival was heralded by a ragged cheer from the waiting passengers. The pub doors swung inwards and there he stood, a Teddy Bear of a man, smiling hugely.

'By gum, there's some traffic on the roads! Stockport's jammed up solid!' He leaned over Annie and kissed her on the cheek. 'By, you're looking bonnier every time I see you!'

Ice formed on Annie's words. 'Am I?'

'Come on,' said Jack, 'I'll show you t'lay-out. I've shifted one or two items.'

But Annie wasn't letting her brother-in-law off so easily. 'You've cut it a bit fine to say the least! Didn't it occur to you to set off a bit earlier, seeing it's Whit Monday?'

'Now, Annie, you know me!' said Jim.

'I should do! I've been married into your family long enough.'

'Ee, I don't know how you stick her, Jack!'

The referee stepped in between them. 'Now, don't start anything! Annie, you get on t'chara. I'll be with you in a minute!'

But Jim had the last word. 'And none o' them Kiss-me-Quick hats, Annie, or you'll never get home!'

At nine forty-eight precisely they were ready for off. Dorothy Greenhalgh slid into the seat next to Len Fairclough.

'D'you mind! I've got one o' them kids next to me and he's started on his sticky toffee!'

'I don't mind, love! My wife might but I don't!'

'She's not here, is she?'

'No.'

'Well, all right, then!'

From her point of vantage on the back seat, Ena was missing nothing. 'Hello, it's started and th'engine isn't going yet!'

Midway down the coach, Annie nudged Jack and directed his attention to Billy and Doreen's animated chatter two seats ahead. 'I hope he isn't going to spend all day with that girl!'

'Now, Annie, leave him be. He's a grown man.'

'That doesn't make him any the more sensible! In fact, judging from some of the grown men *I* know, it's all the more cause for worry!'

Jack, wisely, turned away and watched Arthur Dewhurst wriggling closer to Elsie across the aisle.

'Eckythump,' said Elsie. 'You're taking enough room up, aren't you? Hutch up a bit!'

'I was just getting cosy!'

'Aye, happen you were but I'd rather be comfortable, thank you!'

'You're no lightweight yourself, you know,' said Arthur, ponderously playful.

'Thank you!' said Elsie philosophically. 'I suppose the day's going to be full of little compliments like that!'

The engine roared.

By the time they were passing Salford Royal they were already deep into the second chorus of 'I Do Like To Be Beside The Seaside'. At Farnworth the sun went in and Mrs Hawksworth's youngest wept copious tears. At Astley Bridge the clouds departed and all was happiness again.

Wally chose a pub on the tops for their first stop. The youngsters skipped off the bus and ran, shouting, for their mineral waters. The elder citizens, joints locked by the journey so far, dismounted more painfully but the warm sun soon cured their ills and they gathered in the open air, drinks in hand, to gaze at the panorama which spread before them. Turton Moor and Delph Reservoir and over to Edgworth and Chapeltown and mill country.

'Even the chimneys look attractive on a day like this,' said Annie and, turning for support found Ena offering none.

'There's nowt attractive about a cotton mill.'

'By eck, you're right!' added Martha.

Minnie merely smiled sadly. She'd served her apprenticeship too.

Ena wasn't finished yet. 'And I'm surprised at you, Annie Walker! Seeing you've worked in one yourself!'

Annie smiled the thinnest of smiles and turned back to Jack. It was true. She had tended a loom for three years in her late teens but that was a part of her life best forgotten, together with Cousin Edwin who served twelve months in an Australian gaol for embezzlement and that dreadful time she had been cajoled into playing Lady Godiva in the Clitheroe Co-op Pageant. She shuddered at the thought and turned her mind back to the view.

At eleven twenty-one, as they were crawling past Preston's Fulwood Park, Len started to sing 'I Do Like To Be

Beside The Seaside' again. This time he decorated the song with his well-known impression of a cinema organist, alternately rising to his feet and disappearing behind the seat as he thumped his imaginary keyboard.

'Do you know what these organists do while they're down below?' he asked Dot Greenhalgh during a brief pause in the proceedings.

'No,' said Dot.

'I'll show you!' said Len.

And he did. And Dot quite liked it.

Elsie, who was fond of Len in her way, raised the subject with Dot a couple of hours later.

'What were you and Len doing on that chara?' she asked.

Dot smiled. 'That'd be telling, wouldn't it? And you know what you're always saying? Do what you like but for God's sake keep your mouth shut!'

The thirty-two seater rolled on to the South Shore coach park at ten minutes past twelve. The passengers disembarked and assembled obediently at the foot of the steps, awaiting instructions. Wally allowed a decent pause to elapse then addressed them.

'I want you all back here at half past six on the dot! And I mean here so remember where it is!'

Everyone looked round, mentally fixing the spot.

'Right, I've got it!' said Len. 'We're just to the left o' that old feller in a navy blue suit, white open-necked shirt and a flat hat! Smoking a pipe!'

'You daft thing!' said Dot and turned her attention back to Wally.

'And I'm warning you! This coach leaves this car park at a quarter to seven if there's only me and Minnie Caldwell on board!'

A voice piped up. 'Say there's just you and Ena?'

'Then I wait for help!' Wally smiled at Ena. 'Enjoy yourself, Mrs Sharples! And the rest of you! And don't forget – half past six!'

The group splintered into twos and threes. Elsie sought out Dot.

'Don't leave me with PC 99, for Pete's sake!'

'Oh, Elsie! Len wants me to go with him! '

'Well, we can make a foursome, can't we! And that way I can keep an eye on you! He is a married man, you know! '

'So what? I'm a married woman! That evens us up, doesn't it?'

At the back of the coach, Ena, Minnie and Martha were in serious debate. Blackpool held no mysteries for them yet, year after year, the arguments raged fiercely as to where they were to go.

'I like the zoo,' said Minnie.

'We know you like the zoo! ' said Martha. 'You've been there every year for t'past ten years! '

'Oh, no, I haven't! ' protested Minnie. 'We went to Whitby in 1956, so I couldn't have! '

'Don't waste your breath arguing with this one! ' said Ena to Martha, her hand waving towards a string of animal life heading for the sands. 'She's as stubborn as one o' them donkeys! '

'We'll go to Fleetwood on a tram! ' said Martha.

Ena settled the matter. 'We're going to no Fleetwood and we're going to no zoo! We're going up t'Tower! '

'Up t'Tower?' said Martha. 'It's too windy! '

'If owt's too windy, it's you! ' said Ena. And to the Tower they went.

Lunch had been arranged for most of the party at Harrison's Paradise Café by the side of the Winter Gardens.

The café, under the personal management and supervision of Mrs Ethel Harrison, had provided the mid-day meal for the Rover's trip for as long as most of the regulars could remember. Mainly, it might be said, because of the plaice, chips and peas which were not only delicious, nutritious and filling but also most reasonably priced. Not quite reasonable enough for, say, the Hawksworths who, with six mouths to feed, had brought their own sandwiches which they ate on the sands in the teeth of a stiff breeze which sprang up the moment they sat down and caused the youngest Hawksworth to weep again. Nor could Mrs Harrison's plaice attract Bert and Carrie Pilling who used the trip as a cheap means of visiting Carrie's sister and her husband in Bispham.

But one o'clock found most of the passengers climbing the narrow staircase from the street level confectioner's to the café above.

It was a rule of the establishment that customers always took the table farthest from the stairs. Not, as is normal with such rules, to help the staff but because, so closely were tables and chairs packed together, once seated it was extremely difficult to get out. Only Mrs Harrison and Ruby, her ageing but agile waitress, knew the secret paths through the maze of bentwood and white linen.

But everyone knew the rule. And knew that first-comers gained not only the window seats overlooking the busy street but also the first steaming plates of fish, chips and peas. Which explained why the Pickerings, that well-known gourmand family from Bessie Street, were first up the stairs of the establishment, closely followed by eighteen stone Willie Parkin, his matching wife Dora, and their three gargantuan teenage children. And woe betide anyone who found himself sitting at the next table to the Parkins.

Elsie, Dot, Len and Arthur were amongst the last to arrive. Elsie chose to sit back-to-back with Ena on the grounds that any other seat afforded a view of the old battleaxe and put her off her food. To Elsie's right sat Harry, Concepta and Lucille and, continuing clockwise, the Walker party, Jack, Annie, Billy and, an unwelcome addition as far as Annie was concerned, Doreen. Shuffling uncomfortably under Annie's steady gaze, she bumped her chair against the one behind and turned to smile an apology to Minnie.

'It's all right, love,' said Minnie, 'I can't get settled myself!'

'By eck, you can't!' said Ena. 'Stop kicking your feet about! Anybody'd think you'd got the whole Sahara Desert in between your toes!'

'Oo, I can't bear sand in my shoes,' said Minnie.

'Well, take 'em off and brush your feet with your hand!' said Ena. 'Nobody'll see you!'

Minnie looked round uncomfortably. 'I don't like. Besides, it's all inside my stockings!'

Ena tutted. 'Well, it's your own fault! You should have dried your feet properly.'

Martha joined in. 'I wouldn't mind but it was her idea to go paddling. I'd have settled for a nice sit down on the front myself.' She flashed a tentative look at Ena then added, hopefully, 'Still we can do that this afternoon.'

'Oh, no, we can't!' said Ena. 'As soon as this wind drops and they get that lift running we're going up t'Tower! So be told!'

'Oh, Ena,' whined Martha, 'I don't fancy going up there with it swaying like it does!'

'They take very good care of you, you know!'

'Aye, happen they do but there's always a first time!'

Ena closed the subject. 'Don't worry! When summat happens it'll be to somebody a lot more important than you!' She turned her attention to Minnie. 'And why don't you smile once in a while? Are you frightened of cracking your face?'

'Excuse me, Mrs Caldwell!' It was Doreen trying to get through. Perspiring freely under Annie's continued scrutiny she had decided to take her coat off.

'I'll take it for you,' Billy had said.

'Oh, no, you won't!' said his mother. 'Let Doreen go. She's thinner than you. She'll get through easier.'

They watched her squeeze past Minnie and Martha and head for the brown-painted door marked 'Ladies'.

'Don't call her "thin", Mum,' said Billy, 'She's slim!'

Annie ignored the complaint. 'I hope this isn't serious!'

'What?' asked Billy.

'You know very well what! You and Doreen.'

'I think she's quite a nice girl,' said Billy's helpful father.

Annie rounded on him. 'Yes, but you're the one who likes mustard on chips!'

'What's that got to do with it?' asked the mystified Jack.

'You know very well what it's got to do with it. And shut up, she's coming back!' Annie clicked on her automatic smile. 'Does that feel better, dear?' she asked as Doreen took her place again.

117

Doreen, never too careful about her 'h's, chose an unfortunate sentence. 'Yeah!' she said. 'It isn't 'alf 'ot in 'ere, isn't it?'

The pain was acute in Annie's eyes. 'Yes, it is a little on the close side.'

At the next table, Harry was searching his pockets. They had, predictably, spent the hour between arrival and lunch on the Pleasure Beach. Lucille again, predictably, had spent most of the time pleading to go on the Big Dipper but Harry had been adamant. Which placed Concepta neatly in a cleft stick. A clever girl, she knew that Harry wouldn't dream of taking their relationship to its logical conclusion without the unqualified approval of his daughter. So what was she to do? Support Lucille and risk Harry seeing her as an unsatisfactory step-mother-to-be or side with Harry and lose a necessary ally? She compromised.

'Now, I think it'd be a great pity if we went on the Big Dipper because if we do we won't have time to go on the really special attraction!'

'What's that?' asked Lucille.

'Why, the Ghost Train, of course! Everybody who comes to Blackpool goes on the Ghost Train!'

The compromise had worked. 'Dad, can we go on the Ghost Train?'

And then, after the Ghost Train, Concepta had changed a shilling and handed the magic coppers to Lucille. Which was why Harry was searching his pockets.

'What are you looking for now?' asked Concepta.

'That thing she won on the Pleasure Beach. That gnome thing.'

'The one I won through knocking them tins off that shelf with dusters.'

'*Those* things!' said Harry.

'Those things.'

'Oh, that one!' said Concepta. 'It's here in my bag.'

'Can I have it?' asked Lucille.

'No, you can't!' said her father. 'Not at table!'

'Oh, go on!' said Concepta, looking round and noting that Ruby was still busy with the Pickerings and the Parkins. 'By the looks o' things it'll be another half an hour before we get any food! '

Lucille tapped Len on the shoulder. 'Have you seen my gnome, Uncle Len?' she said. 'I won it myself! '

Len took the plastic pixie and examined it solemnly. 'That's not a gnome,' he said. 'Come here! ' He bent his head towards her and whispered in her ear. 'Don't tell anybody I told you but it's Mrs Sharples with her nightcap on! '

Lucille giggled.

'What did he say?' asked her father.

Lucille transferred the information with another whisper.

'Just watch it, Len! ' said Harry. 'She's cheeky enough without you encouraging her! '

Lucille's eyes flickered from her father to Ena and back. 'Do you think she heard me?' she whispered.

'I hope not! ' said her father.

He needn't have worried. Ena was far too involved in a fencing match with Elsie Tanner. A strange fencing match in which the backs of chairs took the place of foils. The slightest pressure from one chair was answered by the other and they had now reached the point where the weapons were locked together under the full weight of the two protagonists. So it was inevitable that, the physical battle having reached deadlock, the war should become verbal.

'I wish they'd hurry up and get us served! ' said Elsie.

'Some folks are that greedy they can't wait to start stuffing themselves! ' said Ena. To Elsie but looking at Martha.

Elsie needed no go-between. 'Did you say something, Mrs Sharples, or were you chewing a brick?'

'Of course, I was forgetting! You've got a lot to fill up, haven't you, Mrs Tanner? Since you put all that weight on! '

'At least my weight's all in the right places! Which is more than you can say for some folk! '

'So it should be! You take enough trouble getting it

there! What do you say, Martha?'

Martha wriggled uncomfortably. 'Nay, Ena, leave me out of it!'

'Go on! Tell the truth and shame the devil! Tell her she's getting fat!'

Elsie's table was a study in contrasting expressions. Len was stifling a smile. He knew, of old, how much Ena and Elsie enjoyed this in-fighting. Not so Arthur Dewhurst, the intrepid detective. His brow furrowed deeper and deeper as he tried to work out what was going on. Dot was frowning too, but because she *knew* what was going on. All the danger signals were showing on Elsie. The flared nostrils, the tight lips and, several inches lower, the heaving bosom. She placed a restraining hand on Elsie's arm. Elsie shook it off. A devilish smile played around the full, red lips. Dot shuddered. When the words came they sounded sweet.

'Are you enjoying your day out, Mrs Sharples?'

'As a matter of fact, I am.' The reply was cautious.

'Then if you don't want a back-hander you'll keep remarks like them to yourself!'

Ena turned on her superior smile. 'That's all the ignorant can do, you know! Resort to violence!'

Elsie was two inches out of her chair when Dot grabbed her.

'Don't start anything in here, love! Wait till you get outside!'

Elsie subsided to find Arthur looking agitatedly around the room. She switched her aggressiveness to her escort.

'What's up with you?' she asked sharply.

'I was just wondering where it is!'

'Over there at the top of the stairs!'

'Oh, aye!' said Arthur. 'I won't be a minute!'

'You can be as long as you flaming like!' He was still in earshot but Elsie was past caring.

Len, enjoying himself hugely, nudged Dot. 'She's on good form today!'

'I'll show you whether I'm on good form or not!' said Elsie. 'One more word out of her and I'll land her one!'

Dot saw Ena's head twitch and used the restraining hand again.

120

'Never mind *her*, love! What were you saying about him? About Arthur?' said Dot, deciding to sidetrack her friend on to quieter lines. Besides, she thought, it was time Elsie explained a thing or two about this detective chap.

'By eck, he's well named, that one! PC Plod! All he can do is sit there, he never leaves me alone for five minutes and when it comes to the push he's as much use as my Aunt Peg! Does he take my side? Does he eckaslike! He sits there with his mouth open, catching flies!'

Dot smiled. Her little ploy was working well. 'Don't get yourself worked up, love!'

But Elsie was in full flow. 'I pity the woman he marries, by eck I do! He'll handcuff her to the sink!'

'Oh, it's not going to be you then?' said Dot.

'It is *not* going to be me!' said Elsie firmly. 'And mind your own business!' She sensed Ena's nearness and turned to find her staring, point blank, into her adversary's eyes. 'In case you missed that, Mrs Sharples, I said mind your own flaming business!'

Violence could well have erupted but for the timely arrival of Mrs Ethel Harrison. She deftly deposited a loaded plate in front of each of the three old ladies, smiled warmly at Ena and said, 'There you are, love! Just how you like it – not too much batter on your plaice!'

The afternoon was idyllic. Fortified by Mrs Harrison's homely fare and warmed by that personal service and amazing memory which she shared with the head waiters of several of London's top hotels, the coach party emerged into the benevolent sunshine and balmy breeze which, as every Northerner knows, only Blackpool can offer.

Ena and Co, as had been decided, went up the Tower. The breeze was a little stronger than balmy by the time they left the wrought iron lift and joined the knot of sightseers on the observation platform, and the sight of a little boy being rather violently ill in a corner did nothing for the delicate state of Martha's stomach. The mother of the little boy, who was doing her best to hide her son's affliction from the public gaze, smiled apologetically, but too late, at Martha.

'I think we'd better get down, Ena!'

'What d'you mean "get down"? We've only just come.'

Minnie examined her friend with a professional eye. 'I think perhaps we'd better, Ena. She's looking a bit green.'

'By gum, right friends I've got! One can't keep away from smelly animals and the other's sick when she gets a couple of yards off t'ground!' This was a massive understatement, even for Ena. Blackpool Tower rears itself five hundred and eighteen feet above the promenade and the observation platform was almost at the top. Ena waved an encompassing arm. 'Look at that view! Folk come from all over t'world for this view! Go on, have a look – it'll put you right!'

The view was rather impressive. Beneath them stretched the Lancashire coastline from the high rise flats of Liverpool to Morecambe Bay and the Peaks of the Lake District beyond. Behind them lay the bountiful acres of the Fylde, flat as a pancake until, crossing the new motorway, the land rose to the Lancashire fells. And straight ahead, for all the world like a basking whale on the surface of the Irish Sea, the Isle of Man. Even Ena was impressed. And Minnie, always acutely aware of the beauties of this world, sighed with delight. But alas, to Martha, who wished for nothing more than a sight of the Ladies outside Central Pier, the panorama was rather less than breathtaking. Indeed, it was positively harmful.

She stood very still and said, quietly, 'I do think we'd better go, Ena!'

Not having heard Martha speak so quietly for many years, Ena was forced to admit that something was wrong. 'Come on, then!' she said, grudgingly, and they caught the next lift down.

A little farther down the promenade, Elsie blinked in the strong sunlight as the quartette emerged from the darkness of Louis Tussaud's. Arthur had been his usual monosyllabic self and Elsie, inspecting the dummy policeman at the entrance had remarked to Dot, 'Look at *him*! He's made o' wax and there's more life in him than there is in that feller o' mine!'

The four of them sauntered up the prom along the Golden Mile. Whit Monday was one of the most popular days in Blackpool's calendar for in addition to the thousands of day trippers who, according to age, were drawn to its beaches, pubs and promenade benches, the day marked the start of the holiday season proper and already many of the little backstreet boarding houses were proudly displaying their 'No Vacancies' signs.

'Why couldn't they all have stayed at home!' grumbled Elsie as the umpteenth happy holidaymaker bumped into her.

'Oh, stop grousing and enjoy yourself!' said Dot.

'I've got summat to grouse about, haven't I?' said Elsie, pulling Dot back to let the two men walk on ahead. 'What do you say to a swap?'

'A what?' said Dot.

'I'll have Len and you take the arm of the law!'

'Don't be so shameless!' said Dot, her tone reproving but her eyes smiling. 'Len's a married man!'

Two streets back from the promenade, in the middle of Blackpool's shopping centre, another married man yawned as his wife stopped at yet another shop window. Jack was well used to playing a passive role when Annie dragged him out but he had never learned to hide his boredom.

'You're always the same!' Annie would complain. 'I'm never bringing you out shopping again!' But she always did.

Jack watched a little girl dragged screaming from a novelty store and reflected on the strange mystery of the British holiday. There they were, a typical family of four, the blonde little girl howling her misery at the world, her elder brother, sullen and rebellious, grimly absorbing a smack from his red-faced, harrassed mother, while father stood by, outwardly unconcerned but inwardly wishing the earth would open and swallow him. And closing his mind to the terrifying fact that there was still another five days to go. And yet, when they returned to Burnley or Halifax

123

or Liverpool or Stoke or wherever it was they came from, the story would be the same . . .

'Oh, we had a *lovely* time!'

Jack sighed at the injustice of it all and turned to find Annie coming out of a jeweller's shop. His heart sank.

'You've no need to look like that! Unless you begrudge me spending fifteen shillings of our hard-earned money on our only daughter!'

'Now, Annie!'

'You're always the same,' said Annie. 'I'm never bringing you out shopping again!'

'Can I have that in writing?' said Jack. But under his breath.

'I don't suppose for one minute you know where your son is?'

'I don't!' said Jack.

In fact, only two people on earth did know Billy Walker's exact whereabouts at that moment. One was Doreen who was lying beside him in the warm hollow of the sand hill and the other was the grave-faced little boy regarding them unsmilingly from a distance of three feet.

All had gone well with Billy's plans. As soon as he and Doreen left the Paradise Café they headed for the crowds. Soon swallowed up, it was child's play to cross the promenade unobserved and swing aboard one of the resort's proud fleet of streamlined trams. Fifteen minutes later they were entwined in each other's arms in the shelter of a friendly sand dune. And fifteen seconds after that, Billy was undoing the fourth button on Doreen's white nylon blouse.

'I scream!' she had said as the first button popped.

'How loud?' he had asked. Her mouth opened but no sound came. He smiled a satisfied smile. 'That'll do me!' And another button fell victim to his deft fingers.

'Are we all right here?' asked Doreen.

'Course we are!' said Billy and opened two more buttons.

'Hello!' said the little voice. 'I'm Errol!'

Billy raised himself on one elbow and looked at the

speaker. All of five years old, clad in a sand-encrusted, minuscule pair of swimming trunks, clutching a spade in one grimy hand and a gaily-painted tin bucket in the other. Errol, terror of the sand-dunes.

'Go away and play,' said Billy.

'I don't want to,' said Errol with admirable finality.

'Blow you then!' said Billy cheerfully and turned back to the task in hand.

'No!' said Doreen. 'I can't!'

'Why not!' said Billy, 'He doesn't know what we're doing!'

'I know but . . . I can't!'

Billy stared at her tortured face for a long moment then turned back to the infant invader.

'Doesn't your mother want you?' he asked.

'No,' said Errol. Billy wasn't surprised.

'Would you like an ice cream?'

'Yes,' said Errol, no waster of words.

Billy sat up, plunged a hand into his pocket and came out with two pennies. 'Here! Go and get yourself one!'

Errol stepped forward shyly and took the proffered coins. 'Thank you!' he said politely. And remained looking at them.

'Go on!' said Billy.

'My mother says I've not got to have another one yet!' said Errol, and added, gratuitously, 'I've had four!' He smiled at the kind gentleman. 'This is where I have adventures!' he said.

'That's what *I* thought, mate!' said Billy philosophically and left Doreen's side to help Errol build a sand castle.

Romance was having a hard time of it that day. Sitting on the sands, throwing stones at a bottle at the water's edge, Harry was beginning to regret having declined Esther Hayes' offer to look after Lucille. Esther was tied to the house that day, expecting a visit from her brother Tom and having conceded victory to Concepta as far as Harry was concerned, had volunteered to look after the little girl. If he'd accepted, thought Harry, he might at that moment have been doing something more exciting than throwing stones at a bottle. Concepta, however, was quite content. She and Lucille were developing just the right easy relationship to stand her in very good stead if Harry ever did get round to the idea of taking on a second wife.

'Should we have a look round the shops?' asked Concepta, anxious to press home her advantage.

'Why not?' said Harry. Anything was preferable to throwing pebbles.

'Not you!' said Concepta. 'Me and Lucille!' She turned to the girl. 'Who wants men around when they're looking round the shops!'

'Well, we don't!' said Lucille.

'We don't indeed! Shall we see you back at the coach, Harry?'

'Aye, okay!' said Harry and watched them walk away. Idly he turned on his elbow and allowed his eyes to linger on an attractive, bikinied brunette soaking up the sun some twenty yards away. Like Jack before him, Harry indulged in a little holiday reflection. Why couldn't he come here on his own? Esther'd look after Lucille, he could find himself a nice licensed hotel on the front and live the life of Reilly for a couple of weeks. And there'd be plenty of unattached women. Take that one, for instance. A couple of quiet drinks in the hotel bar, a taxi to the Tower ballroom, a few whirls round the floor, out into the moonlight and who knows! After all, he wasn't all that old!

His reverie was rather sharply broken by a muscular young man who sank to the sand beside Harry's dream goddess, handed her one of the two ice creams he was carrying and, leaning over, kissed her on the nose. Harry looked at them sourly, got up and slowly walked away.

Wally's warning had not gone unheeded. By twenty-nine minutes past six the entire party were gathered by the coach. In the event, it was Wally who was five minutes late. Len ribbed him as he unlocked the passenger door.

'That little widow in St Anne's, was it, Wally?'

'Hello, somebody been talking, have they!' Wally grinned as he swung the door open.

Ten minutes later they were edging their way through

126

the back streets of Blackpool heading for the motorway. There was plenty of liquid refreshment aboard and, like travellers since time began, they all preferred, once having set their course for home, to get there in the shortest possible time.

It was a typical Bank Holiday. The sunny warmth of the afternoon had given way to black, scurrying cloud and the occasional splutter of rain as the coach gathered speed on the M6 approach road. The darkening day, with its promise of dark deeds, led Annie to think of her errant son.

'Where's our Billy?'

Jack twisted round in his seat. 'I can't see him,' he said.

'I bet you can't!' said Annie. 'I just hope nobody else can!'

'Nay, you were young yourself once! Live and let live!' Jack gave a little chuckle. 'Do you remember that train trip to Scarborough? You know, when your mill went and we had that reserved compartment? How long had we known each other then – about a month?'

'I remember it vaguely,' said Annie.

Jack chuckled again. 'And coming back we hadn't been out of Scarborough ten minutes before the lights went out! By gum, somebody was crafty! It takes some doing – turning them lights out!'

Annie looked at him, expressionless. 'You mean you don't know who it was who did it?'

'No,' said Jack.

'Oh!' said Annie, and, turning to the window, scratched her nose delicately. Jack leaned forward and, in the fading light, saw that she was smiling.

'It were never you!' he said.

'Somebody had to get you moving!' said Annie.

On the back seat, Billy could well have done with a little of his mother's inventiveness. He and Doreen had boarded the coach first and had headed straight for the back seat. Once settled he had spread their coats over the remaining three spaces and prepared himself to repel all boarders. As more and more passengers took their places in front of them, his optimism grew. He turned to Doreen.

'Hey!' he said.

'What?' said Doreen, turning to him. He kissed her.

It was a long kiss and it was still enjoyable when the shadow fell across his face. Reluctantly he broke away from Doreen and looked up to find Ena glaring at him. Martha and Minnie lurked in the background.

'Are them your coats?' asked Ena.

'Yes, Mrs Sharples!' answered Billy cheerfully. 'We're saving them seats!'

'Oh, I see!' Ena's voice was deceptively mild. 'For them as had 'em on the way out?'

'That's right!' said Billy, still cheerful.

'Then get 'em shifted! We're here!'

Annie had no cause to worry about her son. He had only to move a muscle and three pairs of eyes swivelled instantly in his direction.

'Would you believe it?' he complained to Doreen. 'We get rid of one Errol and we find another three!'

Out of sheer boredom he began to whistle tunelessly but Ena soon stopped that. Then, totally aware of his frustration, she leaned across Martha and tapped him on the arm.

'Plenty of time for canoodling when you see her home, lad! What this coach needs is a song or two! So go on! – get 'em started!'

The coach sang its way down the motorway and through the grey darkening streets of half a dozen Lancashire towns. 'Daisy' echoed across Salford as the coach turned into Broad Street and entered the home stretch. Lucille turned from her seat behind the driver and waved to her father a few rows behind.

'Soon be home now, Dad!' she shouted.

'Aye, love! Soon be home!' He turned to Concepta. She was gazing dreamily out of the window but she turned, knowing his eyes were on her.

'Enjoyed it?' he asked.

'Oh, I have! Very much!'

The singers were growing tired but no less tuneful as 'Daisy' started her last chorus. Harry's hand reached for,

128

and found, Concepta's. He murmured her name. She turned to smile at him.

His mouth was dry but he had little difficulty with the words. 'How . . . how do you feel about marrying me?'

He looked into her eyes and saw the answer.

They kept the secret for three weeks and then, having fixed the wedding date for October the first, Harry suggested they should make their engagement public and Concepta agreed. Lucille would be the first to be told.

Which was why, on that June day when Harry uprooted the rosebay willowherb, he was able to dry his daughter's tears and bring the smile back to her lips. He handed her the wilting flower and said, softly, 'How would you like to be a bridesmaid!'

CHAPTER FIVE

The park was quieter than usual. A dozen or so couples strolled along the sunlit flower-lined paths, passing the dozing pensioners with their attendant sparrows waiting patiently for the crumbs to fall from their slackening fingers.

Deeper into the park, on the walks which surrounded the ornamental lake, it was even quieter. A family of ducks glided past the motionless figure, slumped on the bench, staring, unseeing, into the dark waters. A swan arrived, dismissed the human visitor as unproductive and left.

The crunch of gravel on the path dragged Kenneth Barlow from his reverie. He straightened as a young couple turned into sight around the flowerless rhododendrons and, arms entwined, walked slowly towards him. They had obviously been talking for now they had just as obviously fallen silent, unwilling to continue their intimacies as they passed a stranger. They were seventeen, no more, and very happy.

The boy stopped by Kenneth and smiled politely.

'Could you tell me the time, please?'

Kenneth consulted his watch carefully. 'I make it twenty-two minutes to one although I could be a couple of minutes slow.'

'Thank you.' Another polite smile and they had gone.

Kenneth smiled to himself. A couple of minutes slow! Twenty-two minutes to one! Why be so exact when they had all their lives in front of them. Why not simply say 'It's summer!'? He watched another swan glide by, reproaching him. Reminding him by its own effortless progress that the Paradise where Time has no meaning is the sole preserve of the animal kingdom and that only Man is the Prisoner of the Hour. The boy wanted to know the time because, at one o'clock, he must be back behind his office desk, working to save, to marry, to rescue his girl from her packing department and her twelve-to-one lunch hour. Lucky young devils!

It would have been difficult, with only his thoughts as a yardstick, to arrive at Kenneth's age. He was still not twenty-two yet, mentally, he felt a modern Methuselah. The son of an oppressive family, the victim of a recently-broken affair, the student waiting for his results after what seemed ten lifetimes of study – how could he be only twenty-one years of age?

The affair had been doomed from the outset. He had met her in this very park, by this very lake, on this very bench only three months before. It had been a warm April day and the daffodils had nodded in their hundreds at the water's edge. She was sharing her sandwiches with a pintail duck when he sat, decorously, at the other end of the wooden bench. He hadn't known it was a pintail duck until she told him and he believed her because by then he knew who she was.

'I'm a librarian at the University. That's where I pick up all my useless information! Did you know, for instance, that that was a pintail?'

'No, I'm afraid I didn't! But I wouldn't say that was useless information. I'm sure the duck thinks it very important!'

'It's not a duck, it's a drake. And the only thing he knows is that he's hungry!'

Kenneth smiled. 'I knew I'd seen you before!'

'Are you at University?'

'Modern History,' he said. 'Last year.'

'Good luck!'

'Thanks!' Then, for some reason, shyly, 'I'm Kenneth Barlow, by the way.'

'Oh! Marion Lund. Hello!' He wasn't surprised when she extended her hand. And yet it wasn't a masculine gesture. It was strong, firm, equal. She released his hand and he watched her as she threw her last crumbs to the pintail. She was dark-haired, dark-eyed, not by any means beautiful and certainly not pretty, yet there was an attractiveness stemming from her composure which was new to him. It was difficult to assess her age – he was bad at it anyway – but she was obviously older than he was. Which didn't deter him from inviting her out. And didn't deter her from accepting.

They met, three times a week, for two months. At first their interests were academic, then intellectual, and it was only after a scratch meal and a bottle of cheap Spanish wine in Marion's two-roomed flat that they became physical. It was after that first exciting experience that Kenneth, walking home through the midnight rain, decided with all the wisdom of a twenty-one-year-old that he was going to marry this woman.

He never knew how horrified his mother was when he told her. After a lifetime of compromise, it was easy for her to cover her true feelings, to smile at her radiant son and to suggest that he did nothing drastic until she'd had a chance to tell his father. After all, there were his exams to worry about.

Ida Barlow worried her way through three days before she found the courage to tell Frank. Even then she couldn't face him with the news. She waited until they were safely in bed, the lights extinguished and then, happily, lightly, but with a thudding heart, she told him. She waited, hardly daring to breathe, as he gazed up into the blackness. Then, without a word, he turned away from her. Two hours later they were still both awake. And still both silent.

At eight o'clock the following morning, David pushed back his chair, rose from the table, picked up his toolbag and uttered his ritualistic morning farewell.

'Right! Another day, another dollar!'

The door banged after him. Frank picked up the last round of toast and scraped a black corner on to his plate. Kenneth glanced at his mother, but there was no communication now. She had caught him earlier, as he came downstairs for breakfast, with a whispered 'I've told your father!' but now it was too late. All they could do was wait.

The toast was finished, the last crumb helped in from a corner of Frank's mouth by a horny finger. The last mouthful of tea washed it down.

'Your mother tells me you've got a new lady friend!'

'Yes.'

'T'other one didn't last long. What were her name? Susan?'

'Er . . . no, she didn't.'

'Works in t'University this one, doesn't she? Library, is it?'

'That's right.' So far so good.

'Clever, is she?'

'I think so, yes.'

'And you want to marry her?'

'Yes.' Kenneth began to read the danger signals. For all his faults his father was an honest man and he would never disguise his feelings. And there was a strain in Frank's voice which said that all was far from well.

'According to your mother she's older than you.'

'Yes, she is.'

'How much?'

Kenneth threw another quick glance at his mother. Didn't he know? Hadn't she told him? There was no answer.

'She's thirty-three. Not that it matters.'

It mattered. To Frank it mattered more than any other single fact the world had to offer.

'Thirty-three! Are you out of your mind!'

'Frank, please!' For Ida, the agony was, at last, out in the open.

'Now leave him to me! It's you I'm thinking about, when all's said and done!' He turned back to Kenneth. 'Do you ever think how much your mother's done for you? Does it ever occur to you? Or are you too busy thinking of yourself?' Kenneth stood, anxious to save his mother from yet another scene. 'Sit down, I haven't finished with you yet! Let me tell you something, young feller-me-lad! Your mother goes out skivvying for you! Working all hours God sends so's you can have an education! For what? So's you can spend it on some fly-be-night woman who doesn't give a damn for you!'

133

'That's not true!' The words were wrung from Kenneth.

'Oh, and what *is* true?' Frank glared up at his anguished son. 'I'll tell you what's true! It's true that you want to move out of here the minute you start earning for yourself – that's what's true! With not a thought or a penny for your mother who's worked all her life for you. Or for me, for that matter. Not that you ever had any consideration for me! Is that what you're doing – getting back at me because I can't use a knife and fork proper?'

And so it went on. And on.

It was three days before Kenneth saw Marion again but the tension still showed on his face as she let him in to the little flat. She didn't speak as he walked past her and into the sparsely-furnished living room. He stood with his back to her looking down into the sunlit street.

'Goodbye, Kenneth!' He turned to her, his eyes wondering. 'It had to happen!'

'How did you know?' he asked.

'You told me about your family. And I suppose you told them about me. And they didn't like what they heard!'

'I don't care!'

'Oh, yes, you do! You have to live with them! You . . .' She broke off, looked at him smiling. 'It wouldn't have worked anyway!'

'Of course it would!' He moved towards her but, just as quickly, she moved away.

'No! Please! Believe me, it wouldn't! Haven't you done your sums? When I was a hundred you'd only be eighty-nine!' She waited for him to speak, hoping against hope that he would convince her she was wrong. But he said nothing. 'Perhaps you'd better go.'

'Will I see you again?' he asked.

'Of course you will! But not . . . not like this!

He hesitated and then, without another word, walked past her and out into the street. She could hear his footsteps on the pavement below, could almost sense the relief in them. It was an unfair tug-of-war. Society, convention, the family pulling him one way and, matched against them, one lonely woman. Why was she only attractive to young men? And why did it always end the same way? She sank into the chintz-covered armchair and wept.

Kenneth watched the boy and girl, hands clasped, arms swinging, disappear from sight around a bend in the path. He looked at his watch again. Unnecessarily. It was twenty seconds later than when he had told the young man the time. Another swan looked down its orange beak at him and sailed away.

Perhaps the boy was lucky, he reflected. At least he knew where one o'clock would find him. Where did he work? In that bank perhaps? That new glass and aluminium palace opposite the main gates of the park? Was that where he'd spend his afternoon, making up the post, answering the telephone, his future dull but assured? But what of Kenneth Barlow's future?

'Ring about one,' Mr Green had said. 'We should have the results sorted out by then. And if you've failed you'll have plenty of time to skip the country before night falls! '

A pleasant man, Mr Green. And as good as his word. If he said the results would be out at one o'clock, then at one o'clock they would be out. Kenneth looked at his watch again. Twenty minutes to wait. He stood, suddenly tiring of his long confrontation with the water-fowl, and moved away. The path turned and the vista of the park opened before him.

To his left were the rose beds, the rich yellow of Sutter's Gold standing in relief against the red velvet of Josephine Bruce. Beyond the roses two shale tennis courts, one unoccupied, the other resounding to the cries of two grey-flannelled youths, one of whom, apparently was Rod Laver and the other Chuck McKinley. And in the distance, beyond the roses and the perspiring champions, white-sleeved, plimsolled men played bowls. Kenneth avoided this human activity and struck off to his right and the open meadows of the park. On the grass, just off the path, a little boy, teeth gritted, kicked viciously at a plastic ball and sent it hurtling in Kenneth's direction. Kenneth trapped the ball neatly, though, it must be said, more by

135

luck than skill and kicked it back to the child's grateful father. The man smiled his thanks. Kenneth stopped. Had *he* played these games? Had *his* father acted as retriever for *him*? For David, yes. And, Kenneth admitted to himself, to some effect. His brother had been for some time now, a part-time professional with the County, the local Third Division side – and a talented part-timer too. A couple of Second Division clubs had already put out feelers.

He started to walk again. Things were better now, the atmosphere at home more relaxed. He had never seen Marion again. When, after a decent week's wait, he had strolled into the library, he had failed to find her. A casual enquiry elicited the fact that she had gone. No, they didn't know where. He had wondered why, had conjured up a dozen reasons from a family bereavement to a pools win. Never for one moment had he considered that she might have left because of him.

Work had taken her place. He took to spending entire days in his room, emerging only for the briefest of snacks. One night there had been an apologetic knock at his door. He had shouted for his mother to come in but it hadn't been Ida.

'It's me,' said Frank. 'I was just wondering if . . . if you were short of money. If . . . perhaps that was why you weren't going out. You know what they say about all work and no play! '

Kenneth was touched. This was his first real contact with his father since the row at the breakfast table and he knew how difficult it must have been for him to make the first move.

'Not really,' said Kenneth. 'I can't say I'm rolling in it but . . .'

'Here! ' Frank threw a pound note on to the bed. 'Get yourself out. Go to t'pictures or a football match or summat. You'll study all t'better for a night off! '

Kenneth looked at the note. It was an olive branch, a new era of peace. A refusal would be a rebuff but to accept the money would, he knew, give back to his father some much-needed respect.

136

'Are you sure?' he said.

He had been right. Frank was delighted. 'Of course, I'm sure! Get your bonnet an' shawl on and let's have you out!' And then downstairs in front of a happy Ida. 'I don't want any change, you know! Though if you've enough left for a bottle o' pale ale from the Rover's on your way back, I'll not say no!'

The roar of traffic told him he was back at the main gate. He dragged himself back to the present just in time to save himself from falling headlong over a baby carriage pushed by a chattering, oblivious mother and headed for the telephone kiosk which stood in the shadow of the huge, stone gatepost. He checked the extension number from the scrap of paper he took from his top pocket and dialled the University. In forty seconds precisely he left the kiosk and headed for home. Smiling.

His mother and father were ecstatic. He had, in anticipation, explained the degree system to them so they were fully aware of the fact that a Second Class Honours Degree was an achievement and not some documentary evidence of failure. Within an hour, everyone in the street knew.

'I always knew he was a clever boy,' said Annie to Jack. 'He's the only one in this street I can hold a decent conversation with.'

'Somehow I always saw *you* as a Bachelor of Arts!' said Miss Nugent, shyly. 'You . . . you have that sort of bearing.'

'Really?' said Mr Swindley. 'How very kind! However, much as we may wish it, we can't all be Kenneth Barlows. Not for all of us the heady world of the academic! There are those, like our goodselves, who must serve the cause of commerce!'

Miss Nugent agreed then looked sadly around the empty shop. 'Not very busy, are we?'

They had been together now for four weeks. The part-

137

nership papers had been sealed and amalgamation was complete. Except, that is, nominally. The sign outside still read 'Swindley & Son'.

It had started, as do so many things, in spring. Over their afternoon tea and biscuits, Emily had confessed that business was bad. The multiple baby stores were vicious competition, selling as they did, everything from prams to nappies under the one roof.

As Leonard said, greatly daring, 'One wonders how long it will be before one can obtain the baby itself there!'

Emily, of course, had blushed.

It had been his idea for Miss Nugent to sell her business and come in with him. At first she had been reluctant even to consider surrendering her independence but then, slowly, she became impressed by the common sense behind the thought. After all, two could starve more cheaply than one with the added bonus that one could have company whilst one was suffering. And business genuinely *was* bad. Not only was competition fierce but overheads were soaring and, in spite of the affluence of the times, more and more small businesses were putting up the shutters. And so it was agreed.

Emily threw herself into her new enterprise with a will. As a friend, a natural politeness forbade her from pointing out faults in the Swindley administration but now, as a business partner, only her innate shyness prevented her from speaking her mind. And there were moments when she could overcome even that.

On their second day together, Mr Swindley had emerged from the stockroom with a ragged cardboard box which he placed, with great care, on the mahogany counter. Then, taking his felt-tipped pen, he carefully printed a legend on a square of card and propped it inside the box. Standing back, he surveyed his creation proudly.

'Waste not, want not, Miss Nugent!'

She looked at the card. It read 'Soiled Paper Collars – To Clear – A Penny Each'. She fell silent.

'I found them, lurking as it were, in the inner reaches of the stockroom!'

138

'Yes.' Her tone was uncertain to say the least.

'You appear somewhat dubious, Miss Nugent. Something wrong?'

'Well! My ... my father used to wear paper collars and ... well, he used to throw them away when they got like that. I think that's the idea. When they're soiled you throw them away!'

'Really?' Mr Swindley turned to look at the offending articles. 'Of course! How perceptive of you! I'll dispose of them immediately!' He paused on his way out with the box and looked at her with new-found admiration. 'May I say, Miss Nugent, that I have valued your friendship for many years and I now look forward to sharing your undoubted business acumen. You will find that on rare occasions even I can be guilty of an error of judgement. Feel free at such times to act as guide and mentor!'

'Oh, I will! I will!' said Miss Nugent fervently. Perhaps a little *too* fervently, judging from Mr Swindley's expression as he turned to go.

From such alliances are mighty empires born. And some miscarry.

August had started well. The sun shone brightly when, at noon on the first, which was a Tuesday, Elsie Tanner walked purposefully into the Rover's Return and ordered a gin and tonic.

'My, my, Mrs Tanner,' said Annie Walker, 'you're starting early! Celebrating your holiday?'

'Not exactly! Just drinking to a happy release!'

It was obvious that Elsie wasn't going to enlarge on the theme so Annie didn't press her. However, had she and Jack pooled their information they might well have added their two and two together and got the right answer. For as Jack came back round the bar after a glass-collecting expedition he heard Elsie, as she lifted her gin, mutter something which sounded strangely like 'Here's to the end of PC Plod!' And his ears hadn't deceived him.

Detective-Inspector Arthur Dewhurst was not without his ambitions and when the opportunity to transfer to a more promising Division presented itself, career and romance fought a bitter fight within his sturdy frame. As usual, he took the news, immediately, to Elsie.

'They want me to go to the Midlands!' he said.

'I'm not surprised,' replied Elsie enigmatically.

Arthur gazed at her adoringly. 'You'll never know how much I appreciate the faith you've got in me!' he said.

Elsie hadn't really meant it that way but she summoned up a smile and awaited the inevitable.

And as the inevitable usually does, it arrived. 'Why don't you come with me?'

Elsie counted silently to ten, hoping she was conveying an impression of deep consideration. 'Arthur, I couldn't! I'm not cut out to be a policeman's wife! I just . . . I couldn't bear the thought of sitting alone night after night knowing you were out there with all those murderers and thieves and wondering if you were ever going to come back to me!'

'I'd always come back!' he breathed.

I know you would! she thought. That's the flaming trouble!

But she kept her thoughts to herself. 'Arthur!' He lifted his eyes to hers. 'You're . . . mature enough . . . You're *old* enough to know that some men and women just aren't made for each other. They destroy each other! Tear each other to pieces! And when you know this there's only one thing to do. It takes courage but . . . there's no other way! Think of yourself as Ronald Colman – and me as Greer Garson!' Arthur had never seriously thought of himself as Ronald Colman but it was an attractive idea and he listened even more eagerly. 'You know what she'd say to him?' He shook his head mutely. 'She'd say . . . Go! Search for happiness! And find it! And then she'd take hold of his hand . . .' Arthur offered his paw like a faithful labrador, '. . . and she'd say – Don't look back! Now that the time has come for parting . . .'

'I wouldn't be going just yet,' said Arthur, practical to the last.

'I know you wouldn't!'. Elsie's voice hardened with impatience then softened to Greer Garson again. 'I know you wouldn't! But when the time comes we must remember that you're a man and I'm a woman and . . .' For the life of her she couldn't remember the rest of it. She knew it was from an old Bette Davis film and Bette had been wearing riding breeches but *what* had she said? In the event it didn't matter.

'I know!' he said, and then, in his best Ronald Colman, 'I'll come and say ta-ra before I go!' And he went.

It had been remarkably easy. Why, thought Elsie as she toyed with her gin and tonic, can't it be as easy with that lad of mine? Arthur had called that morning to say goodbye – he took up his duties the following day – and Dennis had practised his guitar right through their farewell scene.

'Has he gone?' he asked when Elsie returned from the front door.

'Yes, he's gone!'

'Good riddance! I don't know what you took up with a copper for in t'first place!'

'Don't blame me!' said Elsie. 'It was you as dragged him in from t'back entry that night!'

'Aye but I didn't know he were a copper then, did I?'

'I see! If you had have known you'd have left him to bleed to death?'

'Course I would!' said Dennis, wondering what sane person wouldn't.

'How did I come to have such charming children!' Elsie, on the point of sitting down, straightened again. 'What's that you're wearing?'

'What's it look like?'

It looked like a suit. A rather expensive, light grey, Italian cut suit. And Elsie said so.

'Ten out o' ten!' said Dennis. 'It's for me nephew's christening! Amongst other things!'

'What's wrong with the other twenty-seven suits you've got?'

'Very funny,' said Dennis, 'I've got four.'

'All right, four!' said Elsie. 'That's one more than your two grandads and your father had between 'em!'

'But my two grandads and my father weren't in show business, were they?'

'You don't need four suits for sweeping up!'

Dennis retained his dignity. 'I am *not* sweeping up! I am on the fringe of a great career. It may not interest you but it so happens I went down very well last night!'

'Oh aye? What did they serve you with – chips and peas?'

'Ha-ha! Highly comical!'

'I bet it's a damned sight funnier than your jokes!' said Elsie.

'Do you know who was in the Orinoco last night?' It was more of a sneer than a question.

'No, go on, tell me!' said Elsie, innocently wide-eyed.

'Only Monty Hyman, that's all!'

'Not *the* Monty Hyman?' Elsie's voice was heavy with respect.

'Have you heard of him?' asked Dennis, somewhat surprised.

'No,' said Elsie.

Dennis turned back to his guitar, disgusted. He was more than touchy on the subject of his showbiz career and had been since the night the manager at the Orinoco, distraught at the non-appearance of the Singing Sylvesters, had pressed Dennis (as if Dennis needed pressing) to take his guitar onstage and entertain the paying customers. And at the end of the night had pressed a fiver into Dennis's grateful hand and said, with a certain amount of awe, 'Do you know, lad, we've never sold so much booze in one night in the history of this club. I'll go farther – in the history of my long and distinguished career on the circuit!'

Dennis, naturally, had taken this as a compliment, blissfully unaware that his audience had lost all interest in him after the first half dozen chords and had turned their attention to drink. The manager, alive to any possibility, persevered with the thirst-making Dennis.

'See that lad' he said to a bookmaker friend one night. 'He's the best salted peanut in the business!'

Faced with the prospect of a nightly spot, Dennis sought to broaden his act. He told jokes, monologues, even introduced a soft-shoe shuffle to his own guitar playing but the effect remained the same. The mere sight of him sent thirst raging round the club. Each night as he mounted the tiny stage, the ash-blonde barmaid shifted her chewing gum to the other side of her mouth, smiled at the gloomy waiters and said, 'Get your running shoes on, lads! It's *him* again!'

And so, with such success behind him, it was difficult to absorb his mother's light-hearted attitude towards his assault on Las Vegas.

He spoke to her, pityingly, as to a child. 'You've heard of Bernard Delfont, haven't you?'

'Yes.'

'And Val Parnell?'

'Yes.'

'Well, bring them up North and you've got Monty Hyman! He's the biggest theatrical agent up here! And he came in last night to see *me*.'

Dennis would have been surprised to know how near the truth he was. Secretly he felt that the redoubtable Mr Hyman was far more likely to be interested in Svenska, the Swedish Stripping Songstress, but he would have gone to his death rather than admit it. As it so happened he was wrong as he would have known had he listened to a telephone conversation between the Orinoco manager and Monty Hyman only a week before.

'Are you telling me your liquor sales are directly related to this boy you've got twanging his guitar every night?'

'Don't ask me why, Mr Hyman, but that's exactly what I'm saying! He's got something! Not talent exactly, but something!'

'Don't knock it, Charlie! It's happened before! It's like ... wallpaper – it's got to be right for you to be happy! Obviously this boy's everybody's perfect wallpaper. And there's another thing! All these performers attack a different part of the human body! Elvis we won't talk about over the telephone but some tickle the ribs, some

143

catch at the heart strings, so why shouldn't this boy dry the throat? I'll come and see him!'

'Don't look at *him*, Mr Hyman, watch the cash register! It'll gladden your heart!'

And Mr Hyman had come and he had watched the cash register and his heart had been gladdened. As had Dennis's when, after his spot, he had been introduced to the great man himself.

'And that's why you bought yourself a new suit? Just because this Hyman feller talked to you?'

'He doesn't talk to anybody! And you've got to look sharp in Show Business! You don't see Frankie Vaughan walking about with his shirt tails hanging out, do you?'

'Well, not often!' said Elsie, and picked up the jacket of the new grey suit from the chair back. 'How much did you pay for this?'

'Money and fair words!'

It wouldn't do to say too much, decided Elsie. After all, Dennis had bought it out of his own money.

'H'm!' she said. 'Very nice!' And she draped the jacket back over the chair so carefully that all Dennis's papers fell out of his inside pocket.

'That's right!' said Dennis sarcastically. 'Empty me pockets! It won't be for t'first time!'

Elsie started to stuff the assortment of letters, bills and photographs back into the jacket. The last item, a visiting card, she glanced at idly.

'What's this?' she asked.

'It's mine!' said Dennis and made a grab for it.

Elsie, pulling the card away from him, read the gold-printed inscription. 'Ricky Dennis – Mr Showbiz Himself – Telephone number . . .' She stopped, looked queryingly at her only son, 'Who's Ricky Dennis when he's at home?'

'It's me, isn't it? It's me stage name.'

'Oh? And since when have we had a telephone number?'

'If you're having a card printed you've got to have a telephone number, haven't you! Any fool knows that!'

'And any fool knows a made-up telephone number when he starts ringing it, doesn't he?'

'It's not made-up,' said Dennis.

144

'Not made-up? Whose is it then?'

'Rover's Return,' said Dennis sullenly.

'Rover's Return?' said Elsie, horrified. 'What do you think you're doing? You can't go round borrowing folks's telephone numbers! There's a law against it! Or if there isn't, there should be!'

'Billy said it was all right!'

'Oh, did he! It's not Billy I'm worrying about! It's Madam Walker – that mother of his! What do you think she's going to say when she finds out you've been taking her telephone number in vain?'

Elsie thought of asking as she pushed her empty glass across the counter.

'Another, Mrs Tanner?' asked Annie. 'You *are* celebrating!'

Elsie remembered the departed Arthur and decided not to spoil the happy day.

'Yes, please, Mrs Walker!'

Annie served her, then excused herself 'to go and prepare luncheon'. Probably means luncheon meat, thought Elsie sourly, lifting her glass and ignoring the glad eye she was attracting from a brawny hod-carrier at the other end of the bar. The telephone rang in the hall. Jack froze in the act of polishing a glass and listened. The ringing continued and with a mild tut he left the bar. The ringing stopped.

'By eck, you can't convince some folk!' said Jack when he came back. 'As if I don't know who lives here and who doesn't! Could I talk to Ricky Dennis!!'

Elsie was suddenly alert. 'Did you say Ricky Dennis?'

'Aye,' said Jack. 'Have you heard of him?'

'I'm sorry to say I have!'

'Some feller called Hyman wants him. So if you see him . . . !'

'Jack!' said Elsie. 'It's a long story!'

It took three more gins and tonics to tell it.

Dennis explained Jack's ignorance of Ricky Dennis quite simply. 'Sorry about that, Mr Hyman! You know what

145

it's like getting office staff. The old feller who answered the phone's a bit hard of hearing! Anyway, what can I do for you?'

It transpired that Mr Hyman could do quite a lot. Unknown to Dennis he looked after the bookings for a number of clubs belonging to the same syndicate as the Orinoco and great interest had been shown in Dennis's strange powers. An allied club, the Grotto, had not been doing too well as far as sales of drink were concerned, and Monty Hyman had been instructed to offer Dennis a higher fee to act, unconsciously, as booster. The Grotto, it appeared, had a rough, tough, beer-drinking clientele and it was hoped that Dennis's magical properties might switch the hoi-polloi on to more profitable lines.

Dennis started at the Grotto the following week and could well have enjoyed a record run had it not been for a quirk of industrial fate. On his fourth night a lightning strike by draymen caused the beer to run out just as Dennis commenced his act. Slow to turn to spirits the customers found they had nothing else to do but listen to Dennis. Which proved his undoing. No one had actually listened to him before and when they did they didn't at all like what they heard. Dennis was booed from the stage and relegated, the following day, to his old position as front-of-house at the Orinoco Club.

But Dennis was nothing if not resilient. 'It's nowt!' he said to his unsurprised but unsympathetic mother. 'Just a stumble on the stairway to stardom!'

August continued to be a happy month. Usually it was regarded with suspicion if not outright dislike in the houses of Weatherfield which, during its apparently endless four weeks, rang with the happy, head-aching laughter of children. Harassed mothers dragged their unwilling and unwanted offspring round the shops, alternately beating off demands for more money and pleas of 'What shall I play at, Mum?' And bitter experience had shown that as

146

soon as the children were sent out to play, August, being August, would conjure rain clouds from a bright blue sky and send them scuttling back indoors.

But this particular August was different. The sun shone, some Russian went round the earth seventeen times in a spaceship, someone else stole the portrait of the Duke of Wellington from the National Gallery, Australia retained the Ashes and Florrie Lindley won £500 on the Premium Bonds.

She knew what it was as soon as she saw the envelope lying on the shop mat. The horoscope in that morning's paper had stated, quite categorically, that luck would smile on her and Florrie could think of no other possible quarter from which it could come than from her Premium Bonds. She had held a block of a hundred ever since they were first issued and, she reckoned, it was high time her number came up. One nervous twitch of her forefinger and the envelope was open.

Never having indulged in great expectations, Florrie would quite happily have settled for twenty-five pounds. She had not even considered anything over fifty. So when she read the amount on the friendly but formally printed letter she almost swooned from sheer delight. Then, feeling that the eyes of the world were upon her, she hurried back into her living room. There she sat quietly, poured herself another cup of tea, and gave the matter some serious thought.

Firstly, what was she going to do with the money? Secondly, who was she going to tell? She decided that number one could look after itself and bent her mind to the second question. Why tell anyone, she reasoned. It was a well-known fact that as soon as anyone won on the pools the vultures gathered on the doorstep. Only they didn't look like vultures, they looked like your friends and relatives. And a lot of the friends were friends you never knew you had. She could just hear that Martha Longhurst!

'May I say how pleased I was to hear of your little windfall! I was just looking at a new tea-set in Granger's window when Ena told me and I thought Ee! how lovely to win summat like that and be able to buy your friends all the little things they craved for! Six pounds fifteen it was, the tea-set! ' Some hopes *she'd* got!

Or that Tanner lad!

'I expect you'll be wiping all t'slates clean now you've won your fortune! ' He'd be lucky!

Or worse still, old Tatlock!

'Do you know how much they expect an old-age pensioner to live on? Well, I'll tell you! – not enough to keep body and soul together! I'll tell you straight, if I came into five hundred quid I'd reckon I were t'luckiest feller alive. And I certainly wouldn't take money off a poor old pensioner for his groceries! ' Well, *I* would, thought Florrie!

The shop bell tinkled. Florrie, still smiling, hurried through.

'You're looking very pleased with yourself! ' said Martha Longhurst.

'Well, I suppose I should! I've just won five hundred pounds on the Premium Bonds! '

It was a week of pleasant surprises. On the Tuesday, Lucille heard that she had passed her eleven-plus and would be going on to Weatherfield Grammar School after the holidays. Harry was delighted – he had, for weeks, been nursing a nagging, secret worry that Lucille was devoting far too little time and application to her studies – and he showed his pleasure by fulfilling his daughter's most ardent desire, to possess a record-player. But every silver lining has a cloud and, as he said to Len that night over a pint . . .

'If I'd had a bit more education myself I might have realized that record players need records to play on 'em! I'd no sooner given it to her than she wanted another ten bob for Billy Fury's latest! '

But he hadn't meant it. He'd given her the extra ten shillings happily enough. In fact, he reflected on hearing Lucille's news, life had been taking a decided turn for the better this year. The only cloud in his blue sky had passed when Alice had left.

It had started with an apparently innocent visit just before Easter. He'd answered the door at seven o'clock one evening to find his sister on the doorstep.

'Hello!' he said. 'What are you doing round here?'

'Oh, I came over to see Cousin Amy and I thought I'd take a chance and see if you were in.' She settled herself in the easy chair and looked critically around the room. 'How are things, then?'

'Oh, fine! Fine!'

'Yes, so I hear!' Her tone was faintly reproving. 'Our Amy was saying! Though how she finds out Heaven only knows! According to her you never go near her!'

'Well, you know how it is!'

'Oh, I do! Or at least I think I do!' Her critical eyes slid from the dusty mantelpiece to Harry himself. 'Thinking of getting married again, are you?'

'Now, Alice, stop jumping to conclusions! You've only been in the house two minutes!'

Her thin fingers flicked at the chair arm. 'You'll have to put up with me, won't you? I've nowt much else to do these days!'

Alice had been a widow for thirteen months. Her husband, Sam Burgess, had been killed at his workbench by a falling light fitment and a bitter Union had fought and won for her a sizeable amount in compensation. But they couldn't replace Sam.

'Still missing him?' asked Harry.

Alice nodded silently. It wasn't Sam himself she was missing. He had been a colourless man. A good provider but little else. But he had been Alice's kingdom, her realm, her only royal subject and this she missed. She could hardly explain it to Harry because she wasn't aware of it herself. But she *was* aware of her loneliness.

'You don't know what it's like, living on your own.'

'Course I do!' said Harry. 'I've had a basinful myself!'

'You've got Lucille. I was never blessed with children.'

'I've got no Lucille now! Not since she's been . . .' He

couldn't bring himself to say 'in care'. Somehow the words were an indictment. As if he weren't capable of caring for his own daughter. All he wanted was for someone to provide the bread and butter necessities of life. To look after her during night shifts, to be waiting for her when she returned from school, to be there in the morning when she left. But as far as caring was concerned, he could supply all that was needed and more. Alice saw both his predicament and her opportunity.

'I'm surprised you let her go! It's not as if you've nobody to come and look after her!'

That had been how it started. Alice became increasingly persuasive and her words made more and more sense to the highly vulnerable Harry. An hour later she left and the following Monday she moved in.

Looking back, Harry knew that there had never been anything he could have put his finger on. Alice was clean, capable, devoted in her way both to Lucille and to himself. And the arrangement had meant that Lucille came home. But there was an underlying presence, a jealousy, a burning desire to turn Lucille and Harry into substitutes for the now-departed Sam. Loyal subjects who would never give their allegiance to any other woman.

On the surface she and Concepta got on well together but Harry sensed the antagonism which sprang between them. In his heart he knew that Concepta's main attraction had been that she would create a home not just for himself but for his daughter. And that need had faded with the arrival of his sister. Alice knew it too. He had waited for Concepta to make a move – to criticize his sister – but no move came. And it was this policy of non-intervention, this apparently negative attitude of Concepta's which turned the scale.

Harry realized that Concepta thought too much of him to create a rift between Alice and himself and he began to see that he needed a woman who would be more to him than a mere housekeeper. Alice stood between him and his needs, and, taking his courage in both hands, he told her so.

It hadn't been easy. Alice fought like a tigress but her

own natural caution proved to be her undoing. Rather than sell the little house she had bought from Sam's compensation, she had let it furnished to a young couple, the son and daughter-in-law of one of Sam's ex-workmates. How, she had argued with Harry, could she kick them out, yet, if she didn't, where was she to live?

It was sheer chance that Harry was at home the night the young man called to ask Alice if he could be released from his verbal contract with her. He had been offered a better job in Preston and they'd found a little flat there. Alice was beaten. Harry felt both saddened and sadistic as he listened to her wishing the boy well. After he had gone, she turned to Harry. 'I'd better start getting my things together. I've no excuse now, have I?'

He had stood silent and let her go, knowing it was the best thing for all of them. When he told Concepta she said, simply and sincerely, that she was sorry. Two weeks later, on the coach back from Blackpool, he had proposed and here he was – a bus inspector with a daughter going to Grammar School and a wedding in the offing. It was a good life.

'Not before time either!' said Ida Barlow. She slid the steaming plate of hot pot in front of her husband and headed for the kitchen.

'Is that all you've got to say?' Frank shouted after her. He turned to David who was looking at his father's plate as if he hadn't eaten for a week. 'Marvellous! You come home and tell your loving family you've been promoted to Supervisor an' all your son can think about is food an' all your wife can say is "Not before time"!'

Ida came back with David's meal and her own. 'What do you expect me to say? *I'm* not surprised you've been promoted even if *you* are!'

'But I *wanted* you to be surprised!'

'All right!' she said accommodatingly. 'I'm surprised! I can't for the life of me think what's come over 'em. I can understand a London football club buying our David but, making somebody as daft as you a Supervisor!'

'Hey, watch it!' said Frank.

'See? You can't have it both ways! I've either got faith in you in which case I expect you to be promoted or I haven't got faith in you in which case it comes as a surprise! Now which way do you want it?'

Frank grinned at his wife's logic.

'Where's our Ken?' he asked.

'You know, I sometimes wonder if I'm not wasting my breath talking to you in the morning! What did I say to you at breakfast?'

'Oh, aye.'

'Oh, aye! Well, that's where he is!'

'Where?' asked David. 'You didn't tell me.'

'He's taken your Grandma to see Beattie. They're having their tea there. And don't talk with your mouth full!'

Nancy Leathers, Ida's mother, had been living with them for a couple of weeks. David and Kenneth had grumbled at being moved in with one another but the little house had settled into a crowded but happy routine. Gran, with her quiet but occasionally acid humour, was always a welcome visitor and the boys had a bit of fun trying to pair her off with old Albert next door.

'Tell you what, Gran!' David had said. 'I'll take one of my girl friends out, you tag along and I'll ask Albert to make up a foursome. Tell him it's a blind date – that'll get him going!'

'It'll get *me* going, an' all!' said Gran. 'And what's this about your girl friend. I thought you were too busy playing football to have girl friends?'

'I lend him a couple every now and then,' said Kenneth. 'I always have too many to be going on with!'

'Yes, that's your trouble!' said the old lady, 'It'd look better of you if you'd settle for one and have done with it!'

'Come on, then!' said David. 'What do you say about this date with Albert?' How do you fancy a jive at the Palais?'

'Go on, then,' said Gran, always ready for a bit of fun.

'But think on, it goes no farther than a spot o' courting! Corporation's only giving me a single flat, tha knows!'

When they did meet, Albert and Nancy got on well. They never actually got as far as jiving at the Palais but they chatted away happily for hours, exchanging reminiscences, and towards the end of her temporary stay Albert helped her move into her Corporation old people's flat on the other side of Weatherfield.

It was during a visit to Albert's that Nancy had met his married daughter, Beattie, who, rather grandly, had invited her to tea. 'We're in a four-bedroomed detached, you know, up the Old Road. Norman's doing very well! Anyway, come and have a look at us, have some tea! Kenneth'll bring you!'

This, it must be explained, was during one of Beattie's less expectant periods. She alternated between believing that her father had a fortune in gold sovereigns hidden beneath the floorboards and a firm conviction that he was penniless and would soon become an intolerable burden on Norman and herself. During the latter phases, one of which was current, she wasn't averse to any eventuality which might relieve her of her responsibility for her father's future well-being. Which explained her attitude to Nancy.

'Are you sure you wouldn't like another sandwich? I can soon cut some, you know!'

Kenneth smiled and shook his head at Beattie. He liked to think of himself as a student of human behaviour and one of his pet theories was that the actions of the body, conscious or unconscious, were manifestations of the workings of the mind. If, he reasoned, Beattie really *was* happy to make some more sandwiches, her body would, by now, be half way to the kitchen. This, however, was not the case. The body, encased in corsets and a pink-flowered dress was still securely anchored to its armchair. This meant, according to his theory, that she hoped he would refuse. So, being a polite young man, he refused.

'How about you, Mrs Leathers?'

'Well, I wouldn't say no!' said Grandma. 'You cut 'em a

bit thin, don't you? Takes half a dozen o' them to make a decent mouthful.'

As Beattie levered herself painfully out of her chair, Kenneth wondered if he might reverse his decision and ask for more himself. He decided against it. And resolved in future to forget his theories when food was at stake.

Beattie's voice floated out of the kitchen. 'Dad's got a lodger from today, you know!'

Nancy shouted back. 'Oh? Who's that then? He didn't mention anything.'

'No, it's short notice. It's young Valerie, his niece. My cousin, that is. Uncle Arthur's girl. Have you ever met my Dad's brother? And Auntie Edith?'

'No, I don't think so,' said Nancy. It was obvious that Beattie was about to launch on a long and complicated family chronicle but Nancy had no fears. The average Lancashire lady of mature years could quite easily absorb a mass of family detail which would have daunted the College of Heralds.

As it so happened, the story was simple. Albert's brother, who had worked himself up through the maze of British Rail administration to the post of stationmaster had been moved up to Glasgow. He and his wife, Edith, had left that day to take up residence there but their daughter Valerie, a qualified hairdresser with ambitions to start her own salon in Weatherfield, had stayed behind.

Albert, always on the look-out for a few extra shillings to supplement his pension, jumped at the chance to take in Valerie as a paying guest until such time as she found a place for herself. Besides, she was his only niece and therefore his favourite and, even more important, she could cook.

'You'll probably be bumping into her,' said Beattie as she brought back the sandwiches.

Kenneth 'bumped into her' that evening. Trying vainly to catch up on the morning newspaper while Gran regaled his mother with a long and not too complimentary description of Beattie's new house as Frank snored gently in the fireside chair, his thoughts began to stray next door. Being a good student he had a strongly developed bump of inquisitiveness and Beattie's description of his new neighbour was, to say the least, intriguing.

'Oh, she's a beautiful girl!' Beattie had said. 'Big eyes and gorgeous hair and a *lovely* complexion! She's very fortunate getting her looks from our side of the family!'

Kenneth was inventive as well as inquisitive. He rose, sighing deeply at the effort, and made for the kitchen.

'I'll pop that cake in to Uncle Albert. The one Beattie sent.'

'Oh, don't bother yourself!' said his mother. 'I'll take it in.'

'Now use your brains, Ida!' said Gran. 'He's not bothered about any cake! It's that girl he's going to see!'

Kenneth smiled indulgently. 'I am going to take Uncle Albert his cake!'

'Oh, stop excusing yourself!' said Gran. 'There's no need. We were just t'same when we were your age. And you can tell us what she's really like when you get back. According to Beattie she's next in line for Miss World!'

Well, thought Kenneth a minute later, I'd certainly give her the Miss Weatherfield title! He had walked out of the front door at the same moment as the smiling, fair-haired girl had left Number One. They stood, facing each other, Kenneth gingerly holding Beattie's fruit cake, and smiled.

'Would you be Kenneth?'

'I would indeed! Would you be Valerie?'

'Yes! Uncle Albert asked me to call and see if Cousin Beattie sent anything.'

'Yes, she did. This cake. I er . . . I was just bringing it!'

The smiles were a trifle uncertain now. He wondered if he ought to ask her in to meet his family, she was mentally tossing up whether to take the cake from him or ask him in to present it personally. Kenneth filled in the gap.

'I er . . . I understand you're . . . going to live here for a while?'

'Yes,' she said.

155

'Oh!' He searched desperately for something scintillating to say. 'Good!'

Which wasn't exactly scintillating but was undoubtedly sincere.

On August the twenty-seventh, the day of Paul Cheveski's christening, summer returned, briefly, to Coronation Street.

'Wouldn't you just know!' said Elsie. 'I buy myself a winter-weight costume 'cos the weather's turning and look at it – the sun's cracking the flags!'

Which, of course, was an exaggeration but it *was* a nice day. At nine-thirty, Dennis, resplendent in his dove-grey Italian two-piece, sauntered downstairs. He executed a couple of male-model turns in the middle of the living-room carpet and turned to his struggling mother.

'Well?' he asked. 'What do you think?'

'I think what I've always thought! You could give me more housekeeping! And give me a hand with this zip. And there's a little hook and eye at the top. Do it up!'

'Aw, Mum, you know I'm rotten at that!'

'I know you're rotten at everything but do as you're told!'

Dennis contorted his mouth and tried desperately to bring hook and eye together. 'What are you wearing this old thing for? I thought you'd bought a new costume.'

'I *have* bought a new costume! And if you can go and have a word with that flamin' weather man on the wireless and get him to fetch that cold spell he promised us, I'll put it on!'

Dennis stood back, perspiring heavily. 'I've done it!'

There was a rapping on the party wall.

'That'll be our Linda,' said Elsie. 'Go and let her in!'

As she repaired her lipstick in front of the flyblown mirror, Linda's delighted cry floated in from the front door.

'Eh, look at your Uncle Dennis! Isn't he a swell!'

'All right, clever! Just because you don't know a good suit when you see one!'

'I'm complimenting you, aren't I, you daft 'ap'orth! If you don't know a compliment when you hear it, Heaven help you!'

Elsie grimaced at her reflection. Why did her kids have to shout at each other even when they were happy?

'There then! Here he is, come to see his Nana!'

Elsie turned from the mirror. Linda stood in the doorway, holding Paul in her arms. The baby's face was purple as, lustily and tirelessly, he screamed defiance at the world.

'He's been like this since he woke up this morning!' said Linda happily.

'Aw, he knows, doesn't he!' said Elsie, gazing with fond adoration at her grandson. 'They know, you know!' And then, chucking the howling baby under the chin, 'Diddums know den? Idda naughty man going to splash water over Nana's lovely little boy!'

'What's he always crying for?' asked Dennis, genuinely interested.

'Don't *you* talk!' snapped Elsie. 'You skriked your head off from morning till night, you did!'

Linda joined in. 'Till he was fourteen?'

'Near enough!' said Elsie, 'He was the only baby I knew who could chew a dummy to bits with his gums!'

'Oo, did he have a dummy?' Linda was disgusted.

'Do you mind?' said the aggrieved Dennis.

The women took no notice of him. 'You know very well he had a dummy!' said Elsie. 'And so did you! And so will that one when he's stopped being a novelty!'

'He won't!'

'He will! You're having it very easy so far, you are! Don't think I don't know who gets up in the middle of the night because I do! And she's not standing in front of me in a moygashel coat, neither! Mark my words, as soon as that husband of yours goes on strike and you have to get up yourself, first thing you'll have nice and handy'll be a little comforter! And talking of your husband, where is he?'

'Where d'you think! Getting himself ready! You'd think it was t'flamin' Coronation!'

'Live and let live!' said Elsie. 'We don't go to church that often! It's an event!'

'And it's an event we'll miss if you don't get a move on!' said Linda. 'Have you seen that clock?'

As Elsie turned away to put the finishing touches to her make-up there was, inevitably, a knock on the front door.

'Dennis, go and see who that is,' said his mother, 'and if it's the Salvation Army tell 'em we gave last week.'

'What did you give?' asked Linda as Dennis trudged, sulkily, to the door.

'I gave 'em a nice smile which is more than most folk get out o' me at that time on a Sunday morning!'

'It's Mrs Sharples!' As Ena was standing next to him, Dennis's announcement was scarcely necessary.

'I won't keep you,' said Ena.

'Good!' said Elsie. And immediately wished she hadn't.

'I've just come to bring t'lad a little present!' Ena smiled triumphantly. If there was anything she enjoyed it was putting Elsie in the wrong.

'Oh, you shouldn't, Mrs Sharples!' said Linda but she took the little cardboard box just the same.

Ena turned her attention to her old enemy as Linda struggled to open the package. 'Where's it happening? St Mary's? Only there's not been a lot said!'

'That's right, St Mary's,' said Elsie, still smarting.

'Know your way, do you?' asked Ena amiably.

Elsie was saved from the necessity of verbal invention by a delighted squeal from Linda.

'Oh, Mrs Sharples, it's lovely! What is it?'

'Oh, it's nowt much! Just a little cross and chain.'

'Is it silver?'

'Well, summat o' that order!'

'Look, Mam!' Linda held out the tiny chain and cross for Elsie's inspection. Elsie glanced at it casually.

'Very nice! Marvellous what they turn out in Hong Kong these days!'

Ena's mouth hardened. 'They're marvellous people, aren't they! A lot of 'em are charitable Christians out

158

there which is more than you can say for a lot round here! '

'You're probably right, Mrs Sharples! And now if you'll excuse us, we're in a bit of a rush! '

Ena turned to Linda, her eyes flinty. 'You've got him up very nice,' she said, nodded at the baby and left.

Linda turned on her mother. 'Oo, you're a right one, you are! Fancy picking a fight on a day like this! And her bringing a present an' all! '

'A present! Don't make me laugh! You know what she was after, don't you?'

'No, I don't! ' said Linda.

'Well, grow up a bit and perhaps you will! '

They were still arguing when they reached the church.

Sheila Birtles and little Doreen Lostock were waiting at Linda's door when the christening party returned to the street. The young, eager vicar had been long-winded in the extreme and Elsie's feet, never hardy, were playing her up rather more painfully than usual.

'What do *you* want? ' she asked the waiting girls.

'We've come to wet the baby's head! ' said Sheila.

'Your Linda asked us! ' added Doreen.

Elsie glared at her daughter. 'You never said anything to me about a party! '

'It's not a party! It's just one or two people coming in for a drink! '

One or two became six and six became twelve and an hour later the party was swinging along happily. Apart, that was, from Elsie whose aching feet were destroying her normal convivial mood. She dragged Linda to one side. 'What did you want to ask them two for? ' she said pointing to Sheila and Doreen. 'They've never stopped knocking it back since you let 'em in! '

'Because they'll come in useful for baby-sitting, that's why! ' said Linda. 'And shurrup or they'll hear you! '

Elsie looked darkly around the happy faces. The Barlows – what were *they* all looking so pleased about? Harry and Concepta – oh well, you could understand *them*! Old Tatlock – if *he* was smiling it must be good sherry! She

159

held out her empty glass for Linda to refill it, 'Where's Ivan?' she asked.

'He's gone for Ena,' said Linda.

'He's what??'

'He's gone for Ena. To ask her for a drink. And don't start again, Mum! She did bring a present!'

'You never learn, do you! You watch! She's spent two bob on a tin cross and for that she'll eat and drink you out of house and home!'

Ena, however, did have her uses. She ate well and she drank well but her faculties remained undimmed. At five past two, with the party showing no signs of abating, it was Ena who sniffed the air and announced, 'Something's burning!'

Elsie flew into the kitchen. The leg of lamb she had presented to Linda so that they could all eat together was sizzling to a cinder. She stared at it, expressionless, not trusting herself to speak, as Linda joined her. And then . . . 'I suppose you realize I didn't have a bite to eat out there. No, I thought, I won't be greedy! Seeing we're going to have roast lamb!'

'Don't cry, Mam!' said Linda, wiping a tear from her own cheek.

'Let's get 'em out!' said Elsie dully and walked back into the noisy living room.

It was Len Fairclough who conjured another drink out of a seemingly hopeless situation. 'Fair enough, Elsie, but we can't go without toasting the lad, can we? Nobody object if I say a few words?' He looked round the silent, flushed faces. 'Right, fill your glasses up and we're off!'

It was a clever move and it worked. When the last glass was charged Len took centrestage and raised his hand for silence.

'Well, we've all had a great morning and the eats have been great and the drink's great but we are in danger of forgetting why we've come! Which isn't difficult when you think the main reason's upstairs in bed. And like Confucius said, out of sight and I don't know what you're doing!'

'I bet I know what *he's* doing!' said Dennis, 'He's getting another nappie ready for his uncle! '

Len waved down the laughter. 'One singer, one song! Dearly beloved brethren, we are gathered here to drink the health of Paul Cheveski, a little lad who was lucky enough to have a beautiful mother and a very glamorous grandma but who had the great misfortune to be born in Coronation Street. 'Cos when you look round and see what this street's produced there's only one toast you can make! He's a helpless little lad – don't let it happen to him! Here's to Paul! And God bless him! '

Harry Hewitt, impervious to Concepta's digs in the ribs, lent his rich baritone to 'For He's a Jolly Good Fellow'. Throwing discretion to the winds the rest of the party joined in and upstairs, in a darkened front bedroom, Coronation Street's newest arrival woke up and began to cry.

Two days after the christening Ida and her mother were sitting in front of the fire, Gran dozing, Ida reading a letter for the third time. The closing days of August had brought a cold snap and Frank had lit a fire before going off to a Union meeting with Alf Roberts. As Ida finished the letter with a smile, the glowing coals dropped in the grate and Gran jerked awake.

'What time is it? ' she asked.

'Ten past nine,' answered Ida then turned her attention back to the sheets of closely-covered paper. 'David's coming up to see us soon. He says they play Bury at the end of September and he'll stay the weekend with us. According to him they should win with Bury only just being promoted to their Division, like, so we should have something to celebrate! '

'I don't know why he wanted to take up football for in t'first place! ' said Gran. 'Seems a daft way o' making a living – kicking a ball about! '

David's rise in the football world had been what the Weatherfield Gazette sports reporter (who also doubled on Council meetings and amateur dramatics) had been pleased to describe as 'meteoric'. He had been spotted

161

whilst playing for his works team and offered a trial with County, the local Third Division side where a crop of injuries to the first team squad soon opened the door to his first senior appearance. He rapidly established himself in the team and it was no surprise to anyone with any knowledge of the game when, at the end of the season, two or three clubs showed an interest in him. County, like many a club in the lower echelons, were at a low financial ebb and they were happy to accept a few thousands for David's transfer to a London Second Division Club. David was more than happy – he was delirious. Football was his life and to be able to earn a living from one's hobby – and from what people were saying it was going to be a very good living – placed him amongst life's fortunate few.

'He's been very lucky,' said his mother, 'but at least he knows it. I'll say that for our David – he won't get bigheaded!'

'Don't count your chickens before they're hatched!' warned Gran. 'Just wait till he gets to Wembley and see how big-headed he gets!'

Ida put her tongue in her cheek. 'Will you be there to see him?'

'Course I will! I'm his grandmother, aren't I?'

Ida sighed contentedly and settled back in her chair. 'You know, I was frightened of this year ever starting! Everything seemed to be going wrong and now look at us. Frank's got his promotion, our David's happy as a sandboy, Ken looks as if he's getting himself settled with a nice girl at last and t'Corporation's finally finished that onebedroomed palace for you to move into! Eh, we're lucky!'

Gran looked at her daughter over her glasses. 'Now, Ida!' she said.

'I know! I know!' said Ida. 'It'll all end in tears!'

CHAPTER SIX

Some days declare themselves at dawn. Storm clouds, gathering on an angry horizon foretell violent and turbulent events, whilst a quiet sunrise, with the dawn light spreading softly over a cloudless sky often heralds a peaceful, happy day. But there are rogue days, deceiving days, days which do not hold to their promise. Monday, the eleventh of September was one of those days.

Harry Hewitt was first out that morning. On duty at seven thirty he left the house at ten past the hour, sniffed the clear air appreciatively and strode happily into Rosamund Street to hail the first city-bound bus.

Rosamund Street was one of Weatherfield's main arteries. It carried a steady flow of mixed traffic towards the centre of Manchester and, even at this relatively early hour, Harry was forced to nip smartly through the skein of cars and lorries heading to and from the city complex. As he reached the other side of the road and joined the straggling queue a buxom, red-faced lady smiled at him and said, 'Thank Heaven you've arrived! Happen a bus'll come now!'

'I wouldn't bank on it, missus!' said Harry. 'They try and keep away from me!'

But even as he turned a bus swung out of Victoria Street and trundled towards them.

'Told you!' said the buxom lady to her waiting companions, 'They hide round that corner and wait for him! They don't care a toss about us!'

Harry stood back to let a couple of new arrivals clamber aboard then swung himself on to the platform. A flustered clippie, a girl in her early twenties, clattered downstairs. 'Pass along inside, please!' And then, seeing Harry, 'Oh, sorry!' New to the service, she smiled nervously and reached for her board.

'Leave it where it is!' said Harry. 'I've not started work yet!'

'Thank Heaven for that!' she said. 'I thought it were going to be one o' them days!'

Ten minutes later the bus turned across the thickening stream of traffic into North Parade and was stopped, almost immediately, by the traffic lights at the Tile Street crossing. Harry glanced down the busy side street and nudged the young conductress.

'How would you like to be one of them?' He pointed towards two smart policewomen swinging round the corner. 'And collect drunks instead o' fares!'

'From what I hear I collect plenty o' drunks on this thing later on!' The little clippie had grown in confidence during the run into town.

Harry smiled. 'Aye, that's true but they'll sober up when they see what they're up against!'

The girl smiled then looked wistfully at the vanishing policewomen. 'All t'same, I wouldn't mind their uniform!'

The two policewomen didn't share her feelings. In fact the uniform had been their topic of conversation since they had met in front of Woolworth's on their way to report.

'Just walk behind me,' said one, 'and tell me if my hem's dipping!' And then, a few paces later, 'Well?'

'Looks all right. But your tunic doesn't fit on the shoulders. Same as mine, it stands out off your neck!'

They were still tearing the designer to pieces when they entered the police station. A young constable grinned at them and turned to the yawning desk sergeant. 'Here they are, Sarge! The Tile Street Tiller Girls.'

'Tiller Girls! They get a damned sight more than t'Tiller Girls! Don't know you're born, you young uns!'

The desk sergeant, a veteran only a year from retirement, never lost an opportunity to mention the new scales of pay which had been recommended, and implemented, in late 1960. But, wise as he was in the ways of men and money, he also knew that he wouldn't be talking to the three new recruits had it not been for these better conditions. And, had he been pressed, he would have admitted

164

that the new intake weren't a bad lot which only proved, whatever the practical side of his job might show, that money didn't attract only the worst side of humanity.

The girls, who only knew the sergeant as a superior and never suspected he could harbour such generous thoughts, turned to the young constable to make some flippant response and found he was taking a sudden and intense interest in his work. A glance towards the door told them why. Sergeant Lancaster had come in. And you didn't joke in front of Sergeant Lancaster.

Three miles away and near to the start of Harry Hewitt's journey that morning, another police sergeant reported for the day's duties. Sergeant Baldwin strode happily into Weatherfield Police Station at the corner of Victoria Street and Booth Street, banged open the counter flap, walked through, banged the flap shut again and thumped Billy Butler resoundingly on the back. 'Come on, let's be having you! Get off your backside and home to Ethel. I've just seen her letting the milkman out so you're all right!'

As did all relieved desk sergeants, Billy yawned. 'Not before time either! And it's not the milkman, it's the coalman!'

As a matter of fact it was neither the milkman nor the coalman but the next-door neighbour, a brawny furnace-man at Weatherfield Steel.

Not that Billy knew. And, reflected Sergeant Baldwin, he wasn't likely to find out from his pals.

As stations go it was a happy one. It is a fact, in the police force as elsewhere, that the farther one gets from headquarters the more relaxed one becomes. And, in terms of administrative importance if not geography, Weather-field was as far as one could get. Which explained the frown on the face of Sergeant Lancaster of Tile Street Divisional Headquarters and the content in the eyes of Sergeant Baldwin of the Weatherfield cop-shop. And yet, within a few hours, the two men were to form links in a chain of events which had no place on such a day.

'The weather's holding up nicely,' said Frank Barlow as he came back into the kitchen from the backyard.

Ida turned her attention from the frying pan. 'I hope you haven't thrown that Marks and Spencer's bag away!'

'You told me to put the rubbish in the bin so I put the rubbish in the bin!'

'I also told you I was taking that shirt back! It's miles too small for you. You went quite red when you tried it on!'

'Eh, be told, Ida! I've been sixteen round the neck for years!'

'And now you're sixteen and a half! You can't eat all the good food I give you without putting weight on!'

Frank smiled and joined Kenneth at the breakfast table.

'Listen to this!' said Kenneth and held up the newspaper to the bright morning light. 'The first goal came from a mazy run and a pin-point pass by David Barlow, a close-season signing, who on this showing should soon make the number eight shirt his own.'

'Let's have a look!' said Frank, taking the paper. He read the report for himself, a happy smile creasing his face then raised his voice. 'Hey, Ida! Our David's mentioned in th'*Express*!'

Ida's voice floated back. 'Is it good?'

'Come and read it for yourself!'

Ida, ever practical, finished preparing breakfast before she settled down, spectacles at the right angle, to read what the *Daily Express* had to say about her younger son. The article finished, she folded the paper neatly, placed it on a chair behind her and said, not totally convinced, 'H'm! Very nice!'

'It's more than very nice!' said Frank. 'It's smashing!'

'What's that about making the number eight shirt his own? I always thought he had his own shirt!'

Father and son looked at each other, then took it in turns to instruct Ida in the intricacies of football journalism.

'You see, Mam, you never just kick the ball past the goalkeeper! You always blast it past the stranded cus-todian!'

'Do you?' said Ida, unimpressed. 'Oh, well, I suppose

they've got to try and make it sound exciting even if it isn't!'

Frank and Kenneth smiled in the face of such devastating truth and turned their attention to their bacon and eggs. Ida watched them, her chin on her hands.

'Eat that bread up!' she said. 'And you'd better get yourselves a good dinner too because there'll be nothing cooked tonight!'

'Why not?' asked Frank.

'Because I'm going out after work, that's why not! So like I say there'll be nothing cooked for you, unless you want to do something for yourselves. If not, there's some cold lamb in the oven. Make yourselves sandwiches – you'll come to no harm!'

'Are you going to see Gran?' asked Kenneth. Mrs Leathers had moved into her old-people's flat only a week before.

'No, your cousin Margaret's there tonight. She's come over from Pontefract special!'

Frank took the last slice of bread and wiped the bacon fat from his plate. 'Where *are* you going then?'

'I'm going to Beattie's. She's been asking me round ever since Mother went and tonight's as good a chance as any.'

'You can take that shirt back for me then,' said Frank, 'seeing you're so sure it's too small for me!'

'Find me that Marks and Spencer's bag and I will!'

The Imperial Hotel occupied a prominent corner site near to the Manchester-Salford border. It was an old-established concern, relying mainly on commercials and tended, unlike its more modern counterparts, to keep many of its staff up to retirement age. Ida Barlow had worked there for seventeen years and, although Frank, when it served his purpose, described her job as 'skivvying' she had long since passed that stage. For the past five years she had been in charge of a section of the kitchen staff, mainly dishwashers, cleaners and kitchen porters. Because of her position, however, she had no need, herself, to get her hands wet, archaic though the hotel's dishwashing equipment was. Being Ida, however, she often did.

167

Elsie Tanner had once described her as 'too flaming good to draw breath!' This was, like many of Elsie's observations, a gross exaggeration. Ida was a simple, honest, hardworking woman who wanted nothing out of life but to be left to look after her family. She was a dying breed and, in her heart, she knew it but there was nothing she could do to change herself. Her standards were too deeply ingrained in her for her to discard them now. A fellow-worker at the Imperial, a gay, forty-year-old divorcee, had tried on more than one occasion to persuade Ida to have a night out with her.

'Come on, enjoy yourself, who's to know! And Heaven knows you deserve a bit of pleasure, the work you put in!'

Ida had given up trying to explain that she derived all the pleasure she needed from looking after her <u>family</u> and her home. And she had never confessed another side of her feelings. Ida, like everyone else, had her daydreams. Only that lunchtime, on her way to change Frank's shirt, she had given herself a little treat and walked through Kendal Milne's on the way.

The store had been filled with shoppers; the little office girls, pressed for time, scurrying round in a search for irresistible bargains left over from the Autumn Sales; the ladies of leisure strolling slowly between the counters, pausing here and there as something caught their fancy. Ida had stopped, ostensibly to examine a bottle of perfume she could never have afforded in a million years, in reality, to look, covertly, at a woman who had stopped nearby. The woman, fur-coated, exquisitely made-up and manicured, smilingly accepted a small, beautifully-wrapped parcel from a glamorous assistant and drifted off enveloped in a cloud of affluence.

Ida gazed after her. Heavens above! she thought, that was mink. Whatever does she wear when it's cold!

'Could I help moddom?' Ida turned to find yet another perfect young lady smiling at her.

'No, thank you!' said Ida. 'I'm just looking!'

That's all she ever did, she thought to herself as she gazed into the glittering window of the King Street jewellers'. The day's work was now behind her. She had left at five-fifteen and, her handbag and her tartan shopping bag securely in place over her arm, she was once more walking through the city on her way to the bus station. She was early. 'Get here about half past six!' Beattie had said, 'That'll give you time for a look round and a bite to eat. I know you won't want to get home too late.'

Ida gazed at a square-cut emerald discreetly priced at £1,250 and worked out that, as it took only twenty minutes by bus to Beattie's, she still had a half-hour to spare, even allowing for the walk at either end. She decided on a cup of tea, partly because she was thirsty and partly because she didn't entirely trust Beattie and her 'bite to eat'. She remembered a conversation with Pat Webster only the week before.

'What would you have done?' her friend had said. 'Here we were invited out to this posh friend's of Arthur's and there's this big good-for-nothing husband of mine asking for his tea! I told him! I said you don't want tea, we've been invited out to supper and you know what *that* means! You've guessed, haven't you! And you've guessed right! Supper turned out to be a cup of weak coffee and a Marie biscuit! As true as I stand here, Ida, my stomach started rumbling at half-past seven and it was still at it at ten o'clock!'

Ida decided that such a fate was not for her. She tore herself away from the jewellers' window and walked more briskly through the busy streets. She paused at a welcoming tea-shop, all dark wood and bull's-eye windows, but a glance at the clientele told her that the cakes would be expensive. And fattening, she added to herself, consolingly.

Her memory hadn't played her false. At the far side of the dark bus station, sandwiched between the 'Admiral Rodney' and a rather dubious bookshop, was a small narrow-fronted, snack bar. Called the 'Bijou Café', it had occupied the site since the opening of the bus station. Ida averted her eyes as she passed the bookshop and turned into the café's dark, warm interior. She paused to adjust her eyes. The sunshine had persisted throughout the day and the sudden gloom left her stumbling over the bentwood chairs which skirted the narrow aisle from counter to door.

'Are you having trouble?' The friendly voice came from the depths of the café as two rather dim light bulbs clicked into life. Ida blinked in the sudden, if ungenerous light.

'Oh, thanks!' She moved more easily to the counter where a thin-faced, sharp-eyed woman in a blue nylon overall stood waiting for her.

'I'm forever doing that!' said the café lady. 'With not going out myself I forget how bright it is out there! You must be as blind as a bat when you first walk in!'

'It is a bit gloomy!' said Ida.

'It's a good word for it, that!' said the lady, whose name was Mrs Maclean although Ida didn't know it at the time, and, rather recklessly, reached behind her and switched on two more lamps. 'Let's have a bit more light on a dark subject, shall we? Now, what can I get you?'

'Oh, just a cup of tea? And I'll have a buttered scone if you've got one.'

'Oh, yes, we have, and very nice buttered scones if I say so myself! Now, how do you like your tea? I always ask because I'm used to making it for them bus lads and they like to stand their spoons up in it!'

Ida told her and Mrs Maclean made the tea precisely to order. The scone was a trifle on the dry side but Ida was never one for complaining, particularly in the face of such friendliness. Mrs Maclean had brought the tea and scone to an adjacent table and had sat and gossiped while Ida ate and drank. The café, it appeared, had only been a part of her life for the past two years. Prior to that she had lived in Oban where her husband owned a small pleasure steamer plying the Western Isles. On his death in 1958 she had sold up, discovered that there were more debts than she had imagined and returned to her native Manchester with barely enough money to buy a small business.

'It was just something to give me an interest in life. I expect you've got a family?'

Now it was Ida's turn. She told her new-found friend about Frank and Kenneth and David and Gran and it was only after looking at a wall poster which bore the picture of an old lady who reminded her, she said, of her mother that her eyes slid over to the wall clock and she said, 'Good

170

Heavens, that's never the time, is it?'

It was the time, Mrs Maclean said and Ida asked how much she owed.

'Just eightpence,' said Mrs Maclean and waited patiently whilst Ida searched her handbag.

Ida looked up, biting her lip. 'You'll never guess what I've done! I've left my purse at home!'

'You're sure you haven't lost it?' asked Mrs Maclean, concerned.

'No, I've never had it out! I always work out all my bus fares and put them in my coat pocket so I haven't needed my purse!' Her head jerked up. 'I remember! I got it out to get a stamp for the letter I'd just written to our David – that's the lad I told you about who's the footballer! I left it on the draining board!'

'Well, don't bother about my eightpence!' And then quickly, because she was a student of humanity and she knew that the Idas of this world don't accept charity from near strangers, 'Drop it in next time you're passing!'

'Oh, thanks!' said Ida, greatly relieved. 'I'd better go and get my bus! Does the thirty-two still go from this side?'

'Eh, love, it doesn't go from here any more! They've shifted it!'

'Oh, no!'

'They can't leave well alone, can they? But don't worry, it's not far. Out of here, turn left and first left again and you're on Gray Street. Follow your nose till you get to that corner where Dolcis is . . .'

'I know it!' interrupted Ida.

'Good! Over the crossing and the stop's just a yard or two further up. The bus turns out of Newgate Street, you see!'

'You're very kind,' said Ida. 'And I'll see you again with the money!'

Ida hurried through the darkening streets. The traffic had steadied to a thin but continuous stream and a light, warm drizzle filled the air. Within a matter of minutes she had reached the shoe shop, checked right and left, crossed the zebra and was at the bus stop. She looked up anxiously at the hanging, metal notice. 'Routes number 8:17:32 . . .'

this was it! She turned to study her flushed reflection in the window of the gents' outfitters behind her and, inside her brain, a mechanism began to tick. Shirts – Marks and Spencer's – Frank – tartan shopping bag. The bag was not on her arm!

She panicked momentarily yet, in that moment, she was capable of a stream of lucid thought. If I go back I'll only miss one bus and I'll have my bag and the shirt and I'm late already so another few minutes won't make any difference! She turned to retrace her steps and, in the act of turning, remembered the superstition wished on her many years ago by a doting maternal grandmother. 'Now think on, our Ida! If you forget anything and you have to go back always count backwards from ten. Because if you don't a big bear'll get you round the next corner!'

Ida ran back to the crossing. She had reached seven when the bus hit her.

Sergeant Lancaster looked across the station desk at the crumpled figure on the bench facing him. The man, dressed in bus driver's uniform, had been looking steadily but unseeingly at the floor in front of him for the past six or seven minutes. The station was quiet and those few officers who passed paid little attention to the man. They were well used to that kind of misery. Sergeant Lancaster, a man of few emotions himself, but who could recognize them in others, bent himself, once again, to his work.

A long, shuddering sigh re-attracted his attention. The man was looking at him, eyes red-rimmed and agonized.

'She gave me no chance!' He'd said the same thing over and over as they brought him to the station but the sergeant didn't interrupt. 'I were doing no more than ten, fifteen mile an hour but t'roads were greasy and . . .' His eyes closed as he relived the moment. 'She ran right out in front of me!'

A car screeched to a halt outside. The man turned lacklustre eyes towards the door as a young constable entered carrying a bundle of clothing. The man's eyes fastened on the woman's coat on the outside of the bundle, followed it, hypnotized. Lancaster noticed.

'Bring 'em round here!' he said to the constable.

The constable, a boy in his early twenties who had already experienced a lifetime's familiarity with sudden death, pushed a typewriter aside and spread the clothing, the few cheap items of ornamental jewellery and the handbag on the table.

'Well?' said Sergeant Lancaster.

'Instantaneous, the doctor said.' His eyes slid to the figure on the bench. 'D'you reckon that's right, what he said? Fifteen mile an hour?'

'It's enough, lad, with a double-decker bus!' The sergeant's fingers toyed idly with the cheap, mud-splattered clothing. 'Who is she?'

'Don't know!'

'Don't know! Nothing in her bag?'

'Nowt much. Just a lipstick and a powder compact and a door key.'

'No money?'

'Not in the bag, no. No purse either. There was a tanner and a few coppers in her coat pocket. And a handkerchief. Oh, and this!'

'This' was an artificial silk scarf, printed in browns and creams with a horse's head motif.

'Where did you find this?' asked the sergeant.

The eyes slid again. 'He had it. He left it in the car when we brought him in.'

The sergeant looked over at the still-slumped figure of the driver. 'I think you'd better get him over to the hospital. I don't like the look of him!'

'He says he's all right,' said the constable.

'They always do! Do as you're told, lad!'

Sergeant Lancaster listened to the police car engine rev up then die away and turned back to the pitiful pile of clothing. His fingers sifted through it, examining professionally, turning back linings, searching every corner of the pockets and the bag but the lad had been right – there was no identification. A woman's cough brought him back to the counter. A thin-faced, sharp-eyed woman with a raincoat over her blue nylon overall. She carried a green tartan shopping bag.

'Hello, there!' said Mrs Maclean. 'Can I hand this in?'

'That depends, doesn't it?' said Sergeant Lancaster, heavily.

'It was left in my place. Bijou Snack Bar on Water Street. You remember? You were there a couple of months back!'

'Oh, aye! Had a few hooligans in, didn't you? Any more trouble?'

The woman's knuckles rapped on the counter. 'Touch wood, no!'

'That's the way we like it! So what have we got here then?' He examined the contents of the shopping bag. 'New shirt! A comb!' He pulled out a couple of slips of printed paper. 'What are these?'

'Receipts from supermarkets and that!' said Mrs Maclean. 'Pays to keep them in case they think you're shoplifting!'

The sergeant looked undecidedly at the bag. 'Don't you think she's more likely to go back to your café?' he asked.

'Well, normally I would but she was in a bit of a state. Pushed for time, you know! I left a note on the door telling her where I'd taken it in case she does come back.'

'Righto then! We'll take it off your hands!' Mrs Maclean was half way to the door when he called her back. 'Just a moment! You'll need a receipt for this!'

'Eh!' said Mrs Maclean, 'You and your bits o' paper!'

The sergeant turned to his desk for the receipt pad and, in the same movement, threw the shopping bag on to the table by the pile of clothing. They were together again. But not in the mind of Sergeant Lancaster.

If there was one comedian who appealed to Frank Barlow it was Tony Hancock. But not that night. He had stared into the fire, barely hearing the dry voice, scarcely conscious of the laughter of the studio audience until, at nine o'clock, the jaunty signature tune had given way to the time signal and the news. He shook his head to clear his thoughts as the newsreader began his nightly chronicle.

'In the Congo today, United Nations forces . . .' Kenneth reached forward and switched off.

'She should be home by now,' said Frank.

'Oh, it's early yet!' Valerie smiled from her armchair. 'And once Cousin Beattie gets started, nothing stops her!'

'You can say that again!' said Kenneth reassuringly.

'All t'same, it's not like your mother!' said Frank. 'If she says she'll be home soon after eight, she'll be home soon after eight!'

'Perhaps she couldn't get a bus,' said Valerie. 'You know what they're like when it's raining!'

Frank nodded but his thoughts brought the pain to his eyes. 'Suppose summat's happened to her!'

'Now, Dad, what *could* have happened to her?'

'Eh, I don't know! You read such things!'

'Dad, look at it logically!' Kenneth leaned forward in his chair and ticked off the points on his fingers. 'If . . . something happens, as you put it, the police are brought in, within a couple of minutes they've got through to the local people and next thing you know someone's knocking on your door. And no one has!'

'I'd feel better if I knew she was at Beattie's.'

'All right!' said Kenneth. 'I'll nip down to the Rover's and ring her up.'

'They're not on the phone yet,' said Valerie. 'I heard her grumbling to Uncle Albert about it the other day.'

Kenneth looked at his father and saw the hope drain out of him. 'I'll go myself then. Is David's bike all right?'

The hope came flooding back. 'Aye! Good lad!'

Outside, in the glistening street, Valerie watched as Kenneth fiddled with his rear light. 'Did . . . did your mother carry anything with her?'

The lamp came on, illuminating Kenneth's smile. 'Now don't *you* start! You know how careful Mum is! She's had her name and address in her purse since she went to primary school!'

Valerie watched him disappear down the dark street and turned back into the quiet house.

Fifty minutes later they found the purse. Kenneth had just got back from an abortive visit to Beattie's. On the wet ride back he had racked his brains for a suitable story for his father. But unsuccessfully. He couldn't find an acceptable explanation for himself but he still clung, and asked his father to cling, to the fact that they had heard nothing and, as everyone was supposed to accept, no news was good news. And then Valerie had come back from the kitchen where she was making a hot drink for Kenneth. The purse was in her hand.

She stood in the kitchen door, the colour draining from her face. 'I found this on the draining board!'

Frank was on his feet. 'I'm going to ring the police,' he said.

This time there was no objection from Kenneth. Together, father and son hurried down the wet pavement to the Rover's Return. A quiet word with Jack and they were in the hallway. Kenneth dialled the number and handed the phone to Frank. 'It's ringing,' he said.

A minute later he was forced to take the telephone back from his father. Asked what Ida had been wearing, Frank's memory had failed him and he had appealed, helplessly, to his son. Kenneth took up the story.

At the other end of the line, Sergeant Baldwin took down the items as Kenneth listed them. Gaberdine raincoat . . . green flowered dress . . . brown headscarf with horse's head. His hand covered the mouthpiece and he whispered urgently to the constable by his side.

'Get me that telex we got from Tile Street. About the woman who was knocked down in Gray Street earlier tonight.'

The constable put the telex in front of him. Rapidly the sergeant checked the particulars against Kenneth's list and then turned back to the telephone. 'Did you say a shopping bag, sir? A green tartan shopping bag?' The question was academic. 'Right, sir! I've got that! Mr Barlow, Three Coronation Street, Weatherfield. I'll send a constable down right away!'

As he put the phone down the constable reached for his helmet.

176

'Shall I go?'

'Hang on a minute! No point in asking questions if we know all the answers! Get me Tile Street! Sergeant Lancaster!' The constable dialled then silently passed the telephone to his superior.

'Hello, George? Jim Baldwin, Weatherfield. We got a telex from you earlier tonight. Some woman, knocked down in Gray Street. I think I've got a name for you!

'What have you got, Jim?'

'Mrs Ida Barlow, Three Coronation Street, Weatherfield. Everything fits apart from one item. According to her son she was carrying a green tartan shopping bag. Could have a shirt in it.'

In Tile Street Headquarters, Sergeant Lancaster swivelled in his chair. The bag was within two feet of him. 'I've got it here,' he said. 'It'd been left in some café by the bus station. I never thought of putting it with the rest of the stuff.'

Back in Weatherfield, Jim Baldwin put the phone down and looked bleakly at the helmeted constable. 'Right, no questions needed! We've got all the answers! You know where the body is, do you?'

'St Luke's?'

'That's right! Take the husband down there.' The sergeant checked his pad. 'Name of Frank.'

The telephone rang again and a woman's voice complained of noisy neighbours.

When the constable reached Coronation Street, Frank and Kenneth were still in the Rover's Return and Valerie had gone back to sit with her uncle. Alf Roberts found him knocking on the door and led him to the pub and through the crowded bar. Silently Concepta lifted the flap to let them through. Alf showed the policeman the way to the living room then turned back to the silent customers, his face stricken. He said all he could.

'She's dead!'

CHAPTER SEVEN

It was fitting that Ena should say it.

'Kenneth, you may be a clever lad but there's some things you haven't grasped yet. We can't just remember the bad things. We couldn't stand it! We'd break under t'sheer weight o' tragedy! We forget, thank God!'

'*I* don't forget!'

'And it's right you shouldn't! But don't blame that lot if they do!'

They were standing outside the Rover's Return. It was Saturday lunchtime, almost two weeks after Ida's death and Len Fairclough had cajoled Ken into coming out for a drink. The pub had been full of football fans on their way to cheer County and it hadn't been long before the singing broke out. Ena, at the snug bar, had watched Kenneth and seen the look of disbelief grow on his face as, one by one, his friends and neighbours joined happily in the song. Suddenly, without warning, he had walked out.

She had hurried after him but there was no need for haste. He was standing outside the door. Doing nothing, simply standing as the black-and-white scarved youths swirled round him, chanting their slogans.

'You can't mourn for ever, lad.'

'It's not . . . just that, Mrs Sharples.'

'Do you want to talk about it?' He looked at her for the first time. She had never been an ogre to him. There were boys of his age in the neighbourhood to whom Ena had been the embodiment of terror. But not to Kenneth. He had never been one of the bullies or the thieves or the liars for whom Ena reserved the fearsome side of her nature. But he had had his troubles and he had taken them to her in the past. She read his thoughts.

'Come and have a cup of tea and tell me about it!'

And over a cup of tea in the dark vestry he had told her,

178

his hands clasped at first tightly and then, as he relaxed, more loosely in his lap.

It had come to a head on the day of the funeral. Frank, desolated by his loss, had been unable to see to any of the hundred and one duties which death inflicts upon the living. The full burden had fallen upon Kenneth's shoulders. Ena's eyes softened as he told her about Valerie and the help and comfort she had given.

The night of his mother's death he had telephoned David in London and broken the news. Two days later a letter had arrived from David to his father. A long letter which Kenneth never saw but which Frank hugged to himself like a lifeline in a stormy sea. All he would tell Kenneth was that it would be difficult for David to come to the funeral but he'd do his very best. On the morning of the funeral, every step on the pavement outside had been David. But he hadn't come. Even as the undertaker appeared at the door of the crowded living room and signified his readiness, Frank had turned to Kenneth and said, 'You go with Gran. I'll take David with me!' And still David hadn't come.

The last mourner had gone and Frank was staring wordlessly into the fire when Len Fairclough came for Kenneth.

'It's your David!' He kept his voice low. 'He's at my place. Wants to have a word with you before . . . you know!'

Kenneth didn't know but he followed Len into the little terraced on Mawdsley Street. Len's wife, Nellie, rose from her seat by the fire and shyly left the brothers together.

'I'm sorry, Ken! I was late getting in. I went straight to the cemetery . . . I saw you all there but . . . I couldn't face Dad!'

'Why not, for Pete's sake! He's been worried stiff! He thought something had happened to *you*!'

'Oh, Lord, I never thought of that!' David hesitated, 'I'm not like you, Ken! I couldn't . . . I couldn't have stood it!'

They had gone home, the two brothers, and Kenneth had watched his father cling to David as if, at last and only now, help had come to him.

The clock ticked quietly on the vestry mantelpiece as Kenneth relived the moment. He lifted his eyes to find that Ena's gaze had never left him. 'I felt like a stranger!' he said. 'And then the next morning, after David left, Father . . . thanked me for what I'd done. He . . . he said that he couldn't have done anything himself and that . . . we couldn't expect too much from David because . . .' The words stuck and he forced them out, harshly. '. . . because he thought the world of his mother!'

He waited for Ena to say the comforting words but they didn't come. He supplied them himself. 'As if I didn't!'

'I should hope you did!' said Ena. 'She thought the world of you!' There was no trace of sympathy in her voice. Nor in her eyes. 'And is that why you're feeling sorry for yourself?'

'I'm not feeling sorry for myself, Mrs Sharples! It's just that . . . no one likes to be pushed into second place! Especially after . . . !'

Ena took advantage of his hesitation. 'Go on, say it! Especially after you'd done all the running about and they'd done nothing! And don't tell me you're not feeling sorry for yourself because you are! Because you're too daft to see that it's summat to be proud of! Lad, there's nowt wrong with finding you've got strength you never knew you had!'

'You're misunderstanding me, Mrs Sharples!'

'I'm doing nowt o' t'sort!' Kenneth half rose as there was a flurry of knocking on the front door followed by the sound of running feet. 'Stay where you are, it's only kids!' Another quieter pause. 'You want your bag o' toffees, don't you? You're the one who's been the good lad and your brother's got the present! Take a tip, lad! Don't spend your life waiting for folk to say "well done!". Just be thankful you can do something well. And be thankful you've earned your father's respect. It may not be what you wanted but it's a damned sight better than nowt!'

Kenneth smiled. 'I don't know if you're right, Mrs Sharples, but you have a great capacity for *sounding* right!'

'I know! I should be t'Prime Minister, shouldn't I? Pass us your cup!'

The days passed and Ida Barlow's tragic death faded from the street memory. Ena had been right – the capacity of the human brain for remembering is only equalled by its undoubted ability to forget those things it decides are best forgotten. In this case the process was accelerated by Harry and Concepta's impending marriage. Fixed for September the thirtieth, both Harry and his bride-to-be had discovered that, however much time you leave to make arrangements, you never leave enough.

Sean and Shelagh Riley, Concepta's parents, flew in from Ireland the day before the wedding and Len Fairclough picked them up at Ringway. He had volunteered only after working out that he could meet the plane, drive them back to the Rover's Return where they were staying, change into his best drinking suit and still not miss a minute of Harry's stag party. Len was best man and very conscious of his responsibilities. His main concern had not been the perennial one of whether or not he would remember the ring but how he was going to ensure that Harry didn't have too much to drink the night before whilst still having a good time himself. Alf Roberts solved the problem.

'Keep looking in t'mirror and if he starts to look like you, stop him!'

Len delivered the Rileys twenty minutes before the pub opened for the final Friday session. It was their first visit to England and, their introduction having been conducted at high speed they were still a little bemused when Annie let them in to the Rover's. And, had they known Annie, they would have realized from her strained smile that they weren't going to get much help from her.

'Oh, how delightful to see you!' she said. 'Do go into the living room and make yourselves absolutely at home!' Which, roughly translated, meant 'Please don't bother me!

I've got quite enough to worry about without you joining in!'

Sean and Shelagh sat bolt upright on Annie's three-piece, glazed smiles on their faces. A phone rang in the hall and was answered. Jack's voice rang through the pub. 'Annie! It's Nesbitts on t'phone! Where d'you want the cake delivering?'

Annie matched him, decibel for decibel. 'Oh, Jack, do use your brains! The Green Vale Reception Rooms, of course! Where d'you think!'

Annie, struggling out of the curlers which the Rileys hadn't even noticed, silently cursed Len Fairclough. Why on earth had he delivered them so early? And, come to think of it, why on earth weren't *they* doing the worrying instead of her? They were, after all, the bride's parents! Though, of course, if the Rileys actually had tried to take a single arrangement out of her hands, she would have fought them tooth and nail.

The bride's parents were still sitting bolt upright when, ten minutes later, Annie led Jack and Billy into the room and introduced them.

'Goodness knows what you'll think of us, leaving you alone as soon as you arrive but we are most terribly busy! Anyway, I'll show you upstairs, then we'll have a glass of sherry and a little chat! Billy's kindly volunteered to sleep down here so you're having his room!' From Billy's expression it was reasonably obvious that he had been told, quite forcibly, to volunteer.

An hour later Concepta returned from her final dress fitting and found her mother and father, still sitting bolt upright, sipping sherry. After the kissing had finished, Mrs Riley explained. 'Mrs Walker was very sorry she had to leave us but what with you being out and Mr Walker and the young boy going off to Harry's ceilidh, she felt she ought to go and help out in the bar!'

'I see!' said Concepta. 'And it's not a ceilidh – it's a stag party!'

'Well, whatever it is!' said her mother. 'They did ask your father but we decided he'd better not seeing he's involved in the ceremony tomorrow morning!'

'Well, I'm hoping Harry'll be involved in the ceremony, too!' said Concepta. 'And he'll be doing his fair share of drinking!'

In fact Harry was doing rather more than his fair share. When he and Len, who was staying the night with him, let themselves in to number seven they were well away. In the interests of propriety it had been decided that Lucille should stay next door with Esther Hayes so the house was quiet and empty. Harry stood in the centre of the living room and smiled foolishly. 'Eh, is that right? Am I getting married in t'morning?'

'You are that, lad!'

'I must be barmy!'

'Well, I warned you, didn't I? Don't say I didn't warn you, 'cos I did, didn't I? Didn't I warn you?'

'You did that, Len. You did that! You warned me!' Harry slumped heavily on to the settee. 'You're a good pal, Len! You are that! You're a good pal! A good pal!' And so saying he fell asleep.

It is to Len's eternal credit that he steadfastly refused to take the easy way out and join Harry in an alcoholic coma. He staggered into the kitchen, sluiced his face in cold water and, painfully mindful of his duties as best man, half dragged, half carried Harry's thirteen stone up to the bedroom. There, with no small difficulty, he undressed his friend and eased him into the welcoming bed. Then, his duty done, he staggered to his night's repose.

Len failed to make it by five feet. He slumped to the ground, gracefully but finally, just inside his bedroom door. When he awoke, in pitch blackness, to find himself fully clothed, he undressed, found his attaché case, fumbled for and discovered his pyjamas, put them on, got into bed and immediately fell into a deep sleep. Ten minutes later, at seven o'clock, his alarm went off.

The wedding went off like clockwork. Len had a hard time keeping himself awake during the service but, that apart, everything went swimmingly. After an early panic the buttonholes arrived, late but intact and even the arrival

183

of Mrs Sharples just after Alf Roberts had allocated all the seats in the leading guest car failed to mar the proceedings. Told that the car was to carry Minnie, Martha, Miss Nugent and Mr Swindley, Ena announced that there would be plenty of room for her as long as Emily sat on Mr Swindley's knee. 'Go on!' she told Miss Nugent behind Swindley's back. 'Grab your chance while you can! You never know your luck!' And with even Ena feeling skittish the day was marked for success.

At the Green Vale Reception Rooms, the serious business of the day, the reception, went without hitch. Even a speech by Mr Swindley containing such happy gems as 'journeying stage by stage to Life's Great Terminus' failed to throw a blight on the proceedings. The food was good and plentiful, the telegrams were readable even in mixed company and the bar opened as soon as the meal was over. And, to cap it all, Elsie found herself a man.

'Let's sit here where we can see everything!' said Dot Greenhalgh as she and Elsie moved into the Tahiti Bar. The only visible claim to the South Seas was the bamboo bar – the remainder of the fixtures, fittings and furnishings were pure North West of England. But comfortable, thought Elsie, as she sank gratefully into a red leather armchair and gazed around her.

'Why does Len Fairclough never bring his wife to these dos?' asked Dot.

'I think it's her as much as him,' said Elsie. 'She's a funniosity. But that doesn't mean to say you've got a free hand! We had enough of you on that Blackpool trip!'

'Oh, go on! It was only a bit of fun!' Dot settled back in her chair.

'You know what?' said Elsie.

'What?' said Dot.

'We should have got ourselves a drink before we sat down. Look at that bar!'

It was evident that the Green Vale had more than one dining room as the bar was filling with an assortment of wedding guests who owed no allegiance either to Harry or to Concepta. The arrival of a totally different bridal couple confirmed the point. As a result there was a three-deep queue the length of the bar.

'Eh, I see what you mean! See if you can spot somebody!'

The girls looked round for a friendly face but most faces, friendly or otherwise were turned hopefully towards the three overworked barmen.

'Who's that with Alf Roberts?' asked Elsie. 'He looks like that cowboy feller!'

'Cowboy! Most of 'em here look like horses!'

'Well, this one doesn't!'

'Oh, I see who you mean!' said Dot. 'Yes, he does, doesn't he?' Her memory took a backward dive into cinematic history. 'I know! Randolph Scott!'

'Yes, that's right, Randolph Scott!'

As always happens if you stare at someone hard enough, Alf and Randolph Scott turned at that moment and looked straight at Dot and Elsie. Alf smiled, whispered something to his companion and the two men began to thread their way through the milling guests towards the girls' table.

'Eh up, we've clicked!' said Dot.

'Hello, Elsie!' It was Alf, smiling down at them. 'Meet an old Navy pal of Len's. Bill Gregory. This is Elsie Tanner. And this is Dot Greenhalgh! Dot's married and Elsie can't make her mind up!'

'Thanks!' said Dot. 'I'll do *you* a favour sometime!'

'Not drinking, ladies?' Bill Gregory smiled down at the two friends. He had bright blue sea-faring eyes, a craggy jaw and a frame to go with it. And a wicked smile, thought Elsie.

'Not from choice!' said Dot brightly. 'We haven't signed the pledge or owt! We just can't get near the bar!'

'Allow me!' said Bill. 'What can I get you?'

Elsie spoke for the first time. 'Two gins and tonics if it's not asking too much.'

He leaned forward slightly and looked straight into Elsie's eyes. 'I don't think you *could* ask too much!' he said. And headed for the bar.

Dot looked after him admiringly, then turned to Elsie.

'How's that for starters, you lucky devil!' Then to Alf, 'Who did you say he was?'

'I've told you, he's a pal of Len Fairclough's. He's a Chief Petty Officer in the Navy. You should see him in his uniform. That *would* get you going!'

Elsie was still gazing at Bill's broad back. 'He's not doing too bad as it is!' she breathed.

'I thought it was only the nice girls as loved sailors! I suppose you're the exception what proves the rule!'

'I suppose I must be if you say so, Mrs Sharples!' They had bumped into each other in Florrie Lindley's shop and for a mad moment Elsie thought of feeding Ena to the bacon slicer. She dismissed the idea on the grounds that Ena would be too tough to be saleable and continued with her order. 'And a little tin o' them shrimps!'

'By eck, he's got expensive tastes!' said Ena as Florrie went nervously about her business. She'd heard some terrible stories about these two and she hoped they wouldn't fight.

'Yes, hasn't he! It's his exotic tastes, you see! There are some of us who've been farther afield than Fleetwood!'

'Oh, aye? Where's your limit? Morecambe?'

'Mrs Sharples, you wouldn't by any chance be working for the *News of the World*, would you?'

'By eck, I'd make a bit o' money if I was! Living in *this* street!'

Elsie had picked up her groceries and was on her way to the door. She smiled. If she played her cards right she could have the last word. 'With ears like you've got, Mrs Sharples, you could earn a bit o' money living in *any* street!' The door was open in a flash and she was gone.

Ena unperturbed, turned to Florrie. 'I hope it works out right for her this time,' she said. 'She's had a rough life!' And then, ignoring Florrie's open mouth and wondering eyes, 'What have you got in the cake line?'

But in spite of – or perhaps because of – Ena's pious hopes, it didn't work out right for Elsie. She had always been a strange blend of optimist and pessimist, forever convinced that life was going to improve and immediately suspicious when it did. And life *had* improved. Bill Gregory was, without doubt, the man she had been seeking for a long time.

'Remember them daft serials we used to read in t'women's magazines?' She and Dot were chatting during a slack moment at Miami Modes.

'What d'you mean "used to"! You still do!'

'All right then, I still do! You know how they talk about the hero? How he's all man and passionate and brave and intelligent? Strong yet gentle?'

'Go on!' said Dot, knowing what was coming.

'Oh, nothing! I was just thinking – it's not just magazine talk. There *are* fellers like that!'

'You mean your Arnold? And PC Plod?'

It ended, as their conversations often did, with Elsie throwing a coat hanger at Dot and the pair of them having a giggle. Then Elsie quietened down and Dot listened attentively as her friend went into raptures over Bill.

They were happy days.

The nights were happy too. Bill, a Chief Petty Officer Electrician, had been sent North for a course at a nearby electronics factory and, consequently, his evenings were free. Like the unlamented Sergeant Dewhurst he much preferred a quiet evening by the fire with Elsie but unlike that insensitive gentleman he knew that Elsie loved nothing more than a night out and once or twice a week they'd drive into Cheshire in his hired Hillman Minx for a drink and a meal. They went wherever the fancy took them and it was inevitable that fate should lead them to the little pub outside Mobberley which Elsie had tried so hard to avoid.

'This is a new one!' said Bill as they pulled up outside.

'Looks a bit dull,' said Elsie.

'Oh, come on! We'll try anything once!'

But for Elsie it wasn't the first time. She had only to close her eyes and she was inside the warm saloon bar, ringing to a mixture of American accents and the chatter of their English girl friends. The silent prayer she offered as she crossed the threshold was answered.

The structure was the same but the people had gone. A strange young couple smiled a welcome from behind the bar and the taciturn farmers had been replaced by the Cheshire set. The E-type owners and their fresh-from-Steiner girl friends. Bill led her to a table in the shadows, then went for their drinks.

'Shall I tell ya how to get change for a bob?'

It was the same table. How long ago? Sixteen, seventeen years? And yet it was now. Gregg was leaning on the table, smiling down at her. Gregg Flint, swarthy, good-looking, Master Sergeant in the United States Army Air Force.

'Shall I tell ya how to get change for a bob?'

He had another sergeant with him. Tall, lean, quiet grey eyes.

'Elsie Tanner, meet Steve Tanner! And if two Tanners don't make a bob I sure as hell haven't got this Limey currency figured out!'

Bill was standing over her, the drinks in his hand.

'Is it all right for you here?'

'Yes, fine!'

And it *was* fine. Steve was gone. A memory three thousand miles away. But Bill was here.

She was quieter than usual throughout the evening but she recovered when, a mile from the pub, the engine coughed apologetically and Bill announced that they were out of petrol.

'Well, I've had a few fellers in me time but you're the first who's ever had the nerve to pull that one!'

Bill blamed the hire firm and they trudged hand in hand down the dark country road. Ten minutes later, on the grass verge at a crossroads they found the telephone kiosk. The light didn't work but with the help of half a box of matches Bill found the number of a local garage who not only promised help but insisted they stay where they were and wait to be picked up.

'I don't know how you do it!' said Elsie. 'It doesn't

sound like any garage I've ever heard of! '

'It's the voice of authority! They issue it with your in-
signia! '

'Oo, I like masterful men! '

'Do you?' said Bill and took her in his arms.

Ten minutes, thought Elsie, was unfair. Long enough
for wanting but not for consummation. She was breathless
when the headlights swept over them and, reluctantly, he
let her go.

'Should I tell him to go away?'

'Why not?' she said.

He smiled. 'You know the old proverb? He who loves
and drives away, lives to love another day! Come on! '

She was still smiling when she arrived home. Linda, who
had popped in from next door for a cup of cocoa, looked
quizzically at her mother. 'Had a good time?'

'Very nice, thanks! '

'You're a bit old for that sort o' carry-on, aren't you?'

'What sort o' carry-on?'

'Turn round and I'll do your zip up! ' said Linda, her
tongue firmly in her cheek.

Elsie was acutely aware that no respectable mother
talked about such matters to their daughters. She tried
desperately to salvage the last few scraps of respectability.
'Heavens above, has my zip been open all night! '

'You'll have to be more careful, won't you?' said Linda.

As her daughter did up the tell-tale zip, Elsie searched
frantically for a change of subject. And found one.

'Did Ivan hear anything more about emigrating?'

Linda fell silent. She had all the characteristics of good
pioneering stock yet her roots went deep and, when Ivan
first mentioned emigrating to Canada her feelings had
been mixed. She knew in her heart that for them, more
than for most, it would be a sensible move to make. Ivan
would allow himself to be accepted far more readily in the
North American melting-pot than ever he would in Britain.
And, as a steelworker, he wouldn't go short of a good job.
She had allowed him to make enquiries and had regretted
it ever since.

'He's had some more papers.' She gave the news reluctantly. 'It looks as though they'd like us. Which is summat new!'

'It's the right thing,' said Elsie.

'Do you want to get rid of us?'

'No, of course I don't! Don't be daft!'

Linda subjected her mother to a long, long look. 'Is it going to work out between you and Bill?'

'Eh, how do *I* know! Why, what's that got to do with it?'

'It's just that . . . I'd feel happier if I knew somebody was looking after you!'

'Don't you think I'm capable of looking after myself?'

'I'm not sure!'

And Linda was right to be uncertain.

Blackpool Illuminations are, in more ways than one, the highlight of the Northern autumn season. This year they had been switched on by the cast of a well-known television programme but the regulars of the Rover's Return decided, in view of the expected crowds, not to make their annual pilgrimage on the opening night. Instead they chose a Thursday evening at the end of October.

Normally a pleasant occasion this particular trip was marred by one discordant note. Annie Walker had slept badly the night before and a series of minor irritations throughout the day built up to a dangerous temper by the time the coach left Coronation Street.

Jack tried his best. 'Come on, Annie, give us a smile! We're on our way to Blackpool!' Annie simply turned her head away. 'Now, Annie! You got your own way – be satisfied! Our Billy didn't bring Doreen with him, did he? It's not as if they're on t'back seat again!'

Annie's tone was vitriolic. 'And it's a good job they're not! They'd have some competition, by Jove they would!' She twisted in her seat and glared towards the rear of the bus. 'Have you seen our Mrs Tanner? A grandmother and behaving like a stupid schoolgirl!'

It was unfortunate that the bus chose to stop at traffic

lights at that moment. Most of Annie's speech, unhampered by engine noise, echoed round the bus and heads swung round from all directions. Bill allowed a moment or two to pass then started to disentangle his arm from around Elsie. But a firm grip on his wrist stopped him.

'Stay as you are! We're not letting that bitch spoil things!'

Annie's barbed remark was to be the first of many. She became obsessed with the now-not-so-happy couple and the more Jack shushed and cajoled the more acid Annie became. For once Ena took a spectator's role.

'Mind you, I'm enjoying it!' she told Martha. 'Though I'm not saying whose side I'm on!'

Elsie maintained, for her, an admirable aloofness throughout. But the outing had been a disaster and the evening continued in the same unhappy vein. As Bill left her that night he was far from his usual confident self.

'I won't be seeing you tomorrow night. A couple of the lads are up from Pompey – they're starting another course next week – and they've asked me to show them round the town. It's their first time in Manchester.'

'I see! It's nothing to do with . . .?'

'Today? You know it isn't!'

And she did know. 'I'm sorry! See you Saturday?'

'Try and stop me!'

They were not to know that she *would* try to stop him. And succeed.

Friday was one of those days. Mrs Dumbarton was in one of her nasty moods, every customer was the wrong shape for the garment she wanted and Elsie got soaking wet waiting for the bus. Dennis, who had been looking forward to a quiet night at home, took one look at his mother and went to the pictures. Elsie soaked her feet. That done she settled down with a packet of cigarettes and the Agatha Christie Dot had lent her the week before and at nine o'clock, confident she knew the identity of the murderer, she turned over to discover that the last ten pages were missing. She went to bed. The rain stopped, a wind sprang up and the window rattled all night.

Elsie awoke the following morning with a nagging headache. Not surprising, she thought, after yesterday. Thank the Lord it was Saturday!

She dressed slowly, gingerly descended the stairs, made herself some toast and a pot of tea and, after the frugal breakfast, took a couple of aspirin tablets. Then she went to the front door to collect the morning paper. It was lying on the doormat, partially covering a letter.

The envelope was blue and cheap but the address was printed in reasonably literate block lettering. Normally, with non-official correspondence (which was rare in the Tanner household) Elsie would play a little game with herself. She would turn it over and over in her fingers, analyse the handwriting, savour the perfume, if any, and from the gathered clues try to arrive at the identity of the sender. But she was in no mood for games and this morning she merely slit the envelope with a stiff forefinger, opened the letter and read it.

She read every word three times before she could believe her eyes. Then disbelief became surprise and surprise turned to fear and from fear grew a cold fury. She steadied herself, walked into the little lobby and simultaneously rapped on the partition wall and shouted upstairs to Dennis.

Dennis was still blinking the sleep from his eyes when he came downstairs. 'What's up?'

'Sit down! I'm not telling my tales twice! We're waiting for your sister!'

Dennis knew when not to argue and instinct told him that this was one of those times. The door banged and Linda came in, dressing-gowned, her hair rat's tails around her head.

'Now what? And I can't stop – I haven't fed him!'

'He can wait!'

'Well, that's a change!'

'Sit down!'

Linda, like Dennis, wondered whether to argue but when she caught her brother's eye the message was clear. She sat.

192

'Have you two been up to any daft games?'

Linda appointed herself spokeswoman. 'What daft games?'

'Have you been writing any letters?'

Linda looked across at Dennis. He shook his head nervously and uncomprehendingly. 'What letters? What are you on about?'

'That's what I'm on about!'

Linda read the letter with much the same rapid change of emotion as her mother. 'Did you honestly think I'd write this muck?' Elsie shook her head wordlessly. 'I should think not!' Linda re-read the last few paragraphs. 'Is it true what it says?'

'You know yourself some of it is! It's true enough I went with Bill to Blackpool on Thursday night, but you don't think I'd get up to tricks like that for all the world to see, do you?'

'I sometimes wonder!'

Dennis was feeling neglected. 'What tricks?' he asked.

'Never you mind!' said Elsie.

'Marvellous! She gets me out o' bed and then says never mind!'

'Oh, let him read it! He's old enough!' Linda passed the letter to her brother.

Elsie's eyes were lack-lustre as she watched her son. Linda leaned forward and patted her knee.

'You know,' said Elsie, 'there's a lot of people round here who don't think much of us as a family. At times I don't think that much of us myself but, God help me, you're all I've got! And I'm all *you've* got!'

'What about Ivan and Paul?' said her daughter.

'That's right, turn your back on me!'

'Mam, I'm not turning my back on you!'

'I don't often ask for anything, God knows. I can handle most things myself. But . . . but that!' She stared with loathing at the letter in Dennis's hands.

Linda was puzzled. 'What's all that about you not being allowed to mess about with men until your divorce was absolute. I thought it *is* absolute.'

Dennis looked up from his reading. 'So did I.'

'And so it is,' said Elsie.

'Are you sure?'

'Course I'm sure!'

'Where's that letter you got from the solicitor?'

'Eh, God knows!'

A quick rummage through the top drawer, that widow's curse of household paraphernalia, and Linda was taking the neatly typed letter from its foolscap envelope.

'*After a period of three months the decree will normally be made absolute and I should be glad if you would call at this office after the expiration of that period so that the necessary machinery may be set in motion.*' Linda lowered the solicitor's letter. 'Have you been?'

'Have I eckaslike been! I thought it was up to them!'

'According to this it's up to you!'

'What do I do then?'

'You go to the solicitors, that's what you do! And you get on to Bill and you tell him to keep out of the way till it's all sorted out!'

Like his mother, Dennis re-read the letter. Then he folded it neatly and passed it back to Linda. 'Who'd write a thing like that?' he said, disgustedly.

Linda adopted the pitying tone reserved exclusively for her brother. 'That's why they make 'em anonymous, isn't it? So we won't know!'

'*I* know!' Two pairs of eyes swivelled to Elsie.

Linda read the danger signals. 'Now, Mam!'

But Elsie was staring into a vengeful future. 'It's just up Lady High-and-Mighty's street, this is!'

Down the street, Lady High-and-Mighty was furious. Her husband, until a few minutes ago happily preparing for the lunch-time session, had fled upstairs in the face of her inflammability. She sat alone in the living room, viciously stirring her tea.

She'd known they were talking about her, of course, the moment she'd entered that corner shop. Ena Sharples could be devious but Minnie Caldwell, Emily Nugent and Florrie Lindley blushed to the roots of their respective hair-dos the moment she showed her face.

Ena didn't exactly make it less plain. 'Well, well, talk o' the devil!' she said.

Annie smiled coldly. 'Has someone been taking my name in vain?'

'You might say that!' said Ena, and, turning to Florrie Lindley, 'Go on, tell her!'

Florrie wiped her hands, nervously, on her apron. 'Pardon?'

'Tell her what you were telling us! About what Elsie Tanner said.'

It was a case of Hobson's Choice. Faced with the possible loss of either Elsie or Mrs Walker as a customer, Florrie could only take one course. Whilst Annie Walker's was invariably the week's largest and most expensive order, Elsie not only concentrated on the cheaper items but was in the habit of transferring her custom to the area's newest supermarket at the drop of a special offer. She always came back but, reflected Florrie, no one could be sure for how long.

'It was yesterday afternoon, just before I closed up.' Florrie smiled timidly. 'I had a shopful of people and Mrs Tanner came in and . . . well, your name was mentioned and . . .' Florrie broke off and looked fearfully at the others.

'Do go on, Mrs Lindley!' Annie, stern-faced, was at her most imperious.

'Well, she said some terrible things about you!'

Annie's tea slopped into her saucer. Impatiently she put the spoon down and stared grimly into her cup. Toffee-nosed old bag, indeed!

Jack came in from upstairs, struggling to fasten his collar. Although it was ten minutes since they had exchanged a word, Annie continued as if there had been no interval. 'Go on, tell me! Am I one to start any unpleasantness?'

Jack groaned. 'Hell's bells, we're not still on that, are we?'

'Yes, we *are* still on that and don't be coarse! Am I or am I not?'

'No, love, you're not!'

Being a simple-minded man, Jack thought that was the

end of the matter. Annie, however, obviously wanted more. She fixed him with an expectant stare and said, 'Well, go on! Is that all you have to say?'

'What else do you want?'

Her laugh was a mixture of hysteria and self-pity. 'So that's the backing I get from my own husband! Mind you, I was a fool to expect any more! I suppose some women are lucky and some aren't, and that's an end of it!' The hysterical laugh again.

Jack strove vainly to inject some authority into his voice. 'Now don't start that!'

'I am not starting anything! If you'd only listen you'd know exactly what I'm getting at! Elsie Tanner had the unmitigated gall . . .' She paused to allow the extent of her vocabulary full rein. '. . . the unmitigated gall to stand in that corner shop in front of Heaven knows who and make the most outrageously libellous statements about your wife! And if you consider me in some way to blame for that then perhaps we'd better start thinking seriously of divorce!'

Jack wasn't unduly disturbed by Annie's threats. Nor did he believe that rancour could live from one day to the next. As far as he was concerned, each sunset wiped the slate clean. 'Nay, Annie, that was yesterday! You've slept on it since. And so's she!'

'I don't care if it was yesterday or last week or ten-sixty-six! I've said it before and I'll say it again – it's the few that bring tone to any district! And Heaven knows it's a hard fight! Apparently I'm up against my own husband!'

Jack groaned inwardly. On the subject of breeding, Annie was inexhaustible. He tried to close his ears, to think of other things, to ponder County's chances of beating the opposition that afternoon. But it was far from easy. Annie's voice had reached crescendo when the door opened and Doreen walked in, reporting for duty.

'So think it over!' Annie was in full spate. 'And while you're thinking, remember it's a straight choice between me and Elsie Tanner!' And with a malevolent look at her life partner, Annie swept past Doreen and out into the bar.

Doreen looked at her miserable employer, admiration

196

growing in her eyes. 'Are you doing a bit on the side with Elsie Tanner?'

'Eh, lass!' said Jack from deep within his heart. 'Isn't one woman enough!'

Mr Swindley would have frowned at the suggestion that he could possibly provide comic relief but provide it he did that Saturday morning.

He was in high spirits when he arrived at the shop. Miss Nugent was already there, hard at work with duster and polish and the mahogany counter shone dark and rich.

'Good morning, Miss Nugent!'

'Good morning, Mr Swindley! Rather blustery, isn't it?'

'A high wind, indeed, but providential, Miss Nugent, providential!' said Swindley as he hung up his Homburg hat. 'One hears much about spring and what happens to a young man's fancy at that season of the year . . .'

'Lightly turns to thoughts of love!' murmured Emily hopefully.

'Quite! But in autumn, Miss Nugent, a young lady's fancy turns in a different direction. Towards more substantial garments! And today, over many a Weatherfield breakfast table, our circulars will be perused with interest! Provided of course, you caught the post!'

'Oh, I did!' said Emily. 'I looked at the pillar box before I put them in!'

'Difficult to do otherwise, eh, Miss Nugent!' said Swindley devilishly. Miss Nugent smiled dutifully as her partner rubbed his hands together with anticipatory glee. 'You must forgive my bounding good spirits this morning. I have a premonition that Dame Fortune is about to smile on us!'

The ting of the shop bell brought him whirling round to the door. It wasn't Dame Fortune, it was Christine Hardman. And she wasn't smiling. 'I've had a circular from you!'

'Indeed you have! It pays to advertise, does it not?'

'Well, it does if you don't put enough stamps on!' said Christine. 'I had to pay another penny!'

'Another penny?' Mr Swindley turned and looked questioningly at his lady partner.

'That's what the postman said!' Christine went on. 'He said it should have been twopence-ha'penny and you only put twopence on.'

'Dear me!'

The telephone rang and it was Mrs Winstanley, one of their most valued customers. Not only had she been forced to pay another penny but had been summoned from a warm bed for the privilege. Mr Swindley's high spirits dropped like a stone.

When they closed for lunch that day, eating was the last activity on the minds of Mr Swindley and Miss Nugent. The firm's good name was, quite obviously, at stake and they faced the still blustery weather armed with a plentiful supply of pennies, the mailing list and a few spare circulars.

'Spare circulars?' Miss Nugent had queried.

Swindley, steeped in the knowledge of human frailty, had explained. 'The envelopes did have our name on. Not all the recipients may have wished to gamble the penny surcharge!'

As Emily and Leonard set out on their errand of restitution, Elsie Tanner sat, glowering, at home. She was working herself into a frenzy, not by the better known methods of voodoo, Dutch courage or drugs but by a continuous reading of the offending letter. For the past hour Linda had sat and watched as her mother's phobia blossomed in front of her eyes. All she could think of to say was 'Now, Mam!' But Elsie didn't hear. She was preparing herself for battle.

In the snug at the Rover's Return, Ena, Minnie and Martha occupied their usual chairs.

Martha leaned forward conspiratorially. 'What do *you* think, Ena?'

'From t'taste of it there's some o' that there fall-out in this stout,' said Ena, examining her glass critically. 'You can't tell me it only drops in milk!'

'No, I don't mean that!' persisted Martha. 'I mean the poison pen letter! You know!'

'Not much chance o' *not* knowing, is there! You can't get down the street for flapping ears. Some folk have nowt better to do than gossip. Personally I'm holding meself aloof!'

'You're what?' said Martha incredulously.

'You heard!' said Ena.

Martha turned to Minnie. 'Did you hear that?'

'Yes, I did,' said Minnie. 'And I don't think it drops in the milk. It's something to do with the cows. And the grass.'

At times, Minnie's mind bore a startling resemblance to one of those old synchronized films where the chatter is three speeches behind the lip movements. She became what the film people call 'out of synch'. Valerie Tatlock once spent an entire evening trying to make some sense out of a conversation with Minnie and she would have had to go on wondering had her Uncle Albert not explained the phenomenon to her.

Ena and Martha needed no explanation. They knew Minnie's idiosyncrasies rather better than their own. They looked at each other, then at their smiling, oblivious friend.

'You've got summat to be thankful for, any road!' said Ena.

'What's that?' asked Minnie happily.

'You'll never get one o' them letters Elsie Tanner got!'

Minnie was on the point of asking what that had to do with radio-activity when the snug door opened and Leonard Swindley's head came round.

'Ah, ladies!' He was beaming at them with Miss Nugent hovering behind. 'You may have received a circular from me this morning!'

'I handed mine back!' said Ena.

'Yes, I thought you might!' said Swindley signalling to Miss Nugent to present Mrs Sharples with another copy.

'So did I!' said Martha, reaching for another circular.

'I didn't know you could!' said Minnie.

'In that case, allow me to reimburse you!' said Mr

Swindley, handing Minnie a penny. 'And I look forward to your valued custom!'

And as quickly as they had come, they were gone.

'That was nice of him!' said Minnie, rising rather painfully from her seat.

'Sit yourself down!' said Martha. 'We're not ready yet!'

'I'm not going for drinks,' said Minnie, 'I'm going to spend a penny!'

'By gum!' said Ena. 'She's no sooner got it than she has to spend it! Easy come, easy go!'

But Minnie was back in her seat and a glance over the bar told Ena and Martha why. Elsie Tanner had arrived.

It was a scene from a Western. The packed saloon held its breath as the protagonists faced each other over the bar.

Annie spoke first. 'What can I get you, Mrs Tanner?'

'I don't want anything to drink, thank you!' Elsie's voice was dangerously quiet. 'I've called about a certain letter I received this morning and I'd like to know what you've got to say about it!'

She threw the crumpled letter on to the bar. Jack reached forward for it but Annie pushed his arm away.

'Just a moment, Jack! I've got two things to say, Mrs Tanner. The first is that I wouldn't soil my hands writing a thing like that and the second is that I'm downright disgusted that anyone should think me capable of it! And while I'm talking I'll say something else! I've stood in this public house and I've heard my name linked with that letter not once but a dozen times. I've seen my own husband and my own barmaid trying to keep the customers from telling me!'

Behind her, Jack sighed, a mixture of sadness and relief. The word had come to him from old Albert who had heard it from Dennis and the news had spread like wildfire. He and Doreen had hoped that Annie had been spared the whispers but they had been wrong. She had heard every innuendo and suffered. In silence. His hand went out to hers but, taking it as restraint, she shook it off.

'No, Jack, I've a right to speak my mind. I've been accused in public and I've a right to defend myself in public. I did *not* write that letter, Mrs Tanner, and if you'll take my advice you'll go back home and you'll pull yourself together. And when you've done that perhaps you'll have the decency to apologize!'

Annie's attack was devastating. Elsie stood there, stunned, knowing she was wrong. She blinked back the hot tears and, turning away from Annie, found herself looking into the eyes of Ena, the old enemy.

'Before you say owt, Elsie Tanner, remember this! You know me of old. And you know that if I believe in summat I'll sign my name to it!'

The silence was absolute. Elsie was hemmed in, a prisoner of her own impulsiveness. She looked around wildly for some avenue of escape and, seeing her distress, Len Fairclough took her arm.

'Come on, love, I'll see you home!'

But when the tigress is hemmed in she doesn't allow herself to be meekly led away. 'You take your dirty hands off me!' She spat the words. 'You've been a bit funny these last few weeks, haven't you?'

She was right. Len had been 'funny' for the past few weeks but this was no time to tell her why. No time to tell her that Bill Gregory was a married man. No time to describe the rows between Bill and himself or to admit his failure to persuade his friend to tell the truth. No time to add more troubles to that troubled face.

'Steady now!' he said. Gently.

Her reply was far from gentle. Nor was it just to him. It was to the listening customers, the street, the whole world if it cared to listen.

'Steady!! What do you mean, steady!! Whoever wrote that letter wasn't steady! They didn't care what they did to me, did they?' Her eyes swept round the silent on-lookers. 'You're all the same! Every damned one of you!'

The door swung after her then came to rest. Only Annie moved.

'Doreen?'

'Yes, Mrs Walker?'

'Get a quarter bottle of brandy and take it round to Mrs Tanner's.'

'Yes, Mrs Walker.'

Doreen moved to the spirit shelf like Prince Charming through the enchanted castle. Annie became aware of the tableau around her.

'Do please carry on drinking! ' she said. 'We can't afford to let this sort of thing affect business! '

With a great gust of relief the enchanted courtiers came back to life.

CHAPTER EIGHT

The Monday after the incident at the Rover's Return Ivan heard, officially, that he, Linda and Paul were to sail to Canada on December the sixth. The *Manchester Trader* would take them to Montreal and they would then travel by rail to Toronto where lodgings had been arranged for them. A job was waiting.

There was a great deal to do and Elsie's involvement in her daughter's problems had the happy effect of taking her mind off her own. She helped Ivan and Linda sell their furniture, she took over the sale of the house, she looked after Paul when the young couple made their farewell visits to friends in Warrington and in the Polish community of South Lancashire. Ivan, for all his faults in Linda's eyes, was a thrifty husband and he had saved enough to tide them over the first few difficult months. Nonetheless, as he told Elsie, the sooner the house was sold the better.

During the following weeks, quickly though they passed, Elsie still found the odd moment to ponder over the anonymous letter. The sender's identity was still a mystery but the effect had been salutary. Elsie had visited her solicitor and was now waiting for her decree absolute. Bill, warned off by Len until things cooled down, was conspicuous by his absence.

'Don't see much o' that boy friend o' yours these days,' remarked Ena on the street one day.

'No,' said Elsie.

'Putting your house in order, are you?'

'You could say that, Mrs Sharples!'

'And not before time neither!'

Ena had her own problems. Yet another clash with the Mission Committee over her intemperate habits had led to her dismissal from her post of caretaker. Martha, the fair-weather friend, had raised every objection she could muster as to why Ena couldn't possibly move in with her and, inevitably, Minnie had provided shelter. They were currently living a cat and dog existence in Jubilee Terrace in the brooding presence of Minnie's unseen but dominant mother.

Leonard Swindley had done what he could to bring about a reprieve. In his way he respected Ena though he was happy at the thought of losing that constant grumbling which she considered her inalienable right. In the event he lost nothing. In appointing Albert Tatlock to the position of caretaker at the Glad Tidings Mission, all Swindley changed was the grumbler's sex.

On the morning of the sixth, Ena and Minnie, glad to get away from old Mrs Caldwell's imperious rappings on the bedroom floor, walked under the mossy, dripping viaduct arch and into Coronation Street. They were not alone. The street was thronged with well-wishers, gathered to say their farewells to the migrants. A cheer went up as Ivan, carrying Paul, emerged from Elsie's house. He allowed the cooing women to fuss over the little boy as Dennis and Len packed the latter's van with the last few pieces of the Cheveskis' luggage. He smiled as the men in the party chipped in with their bawdy warnings about Canadian women. He promised to write to a dozen people he hardly knew.

Inside the house all was quiet. The last minute pandemonium was over and now it was simply mother and daughter. Alone and, after years of saying too much to each other, not knowing what their last words should be.

'Go on!' said Elsie. 'That boat's not going to wait for you!'

'Come and kiss Paul!'

'No! I've said goodbye to him.'

'Oh, Mam!' There were no visible tears but both women were trained to hide them. 'I've got to go with him! I've got to! He's my husband!'

'I know, love! And keep remembering that!'

A flicker of a smile. 'I'll write to you!'

'You'd better! Go on!' And Elsie pushed her only

daughter out of the room, out of the house, to the other side of the world.

She looked for a cigarette as she heard the van start up and the cheering begin, and failed to find one. The cheering died.

'She nearly took our back door key with her!' It was Dennis.

'Put it on t'mantelpiece!'

'Want a fag?' He was offering her one from a new packet.

'Where d'you get them from?'

'I bought 'em!'

Elsie managed a brave, wry smile. 'Eckythump!' And then she started to cry.

Heaven knew why it had to be that night. The woman herself couldn't possibly have known.

Len had taken Elsie for a drink. The various rifts had been healed and Elsie, had she taken advantage of the many sympathizers, could have drunk free gin and tonic until the small hours. But at nine o'clock she excused herself. 'I'd better go while I can still stand up! By eck, it's not easy *having* kids but it's a damned sight harder getting rid of 'em!'

She had barely returned to the quiet house when the knock sounded at the door. And there she was. Arnold's girl friend, Madam Toffee Shop, as large as life.

'I was in the neighbourhood and I thought I'd call.'

'Oh yes?' said Elsie guardedly.

'I was wondering if you'd done anything about getting your divorce made absolute. Me and Arnold can't wait for ever, you know!'

And there it was! The blinding flash of light! The truth!

'Did you by any chance write me a letter and forget to sign it?'

'A letter? No!' She wasn't a very good liar. 'Why should *I* write you a letter?'

'You've just told me why!' said Elsie. 'And if it's any

205

consolation, it worked! I've been to the solicitors and they're dealing with it. Any day now you'll be able to get what you deserve! The pair of you!' Elsie advanced, smiling. 'Now get gone before I tear your wig out by its roots!' Madam Toffee Shop fled before her.

It was a typical Christmas. Full of drunkenness, family rows and stomach ache. But there were pockets of festive spirit. The romance between Kenneth and Valerie Tatlock had deepened into a happy permanence and it was the girl who, more than anyone, made Christmas bearable in the Barlow household. It was inevitable that the memory of Ida should be at its strongest at such a time but David's brief visit and Valerie's happy attentiveness helped the family through a testing period. Generally, however, Christmas came and went, adding neither scars nor lustre to the year.

The last few days of 1961 followed the time-honoured pattern. Faces on the television, voices on the radio, masses of words in the columns of the Press all dealt in the same commodities – recriminations on past misdeeds, hopes for the future. Next year everyone would be holidaying on the moon, peace and prosperity would return to the world, Burnley would win the F.A. Cup. And the people of Coronation Street looked, listened and read, believed what they wanted to believe and assembled, dutifully, on New Year's Eve to observe the twin ceremonies of absolution and a fresh start.

Ena played the piano, dragged for the occasion from under its shroud in the Select, Albert delivered his favourite monologue blissfully unaware that it was no one else's, Concepta sang an Irish song and Len led the assembled company in a burst of boisterous if off-key community singing. Then Alf Roberts, who had been appointed Master of Ceremonies, raised his voice above the hubbub.

'Ten to twelve! Get your skates on, Harry!'

The call was taken up. 'Aye, come on, lad!'

Harry groaned. 'Aw, not again! Haven't you read what

it says in the papers? Coldest spell for seventeen years! '

'Give him a Scotch, Jack! ' shouted Len. 'We don't want him freezing up on us! '

'And give him that noggin while you're at it! ' said Annie. 'He can't let the New Year in without a drop of whisky in his pocket! '

'Why wasn't I born a redhead! ' moaned Harry. 'Why does it have to be a dark-haired feller?'

'Heaven knows! ' said Elsie. 'But it has so that's an end of it! '

Concepta passed Harry a small screw of paper. 'There's your salt! Put it in your pocket! '

Harry obeyed and followed it with the small bottle of whisky which Jack handed to him.

'I'll tell you what I haven't got,' said Concepta, 'and that's a piece of coal! '

'Don't worry, I have! ' said Ena, digging into her handbag.

'Never without a piece of coal in your handbag, are you, Ena!

'Less o' your jokes, Len Fairclough! I might be short in some respects but I know what's right and proper on a New Year's Eve! '

At last Harry was prepared for his vigil, primed with all the regalia of the first footing. Had an opinion poll been taken in the public bar it would have produced near unanimity on why salt, coal and whisky were necessary ingredients of the ceremony. The popular explanation would have been that they symbolized food, drink and warmth for all present in that house throughout the ensuing year. But there would have been no consensus regarding the other necessity – that the man who first put his foot over the threshold at the beginning of the year must have dark hair. The roots of that belief lay buried in the realms of folklore. But it was the rule and Harry was dark and there he stood, ready to go.

'Right! Out you go! ' It was Alf again.

'Have a heart! ' said Harry. 'It's not five to yet! '

'That clock could be slow,' said Annie. 'Better to be sure than sorry! '

A casual observer from another planet might well have wondered what would have hit the Rover's Return had Harry been caught on the premises at the stroke of midnight. A thunderbolt, apparently.

Harry bowed to popular opinion. The air was bitter and the frost formed on his cheeks after a half dozen paces. He hunched his shoulders against the cold and walked up the street towards the shop and some shelter from the hostile wind. As he drew level with the Tanners' he saw the faint red glow from under the black viaduct arch. He walked on and a shape materialized behind the glowing cigarette.

'Tommy?'

'Aye!' It was Tommy Seddon, the ironmonger from the corner of Mawdsley Street and Viaduct Street. 'Got you at it again, have they?'

'Aye, muggins, as per usual!'

'Got your piece of coal, have you?'

'I have that!' said Harry. 'Have you?'

'Oh aye!'

'And your salt and your drop o' whisky?'

'Too true!'

'Oh well, nowt much can happen then!'

Nowt much can happen. Harry looked back into the dark street with its dim pools of light. He saw them all. The new woman at the shop. Elsie daughterless, Christine motherless, Ena homeless, the Barlows womanless. And himself with a new wife and the Cheveskis with a new life and the Walkers with a son back at home. Nowt much can happen! He smiled into the unseeing darkness.

'Come to think of it, I said t'same thing last year!'